iN ENEMY HANds

Émile opened his eyes to the sight of two very unpleasant *flics* standing over him, one with a drawn softknife, the optic fibers stiff with power. He didn't need the green-uniformed man to touch the bright filaments to his skin to know that they would burn through him as if through butter, but the *flic* made double sure. The pain was so intense that at first Émile couldn't feel it, and then it exploded through the back of his hand and up his arm. Although the softknife never went beyond the elbow, he could feel the nerves reacting into his shoulder and chest.

He hated pain . . .

Blind Justice

S.N. LEWITT

ACE BOOKS, NEW YORK

This book is an Ace original edition,
and has never been previously published.

BLIND JUSTICE

An Ace Book / published by arrangement with
the author

PRINTING HISTORY
Ace edition / April 1991

ISBN: 0-441-71843-4

Ace Books are published by The Berkley Publishing Group,
200 Madison Avenue, New York, New York 10016.
The name ''ACE'' and the ''A'' logo
are trademarks belonging to Charter Communications, Inc.

PRINTED IN THE UNITED STATES OF AMERICA

10 9 8 7 6 5 4 3 2 1

For Sue Stone and Mary Allen, for handholding extraordinaire, and with thanks for inspiration to Leatherwolf for "Princess of Love"

CHAPTER ONE

It was like the Last Supper and Émile Saint-Just was certain that someone was going to die. They broke out the good Château Moullage '39, all three bottles that Jean-Louis Marchand, the purser, had been saving to celebrate the closing of a sale. "But if we get caught we cannot permit them to drink it without appreciation," Jean-Louis had announced with just a slight catch in his voice.

Émile could well understand that. Common knowledge said that no one who was truly Justica could speak a civilized tongue and they had no appreciation of good wine. And he had to admit he was pleased. As the lowest-ranking apprentice on the Free Trader *Mary Damned*, under normal conditions he would not have had any opportunity to taste the fine vintage.

The Captain had even decided to let the ship run on comp so the entire crew could attend dinner together. Not that the wine was the only glory of the evening. Paul Foncier, who normally acted as first apprentice in navigation, had indulged his hobby and ship's stores to the fullest, producing a stuffed trout in puff pastry and champagne sauce that surpassed anything Émile had ever tasted in his life. Until Paul served the white chocolate mousse for dessert. That was even better than the *beignets* from the Café de la Montagne in the Quartier du Paris.

Then Captain Sarrault rose and proposed the first toast, to the Académie Français as always. The crew of the *Mary Damned* might be colonials twenty light-years from Earth, but they followed the dictates of the Académie all the more avidly for it. And while Republics and technologies rose and fell, the Académie Français was one of the few eternals in the universe.

1

Tears came to Saint-Just's eyes as he thought of the long
and constant history of the Académie. Without it the traders
might come back to their own future to find that they couldn't
even speak their own language. No idea was more frightening,
and so the Syndicat's loyalty to the Académie was perfectly
reasonable. Not at all a conceit of light-runners with intellectual
pretensions, as some planet-bound members of the university
community had claimed in *L'Ami du Peuple*, the most presti-
gious Quartier newspaper.

Then they toasted the Syndicat, and the Captain toasted the
crew. And then Chief Rimbeau toasted the Justica *flics* who
would shortly be after them. And the Free Traders of Beau
Soleil who refused to go along with the dictates of a uniform
Justica that had tried to impose authority where it wasn't
wanted.

And so the Syndicat had offered the *Mary Damned* the honor
of being the first Free Trader to openly defy the Justica. Naturally, there was no question that Captain Sarrault would accept. She had great experience running around the tax *flics* who
were so much bother and completely useless, Elisabeth Sarrault
did. Which was why she was in command of the most notorious
vessel in Syndicat history. And the *Mary Damned* was destined
to become even more infamous in the annals of the Justica
when they had made this run across the Void.

Still, Émile could feel some tension under the bravado. The
fish had been perfect and the mousse lighter than helium, but
somehow they all turned to solid stone in his stomach. Even
being seated across from Catherine des Musées, second apprentice and arrogant redhead, did not distract him from watching for the final moment.

For all the Justica were arrogant and uncivilized, they were
unfortunately efficient at what they did. Collecting taxes, dictating policies to perfectly sufficient colonies and capturing
drug runners were among their fortes. There was a chance the
Mary Damned would get through, but Émile would not be
willing to put money on that possibility. Captain Sarrault had
made it very clear when the proposition was first brought that
they were to be something of a test case. The circumstances
might enhance the piquancy of the dinner, but Émile was not

able to appreciate the addition. His appetite had deteriorated as they reached the designated point.

At the Captain's signal the *Mary Damned* cut her lights. There was nothing to show against the invisible depths of space where no Zones held influence and the Justica patrolled only rarely. Captain Sarrault had every intention of making the Justica look like fools and come out untouched.

"I certainly do not want to be remembered as the first Syndicat captain to lose a ship to the press gangs," she had said dryly when first explaining what they were going to do.

Émile watched the on-line galley displays as one by one the engines shut down. Going black out of the Zones, running cold by light far from the traffic lanes was something even Free Traders did not do. The *Mary Damned* was the first. It made Émile proud. He rubbed his thumb unconsciously over the deeply engraved ship ID on his Syndicat cuff. He had only been accepted by the Traders a year before. Now he had an apprentice berth on the proudest lady in the fleet.

Still, once they had left the plan filed with the Justica offices and started running black, everyone aboard began whispering and being careful not to bounce too hard on the bulkheads. Not that the noise mattered. Double hull construction and vacuum made certain of that. But habits bred into humanity since its emergence from the ice refused to die. Clandestine meant hushed voices and deep shadows.

They were running the long way through the Dark, loaded with fifty liters of sadece senin, the pure extract of the sadece milk that brought Beau Soliel more in trade than the rest of her combined products and services. Sadece senin was the life and the blood of the Syndicat, the trade, and the people of Beau Soliel. It was also extremely illegal in the uniform Justica, unless it was excepted for experimental and medical use with permits and taxes and destinations affixed.

"But why is it illegal?" Émile had asked when he had first been taught the Justica rules of trade and transshipment. The whole idea seemed absurd. If sadece senin were harmful then the entire population of Beau Soliel would be afflicted. After all, though they did not use the refined senin except for interface, their entire atmosphere was constantly being permeated by sadece gas, that little belch the flowers used to draw their prey.

Indeed, it was only because space was limited and they wanted to maximize the profits that the crew of the *Mary Damned* did not touch the merchandise on the journey. Sadece they used was sadece they could not sell, and it sold for a price that made even the terrible expense of bringing it from a gravity well half way through the visible stars well worthwhile.

One of the reasons that the *Mary Damned* and Elisabeth Sarrault had been chosen was that the ship's AI was more perceptive than most and Sarrault could actually fly realtime. She didn't need interface for most functions, like the bargers and Zone drones who had adverse reactions to the dark senin used for deep contact. And it was the dark senin they were shipping, the best, the most expensive, the most infamous substance in the universe. There were places where Justica rumors were that it was fed with human blood.

Like any proper Syndicat vessel, the *Mary Damned*, officers and crew, couldn't be bothered with permits and destinations that cut the profit nearly ninety percent. Even Émile Saint-Just, the newest member of the crew, had acquired the requisite attitude—that the uniform existed merely to provide the Syndicat with amusement. While it was good to score profit points off the Justica, it was even more gratifying to count coup with elegance that showed the entire uniform how unimaginative and utterly vulgar the *flics* were.

Just like the British whore for whom she'd been named, the AI and crew would rather go down than run and hide. And the original Mary Damned did go down, refusing to leave her pleasure house on the Rose Plage when the tsunumi of '39 struck. Her body was never found, and children whispered about her ghost.

Now Saint-Just's cuff, still new and bright, bore the incised device of the *Mary Damned*. Coded to the ship and his rate, it seemed heavier somehow, as if data had mass. Naturally he knew that was pure romanticism, but he couldn't stop looking at the design. Two black circles pierced by an arrow, not much to look at unless one knew what it meant.

"Now, you see, we're dark and low," the Chief had explained to him when he returned to his station on the late watch after the last helpings of mousse had been consumed. "The only way to spot us infrared on our position is on our tail. But the wake chills down fast and our position changes enough that nothing should show at all. And if it does, well, with a signature this low and on this course, we should show up just like a Justica drone on their scopes. Check the settings and learn them."

Émile had blinked to keep his eyes open. He hadn't done anything but watch the board on this low setting for hours now and he was getting glazed. Pulling the dead shift six weeks out had been bad luck. Out of a crew of eighteen, only three people were needed on the graveyard monitor. No chatter in the optics, no gossip in the hall. And no interface either.

He had only experienced real interface once, when he was printed in the Syndicat's central Mass. That experience had both seduced and scarred him, and when he had won his berth he had been a little apprehensive of doing it again. But in his current job that was not required. It was not even wanted. No, all he had to do was stare at visual output that remained as static as anything ever pencilled by a street artist doing portraits for tourists on the Boulevard Lafitte.

He swallowed the dregs of the *café au lait* left from breakfast, sitting separated on the monitor ledge. It was turned, soured. He went to the head and poured out the rest, taking his time and stretching his legs before going back to his position.

Running this low made being an apprentice monitor evil work. But necessary, he told himself again. If not for the ship and Syndicat, then for his career. Everyone started as an apprentice monitor, even those with more training and time in the Palais. Look at Paul. He had been a full chef at one of the exclusive restaurants on the Boulevard Lafitte and then had spent three full years at the Palais Syndicat studying energy systems. He had signed on as an apprentice monitor, having passed the second rating test. It was just part of the job.

But boredom struggled against awareness minute by unchanging minute. Trying to focus, he found his eyes wandering, and his mind would not stay on the plotted course. Not even on the games he called up to keep himself awake. Saint-Just found more time just slipping, spent on thoughts of *beignets* and red-haired Catherine.

She was senior to him and so barely acknowledged his existence. That was to be expected but it still hurt. She was tough and smart, which only enhanced her perfect features and milk-white skin. While he knew it was no use, he still had some small hope. She had already acquired the layer of control that marked her as a trader more surely than her incised cuff. So under that smooth arrogance she could well be hiding some attraction for him as well. And there was plenty of time. They were only six weeks out.

And those six weeks had not been at all what he had expected. He had always imagined trader life as more, well, exciting than this. The romance of the long-haul ships and the life on the Zones where time played evil tricks on everyone, including those who stayed. He had not been seduced by the way traders had to leave everything behind when they were accepted to the Palais, the better to buffer them from time-shock. His parents were not happy to see him go but they didn't protest either. It was more like leaving a prologue. He had always known that he belonged out with the traders; he remembered no other ambition.

And so sitting dead shift hour after hour, watching the steady red and blue specks march in orderly progression, was unfair. After all, they were jumping the lines, going illegal, cutting the Justica domination. They were hauling sadece senin to the market source, keeping away from prying eyes that were more interested in collecting their tax than in any health or moral issue the drug seemed to precipitate. There should at least have been a little affair with an exotic or maybe even an alien, although those he had seen did not seem compatible with humans. But so far he had not even been into a Zone, let alone tasted the vaunted pleasures thereof.

And then the flat voice broke the silence. "Sensing, passive return," the computer informed him.

Émile held his breath and let it out slowly. Get the Chief, he thought, get the Captain. Sound the alarm. But the alarm would take them off passive, and perhaps they could still pass in the dark. Maybe the intruders wouldn't bother any more, assuming them to be a drone and passing by. Not that anyone believed in such luck, but Émile grasped it as a thread of hope.

And then he panicked. He left his post, pushed himself down the darkened halls, his cuff clanging on the handgrips that lined the tube. He didn't even notice the noise. All he knew was that he had to get to Rimbeau, get someone to take over. To do something.

It wasn't easy getting into Rimbeau's stateroom. The lock refused to budge until he used the cuff code. He woke the Chief by hand, shaking him in the dark of his luxurious private quarters. "We've been seen," he whispered.

Not that a probing could pick up voice, really. Just that the discipline of silence had been so deep in him that he echoed the ship's condition. And so the Chief's howl startled him and he fell back.

"I'll get the Captain," the Chief said, pulling on his overalls. "And the mate and the second. You get the bosun and Jean-Louis and the other apprentices and make sure everyone is in the galley. *Vite, vite, vite.*"

For the first time in weeks he felt awkward propelling himself through the halls. He had been so proud of his skill so recently, and now it was all abandoned. He kicked and spun like a gravity addict, unable to get his bearings before he lurched again.

Nothing was any good. He clung to one of the grips and made himself breathe. Long, deep breaths to calm down. They had been spotted. There was still a little time. Time enough to do it right the first try because there wasn't enough time to do it again. Forget the whole picture, a voice in his head told him. One thing at a time. Nothing more. First get the bosun and the purser and the other apprentices.

That was easy. The bosun and the purser shared the aft stateroom and the other apprentices had nets strung down the lower corridor. Rimbeau had told him to get everyone who slept in one general area. Very sensible.

He made himself use the grips. It was slower, but not so bad as getting caught in a spin. Grip by grip to the hatch that opened on heat recognition. Through the hatch, use the grips, don't think about where anything is. One inch at a time. One job and then the next. On and on, bit by bit.

He was in the apprentice sleeping corridor before he recognized it. He didn't bother to look at whom he was shaking awake. There was no time for anything but survival. Suddenly Émile wished it was boring again.

Catherine didn't scream or demand explanations when she woke. She listened to his three words and nodded immediately, then volunteered to get the bosun and the purser while Émile got Paul, and got down to the galley.

The galley was the only place large enough to hold a meeting of the entire crew. Six tables were bolted to the unfinished deck, each surrounded by eight similarly bolted stools. Not all the stools were full. The *Mary Damned* ran light. More mass for cargo, fewer divisions of the profits.

"We're pretty sure they know we're not a drone," the Captain began. Her eyes were weary and her shoulders sagged against the knowledge of the Justica. "We've checked the records and they've been probing every six seconds. Too frequent for something unsuspicious, just under the mark for immediate reporting. They started slow, every thirty seconds, so we weren't alerted. Have to change the program on that. Now we can expect that they will try to board and take us by force. Everyone had better be armed. If we can overcome the boarding party, then we might be able to use them as hostages to get away."

"What about outrunning them?" Catherine asked.

Sarrault shook her head with profound sorrow. "We can outrun their ship but we can't outrun their guns. That's the problem."

"We should be able to get off a shot or two ourselves," Chief Rimbeau muttered.

The Captain smiled at him. Everyone in the galley understood. Their one little peashooter against the real guns of the Justica was a joke, nothing more. Oh, it came in handy enough when they had a drunken run-in with an arrogant Independent or a mine trap, and applied with real skill could even deflect a high-vee drone or Void-rock. But face to face with a real enemy, they were as good as unarmed.

"Why don't we have real guns?" the environmental section head asked no one. As it was, their little garbage gun endangered their Justica license. And the license, while perhaps not a strict necessity, did make operating in the Zones much easier.

According to the uniform Justica, only the uniform could keep weapons.

"Now that all the irrelevant comment is done," the Captain said dryly, "you will all arm yourselves with something useful. Knives, wrenches, the welding laser. We will see if we can't talk them into not coming aboard and just letting us go by. We can hope for that. We'll have to dismantle the peashooter. Rimbeau, take care of it.

"If they board, everyone wait in the hold behind the crates. And I mean wait. There's no guarantee that they will catch us doing any worse than jumping the lines of traffic. That's a minor violation. Possible that we can fake a nav error or something."

Michel Cherin, navigator in spite of being the Captain's lover and not because of it, crossed his eyes eloquently. "I can try," he said, sighing. "A few degrees perhaps they would have believed. But I would have to be a certified moron to let it go this far."

Sarrault shook her head indulgently. Émile wanted to make a rude noise. In his six weeks aboard the *Mary Damned* he had come to the conclusion that the navigator was vain enough to prefer that they all face a Justica trial than anyone should think he didn't know his business.

The Captain shrugged fatalistically. "If we can bluff, it would be better. The boarding party will have to come through from the lock to the bridge. The officers will pretend to cooperate, so the boarding party calls off suspicion. Then, after they have checked in, and only if they go to inspect the cargo, then we hit them. If they don't check the cargo, then they have nothing to charge us with. We only fight if we have to. *Comprendez*?"

Saint-Just understood just fine. Growing up in Huit Fleurs with the *clochards* of the Quartier du Paris, he knew it was better to try and talk his way out of any situation. That didn't mean the *clochards* couldn't fight. Only that he had learned that it was more important to win.

But because of the undesirables in the Quartier he also had some little experience with a softknife. He went to his locker, shared with the two other apprentices, and pulled his personal knife from his compressed stowage compartment. He had charged it before he had left, but he checked the indicator anyway. Back in the Quartier one never was too sure of anything.

The charge was still high. He touched the short tang and watched as the fiber-optic filaments quivered and then tensed with power. Then he shut it down before he maneuvered back to the cargo bay. No sense using up good energy before the enemy even showed.

He joined Paul and Catherine in the cargo bay, anchored to the strapping on a carefully secured stack of bolts of hand-painted silk. One of Beau Soliel's better export items. Naturally the sadece senin was the most expensive, but since it was illegal they always carried permitted goods as well, to shut up the Zone authorities. It made customs checks a little less expensive.

Catherine was watching him. He felt her eyes on him and brought up his hand casually displaying the softknife. Catherine's dark eyes widened in surprise. Émile smiled. He couldn't tell whether her expression was revulsion or respect, but that didn't matter. She had noticed him and had seen that he wasn't merely any first-out apprentice.

No, even Catherine had to know that only in the Quartier did they use softknives. He would be proud to show her, later, the thin lacing of white scars that ran over his ribs and belly, thighs and shoulders. When they were alone, finally, he would show her, so that she wouldn't miss them in the soft light. Since he had become a trader the scars had faded into skin that was no longer tanned. Like every other runner he had worked hard to acquire the pallor that marked an outgone trader.

"Are we all here?" Jean-Louis asked nervously when he arrived. He was young and his nails were chewed down to the quick. Émile judged that this was his first trip as a full member of the crew. "Good. Then I want you all to hide over here." He indicated several large cases stamped as exotic foodstuffs. "The Captain said that I'll be responsible for leading the boarding party around storage. So I'll take them here, and show them this." He indicated a fairly enclosed area, boxes making a canyon that was cut off at one end. There was plenty of good hiding to catch enemies from above and behind. Émile decided that he had just a touch more respect for the purser.

"I'll stay here while you all hide, and then I'll look around and see if I can see you," Jean-Louis instructed.

Émile shifted two boxes of sadece senin, pushing the upper one out just enough to provide a small ledge. The sticky cord that kept the cargo in place tore and a length hung from the bottom of the upper box. Sloppy. Jean-Louis would never allow any cargo to be less than properly secured. But the Justica didn't know the purser and Émile figured the arrogant fools most likely did think that Free Traders weren't as careful as they were.

He lay flat on his belly in full view of the room holding the corner of the crate. One thing he knew for sure was that people almost never looked up. Even in zero-gee most preferred to pretend there was some local horizontal, no matter how arbitrary. And in his sturdy tan overalls he blended nicely with the packing.

"I can see you," Jean-Louis said.

Émile sighed, took a small carton and wedged it into the gap. Then he crouched behind it on the ledge created by the box underneath, his toes on the sticky rope surface holding him in place. "Now?" he asked.

"Wait," the purser answered. Then the officer cut the dangling rope, adjusted the boxes and inspected the whole effect. "Well, I wouldn't pass on it myself," he said reluctantly. "But it's not too bad at first glance."

Catherine found a spot between the silk bolts, a wrench on her belt and another in her hand. Émile could see her clearly from his perch and was pleased at her position. She was ready to close in from behind. He couldn't see Paul at all. The senior apprentice, with the long chef's knife he had brought aboard from his days as an artist and had never let anyone else touch, had opened a spare crate and hid inside. Honestly, Saint-Just wondered how Paul planned to get out. Or maybe he just planned to slip the knife through the slits in the crate. That would work perfectly well if any of the boarding party happened to get close enough.

Émile tried to smile encouragement at Catherine, who looked rather pale. Somehow it all seemed unreal and strangely funny.

He didn't honestly believe that they were being boarded, not at all. This was some elaborate joke, some farce that would end in a tangle of mixed identities. This was not a fight. He had left the violence when he had left Beau Soliel.

CHAPTER TWO

Émile awoke in a Justica holding pen, separated from his shipmates. He had a vile headache. Worse still, the cuff was gone. He felt around his arm. There had to be some kind of mistake. No one could take that from him, no one had the right.

"Whatcha in for, kid?" a man who looked old enough to be his grandfather asked.

"In for?" Émile asked, dazed. His head swam and his stomach protested strongly. At least no one had offered him food just yet. "I didn't do anything."

The old man grinned unpleasantly. "Well, you'll find out at your trial, I guess. They don't press anyone until they get a fair and speedy trial. By the numbers." Then he laughed hoarsely and pulled up his sleeve. A series of numbers had been marked in his arm. "Like I said, by the numbers. And if you got any skills at all you'll get life. Like everyone else."

He wished the old man would shut up. He didn't understand the Lingua Justica terribly well and the sound of it made his head worse. He ignored the man and pulled the blanket over his head. It smelled strongly of disinfectant, which he ignored. He slept again.

The next time he woke up he felt better. Catherine was sitting next to him and she had no cuff either. Her bright red hair lay limp on her shoulders. Émile thought it looked like a defeated flag.

"What happened?" he asked.

Catherine groaned. "Paul's already been tried. You're on the schedule, over there." She pointed to a screen secured

behind mesh. Émile saw his name and a time and date that
meant nothing to him.

"But how did we get here?" he asked.

Catherine's eyes widened. "They drugged us. Just opened
up the gas and hauled us off."

Rage burned in Émile's heart. "But they had no way to
know," he protested. "They have absolutely no honor. We
have rights."

Catherine laughed harshly and spat. "Yeah. Honor. Rights.
You've been out a long time; you didn't hear the old man.
That's how they get their crews, you know. The Justica Outtimers. Criminals. And if they don't have enough real criminals
to sentence to their prison ships, they send out press gangs.
They didn't know who we were or what we were carrying, and
they didn't care. Just trained humans to do the dirty work of
their little empire, and for free at that."

"I will protest," Émile said.

Catherine shook her head. "Only one way out, little brother.
When they ship you out. Open the face plate before the airlock
cycles through."

Without the cuffs they were nobody. They didn't belong
anywhere. He wanted to tell her that it wasn't that bad, but he
was afraid that it was.

A single tear tracked down her milk-smooth cheek. Saint-
Just raised a finger to brush it away. He wanted very much to
comfort her, to tell her not to despair. But Catherine was already
tough, already had the shell of a trader. There was nothing he
knew to say.

His trial lasted fifteen minutes and he didn't even know it
had begun until it was over. Three people sat in front of him
at a long bench, asked his name, his membership in the Syndicat
of Free Traders from the ArianeSpace colony Beau Soliel. His
age and his training and specialization in the Syndicat. And
then they pronounced sentence. Ten years labor in the outbound
lanes.

He was assigned to the *Constanza*, an ice miner refueling
the exploration ships of the Justica. He was shipped out directly
and was not even permitted to talk to Catherine before he left.
He never found out if she had relented from her despair. Anger

alone sustained him through the first weeks of transit until he was delivered to the ship that was his prison. Anger substituted very nicely for the fear he couldn't admit.

When he arrived on the *Constanza* he was assigned a berth in the aft net corridor along with maybe twenty others. So very different from the Syndicat, where only apprentices were in the corridor, and then there were only three or so of them. Everyone else got staterooms, even if they were too tiny to stretch out in and each was assigned double.

They had taken his tan overalls, his good watch, his sapphire earring, and his money (three hundred francs) as well as his cuff. There was a list of his belongings that he had to print that promised that everything that had been taken would be returned when he was released. He noticed that no one mentioned the Syndicat cuff and his heart raced. No, he told himself carefully, the officer had said *everything* quite distinctly, and the computer had translated into French so there was no question as to meaning.

His clothes were replaced with a dark green uniform worksuit that had a number stenciled in black over the left pocket. The fabric was stiff and heavy and the thing didn't fit well at all. It was far too big and chafed miserably whenever he moved. He also was given a pair of soft mocs that were a little too small. The officer, echoed by the computer translation, said they would stretch.

Thus attired, he was thrust into life on the prison ship with his first meal. He used the handgrips to propel himself through the hatch to the galley, which wasn't at all pleasant the way the one on the *Mary Damned* had been. The stench that rose from the trays was not anything he associated with food.

The people all around were a strange assortment, different colors and faces and body types from what he was used to. It seemed as if many of the larger men had created a uniform of sorts, their heads shaved, with strangely stiff tattoos on the scalp. When one of those men passed by, jostling another prisoner out of line to get seconds, Émile realized that the tattoo had been made by using melted plastic instead of ink in the skin. The plastic colors were strong primaries, nursery-school shades. On the prisoners they mocked and threatened together.

"Well, you gonna stay there and become a strut on the hull or you gonna eat?" A heavy older woman taunted him in such a heavily accented version of the Lingua Justica that he barely understood her.

He got in line, more to avoid her moistly malodorous aura than to eat. What he found in the tray under the plastic dome was distressing. He had no idea what it was. And to add insult, there was only a spoon to eat with. Émile managed to force down the first few bites but could not continue. No bread, it seemed, came with dinner. Nothing that he could identify as bread, anyway, and that more than anything else made Émile overwhelmingly depressed.

He had been braced for evil. This was, after all, prison. And a foreign prison, too, where no one spoke a word of French. The Lingua Justica flowed around in all accents too quickly for him to catch much of it. But no bread with a meal—that was unthinkable. On Beau Soliel even the worst offenders had bread to eat.

Hungry and nauseous at the same time, Émile dumped the entire tray down the disposal chute. He was of half a mind to follow it, if only the chute hadn't been so narrow. Catherine's solution seemed very reasonable now.

"You Émile Saint-Just?" a large man behind him asked.

Émile didn't bother to turn. "How did you know?" he responded.

"We don't get new faces in here often," the man said, and his voice was both soft and somewhat cultured. Émile was impressed. "You're on the work list under my crew. Thought I'd introduce myself before you actually showed up tomorrow. So you wouldn't be so isolated."

Émile shook his head. He knew it was more polite to say something about the kindness, but he didn't have the strength to face anyone. And he didn't want to make the effort to find the words in the unpleasant language that was common here. So far he had not heard one accent that indicated another speaker of *la belle langue* among what seemed to be nearly a hundred or so who crewed the ship.

"Is there anyone else on this cursed ship who speaks French?" he asked miserably.

The big man did not answer right away. "Information like

that costs around here,'' he said finally. ''The Hounds have a pretty good data gang going, but they're only connected in the usual. You want something a little more specialized, you come to me. But, well, for a first day here, I'll give you that information. And the answer is no. I've never heard of anyone speaking French. Or from any of the Ariane colonies on this bucket.''

Émile hissed but said nothing. Strictly speaking, the Justica didn't really have any authority over the ArianeSpace colonies. Even if there were only half a dozen of them, three speaking French, two German and one Italian, they were still technically under the jurisdiction of the European Economic Community that had sponsored them.

Trade treaties stated that any infractions in nonterritorial space were to be handled by the original countries of Earth whose flags the colony ships flew. Those laws were still on the books, antiquated, like the laws that stated that colonial governments could not be seated until their credentials were approved by their sponsoring administrative national/multinational group. In practice that had become a joke. By the time a government for Beau Soliel had been approved by the EEC, their grandchildren would be in power. Thirty years each way for communications meant that four or five constitutions could be written and fall by the time there was any word.

So while Beau Soliel could complain along with the other ArianeSpace colonies, and had at one point considered doing so, they could not remove the Justica from their self-appointed role as enlightened imperialists. Émile knew that much history. More, he knew something about reality, and the law of the street was that the big guy usually won.

The next morning he reported to his labor delegation. The work itself was hard and frequently dangerous, but no more so than on any ship out of the Zones. He was assigned to apprentice on the ceramic superconductor links that laced the outer hull. It was interesting, a high-level specialization in the Syndicat and even on a prison ship. It took some intelligence, too, which meant that there weren't any members of the prison gang on the detail. Not a one of the six assigned to the hull had the bright plastic insignia melted into their skins. And he wasn't a miner, going down the gravity well and hauling blocks of ice out of the environment.

Besides, his supervisor was Hugo Gorvitz, one of the few prisoners who seemed to command a silent respect from not only the other inmates but even the few Justica officers aboard. Gorvitz was a huge, bearish man with a penetrating mind and a technical competence that rivaled anything Émile had ever seen. The first day they were out on the hull, Gorvitz had pointed out the sickly green veins that ran across the hull.

"Isn't the exposure dangerous?" Saint-Just asked.

Gorvitz threw back his head and laughed deeply. "Makes our lives real easy, kid," he said. "We don't have to worry about cooling materials unless we get in close to any system. Which we don't because we're outbound, but that doesn't matter. Comes in close and we just cover it all up in reflectives. Doesn't even have to be strong stuff. Just enough to keep the light off. No, what we have to worry about here is the actual electron stream and breaks in the line. And keeping the power feeds clean. You won't be doing that for a while, though. Right now I just want you to take a good look at that color. Memorize it. Any deviations from that shade and we link up a new segment. Then you'll get a chance to mix up a batch in the oven. Just like Christmas cake."

Émile Saint-Just looked out to the stars. They were outbound, and there were only a few and those faint. He wondered about Catherine then, vitally aware that Gorvitz couldn't stop him if he chose to open his mask now. To die. It would be so very easy, so very painful, so elegant and final.

He had known he had to be a spacer since he was ten years old and his parents had taken him down to the Blessing of the Ships. Every year at the port was a grand outdoor Mass under the raging violet sky of Beau Soleil. Half the city went to pray and the other half went to sell them things. Temporary stalls and tables were set up against the pink and turquoise and citron-yellow buildings of the port. His father had bought them all sugar *crêpes* twisted into paper cones and extra large cups of frothy orangata that somehow tasted better out at the port than on the fashionable Boulevard Lafitte for twice the price. There had been cheap trinkets for sale, too, fragile and shiny imitations of Syndicat cuffs and religious medals and squirt guns and wind-up ducks that swam around in a bucket. Papa, in an unusually generous mood, had bought him one of the light fake bracelets and he had worn it for months, until the finish had oxidized and turned his wrist black.

The Mass had been held out on the barge lanes themselves. There was no danger, his father had assured him. All the barges were in Port for this occasion. It was their own festival and celebration. Around the platform that had been set up as an altar were several models of the Syndicat long-haul ships, all decked out in flowers and ribbons with their names painted brightly in gold and silver and copper. He had joined the crowd before the Mass going up to them and reading off the names. They were so brave and bright. He had reached out to touch, to stroke the glittering fiber arrays that rode the lateral banks.

"No, no, no." Maman had taken his hand gently and held him back. "They aren't just models, Émile. They're the AIs for the new ships. The ships are too big and aren't made to come down to atmosphere, so they are in models to be baptized before they go out."

Émile knew about baptism. He was ten and Sister Marie Bernard de l'Ange had already explained it in catechism. It seemed reasonable that someone brought the AIs down and did them all together, since they didn't have parents and a parish and godparents to make arrangements.

Just then there had been a blare of test-music from the loud-speakers and they had to scurry around to find places on the large open field. Since they had been up by the models, all the good places had been taken and they were way in the back. His father had lifted Émile on his shoulders so he could see it all.

The regular Mass part was mostly boring. Not that his family ever went, so he didn't understand it very well, and the loud-speakers distorted the sound so he couldn't even hear clearly. But when the priest turned around and sprinkled water on the models and the barges, the fiber-optic bands had flooded with light. AI to AI to the barges and even the small Zone drones and the ferries, arcs of colored brilliance interlaced and created a sparkling lattice. The priest finished, and the people all surged forward again under that canopy of light that Émile could see was the ships' own expression of joy.

Then his father had bought them more *crêpes* and *sorbet*, and Émile decided before the long ride home that he would join the Syndicat. He had overeaten and gotten a stomach ache but that didn't dull the wonder and the desire.

He didn't want to take Catherine's way out. Not now, not yet. He looked out one more time into the empty darkness and saw Gorvitz's dark gaze on him. The big man was watching, curious, waiting, and Émile realized that he was being given the choice. Catherine couldn't have been the only person to take the easy way. If she even had. He met Gorvitz's eyes through the clear shield and then firmly focused on the hull, on the work at hand.

Except for the gang members, the other prisoners were generally interesting. There was Lee Xi Chu, who ran the ice tugs, and the doctor, a wizened and bent woman who looked like a storybook witch but was brilliant when she was coherent. Mostly she wasn't, muttering to herself and staying in the sick bay doing experiments even when she had no patients.

And there was Pauli Tree. At least that's what she called herself, although Saint-Just suspected that it was just one of several names. She had been a safecracker and thief, a break-in artist of the first rank to hear her tell it. Émile only half listened to her stories, certain that most were exaggeration. He liked her attitude, her confidence. It reminded him of Catherine and of the other women he had known in the Syndicat. If she exploited her position as the most attractive woman aboard, he didn't really care.

There were only two officers, and the rest of the crew saw them rarely. Their major link to the Justica proper was the assignments board and the heat sensors that plotted the position and emotional state of every prisoner aboard. But even then the officers stayed well out of it.

He had been aboard the *Constanza* for nearly six months when a new prisoner was brought aboard. Émile didn't see him at all at first, only heard the hushed rumor around the galley. That he was from Leemo or Court Zone, somewhere real heavy Justica, and that Justica was his first language.

"Got to watch for that one," Fox said. Fox was one of the older Hounds, and not one of the brighter ones. Not that any of the Hounds of Hell, the prison gang, were exactly university material. But Fox usually didn't say anything at all unless he was put up to it by Shadow or Frag, who passed as heavy brain as far as the gang was concerned. So Émile didn't bother with Fox's warning any more than he listened to anything Fox had to say.

Besides, the Hounds were mostly drawn from Old Program worlds, early colonies settled by independents who wanted their own claim worlds. Very standoffish and not very social, they were a culture that personified what Émile thought of as uncivilized.

He had come to that conclusion at the end of his first month aboard, when one of the younger Hounds called Ice had told him to keep away from Pauli. It was during recreation, which was when everything happened on board the *Constanza*. Even the Hounds weren't stupid enough to take risks in hard vacuum. But the single oversized common area that was the gym and prison yard and recreation hall all at once could have been designed to instigate trouble. There was too much going on, too many noises, and conflicts about entertainment and music and all the things free people beat each other raw over.

So he'd been listening to some musical thing he didn't understand and Ice came over and ordered him away from Pauli. Ice was maybe only two years or so older than Émile, muscled and filled out by age and genes and hard living. But even large muscles and an imposing tattoo in hot pink and yellow and turquoise served only to fuel Saint-Just's pride. "I think the lady in question has some say in the matter," he replied coolly.

The Hounds surrounded him, Fox and Chicken and Frag and Shadow, faces that Émile couldn't read. All of them with their shaved skulls decorated with burned-in plastic designs. Pauli told him that they were done with melted toothbrushes. Given the state of the Hounds' teeth, those teeth they still had, Émile was not surprised they had chosen to sacrifice oral hygiene. Even Ice, who was one of the most presentable of the gang, was missing an incisor and had chipped two others.

One of Ice's oversized meat-paws clamped on Émile's shoulder and the next thing Émile knew was that blood fountained from his nose. He didn't remember the blow, only the laughing gang members. He spit and his saliva was pink. He wondered if he was going to match Ice's gap-tooth smile.

"So what do you say, skin virgin? You gonna take some well-meant advice?"

Free Trader just took over. Memories of Elisabeth Sarrault and Michel and Chief Rimbeau all combined at once. Émile steadied himself on a handgrip and narrowed his eyes with contempt. "Softknives," he sneered. "Or don't you know how to use one?"

He had been ready to back it up. Not that he wanted to fight the Hound. There were too many of them and he would most likely lose. But he would lose a lot more by backing down, and there was no way he was going to permit this half-wit to show him up. He would think of something before the next rec.

And then the other Hounds laughed. Frag and Shadow and Fox and Chicken, their faces screwed into something aping humor, that was a terrifying sight. Émile almost thought they were having seizures.

"Well enough," Frag said. "Let him go. Good enough for me. Kid, you want a tattoo?"

Émile had wanted to say something about preferring his teeth and bit it back. Instead he answered steadily that he was simply not interested. Ice had clapped him on the back, hard enough to shoot him halfway across the rec into two older prisoners playing chess.

Hugo Gorvitz explained enough about the Hounds later. "The Hounds," Hugo said, "are useful. To each other because they need the structure of a firm hierarchy and the identity of their own place in it. Old Program worlds are like that. You're born into a certain segment of society and you know exactly what is expected of you for the rest of your life. In a way the Hounds are all rebels, since all of them found their way into crime and out of there.

"And they're very useful to me," Gorvitz added.

Émile understood. He had seen the large man manipulate the gang members on more than one occasion. It was a skill that Émile was trying to learn by emulation. The incident with Ice had bought him the gang's wait-and-see. He still didn't have their respect. Nor did he care. His desire to talk to the new prisoner and maybe find out what had happened to the rest of the crew of the *Mary Damned* was much more important than anything the Hounds could want from him.

The new prisoner was male, dark skinned and cast with the mixed characteristics Émile had seen in passing on a few of the prisoners and all the Justica officials. The Justica had a strong dislike of any ethnic/racial group that had kept some identity beside the officially approved Justica. So far as the Justica was concerned, such an identity was elitist. Émile believed wholeheartedly that being *anything* particular was better than being Justica, and was more than certain that he was a member of that superior breed.

But so far the info on the Justica connection seemed accurate. Émile approached the man carefully. He was older than Émile, fully muscled and powerful. His face was completely emotionless.

"I am Émile Saint-Just of Beau Soliel," Émile introduced himself carefully. "I had wanted to know if you had heard anything about my former shipmates, or knew anyone in Justica custody from my homeworld. Or if you had any news at all about Beau Soliel."

The man smiled unpleasantly. "It'll cost you," he said.

Émile had expected this standard answer of prison life, although from someone newly incarcerated it indicated that perhaps he had prior experience. "Let me hear what you got first," Émile countered.

The new prisoner shrugged. "Not a lot. Nobody hears anything about Beau Soliel anyway. Not that important. But I did hear about someone named David Rimbeau while I was in the holding pen. And someone named Jean-Louis Marchand. That interest you?"

Émile nodded and swallowed hard. Just hearing their names was painful. He wasn't sure he wanted to know much more. "What do you want?"

The man thought for a moment. "Gorvitz," he said. "I want to know his connects."

"Can't do," Émile responded. "Gorvitz is tighter than a hull in vacuum. Can't get it from him no way."

"But you're his boy, aren't you?" The man's eyes glowed with innuendo. "So you can get it."

Émile was so infuriated that he was ready to swing at the stranger immediately. Not so much for the assumption about

his relationship to Gorvitz as for the one about how he would
be willing to use it. His honor did not bend that far. And then
he decided that he had no choice but to let the affront pass for
now. This person was not important. What he knew was. There
would be a way, later, to avenge the insult.

"Tell me what you know," Émile said evenly. "I'll get you
something useful. Cigs to trade with the Hounds. Or a softknife."

The prisoner licked his lips at the mention of the weapon.
"Marchand was sentenced to twenty years aboard the *Carmel*.
He didn't resist and was transferred last I heard. Rimbeau, that
one was a Drive Chief, right? No way the Justica's going to
lose those skills. He got life aboard the *Lowsten*, outbound.
But there was something else about him. I didn't pay too much
attention to the gossip. But—let me think. Yes, I believe there
was some kind of accident aboard that ship that blew the mains.
Something like that. No survivors, of course. But as to whether
it was before or after your shipmate got there I couldn't say.
You know how time plays tricks outbound."

Émile didn't respond. He could only think of Chief Rimbeau,
careful and gentle with his instruments, lovingly setting them
just out of synch. Just enough to record his protest, as it were.

Then he insisted that couldn't be true. Rimbeau loved his
machines, would never willingly destroy them. But David Rimbeau had loved his life, too, Émile knew. And without the
Mary Damned there was nothing else. Not for any of them.

"So when do I get my knife?" the new prisoner asked.

"It'll take a little time to make. I've got a gym period
scheduled for the day after next. It's on the board. Come by
then."

Émile didn't want to see anyone. All he could think about
was his old Chief calmly making a decision to kill himself and
an entire crew of prisoners. David Rimbeau would do it ra-
tionally, carefully, being sure that the majority of those on the
Lowsten were in agreement. Not like Catherine might have, in
a fury, but a gentle and considered operation that was no more
than sense. Saint-Just didn't know why he didn't agree, but he
found himself furious at Rimbeau.

Shadow, the head Hound, sought Émile out that night. "You

didn't come to dinner," he informed Saint-Just. "You talked to the new guy."

"It isn't your business," he answered Shadow evenly. When dealing with the Hounds it wasn't a good idea to show any emotion at all. They sensed fear, which was why Émile decided they were called the Hounds. Like the dogs they were.

But Shadow wasn't threatening, taking on any poses. Ice was with him and hanging back respectfully. "Anything strange about this person?" Shadow asked almost politely. "He say anything that makes you think he isn't right?"

Suddenly Émile trusted Shadow, at least on this. He told the Hound leader about how it was very strange that someone so new would know about Gorvitz and his connections, and that he should have heard of two of Émile's shipmates.

Shadow listened intently. Obviously this much concentration was difficult for him. He thought for a long time, relying on Ice to keep him anchored to the grip while he considered. Then he came to a conclusion. "The guy's a narc."

Émile swallowed. He hadn't thought of that. He'd heard of narcs, of course. When they were found out, they were spaced during a work assignment. That was the safest way to get rid of the body. But he'd been so proud of following Gorvitz's example that he'd never thought of an informer planted on them.

"Why?" he asked.

"You ask Gorvitz," Shadow said. "And we expect you to deal with this scum." Shadow left.

Ice lingered for a moment and gave Émile a look that was close to fraternal. "Newest guy always gets the dirty jobs," he said sympathetically, before he followed Shadow one more time.

The next day he asked Gorvitz about getting a minizap battery. Hugo looked at him quizzically and then smiled. "You're gonna want some fiber optics, too, aren't you? Been a long time since I made one of those babies. Planning to test it out on someone?"

Émile didn't respond, but that didn't stop Gorvitz from making guesses. "The new guy, right? And the Hounds are in on it too, I'll bet. Well, supplies are no problem. But it'll cost you."

Émile rolled his eyes. "What do you want?" he asked by
rote.

Gorvitz studied him carefully. "I want you to take the informer out. Not set him up for the Hounds. They've got too
much power already on board. And I need you to do it. For
you."

Émile didn't understand the bargain but he made the softknife. Completely harmless when the power was off, not much
to speak of when it was on. Except at the very tips of the live
energy fibers that glittered with deadly light. The whip end
hung softly in zero-gee, the fibers reaching out to their full
length. Gorvitz made the grip from ceramic and they baked it
in the oven; then Saint-Just covered it with layers of adhesive
bandages.

Stupid of the Justica to place schedules on prison gyms.
After so long in the business they should know about that.
Émile thought it was more likely they didn't care. Only two
officers aboard the *Constanza*, and he hadn't seen either of
them down in crew zone since he had been aboard. So what
did they care that the gym automatically entered his ID on the
screen schedule, a perfect announcement to the informer that
he was alone?

Riding the pressure wheel, he didn't see the new prisoner
come in. Didn't know anyone was there until the resistance
got so high that he couldn't push the platforms jumping with
both feet. It just launched him off in another direction, across
the open center of the gym toward the construction corner. He
caught one of the struts and twisted to face the new prisoner,
who waited for him there. It was an impressive show of skill.
Just as he had intended.

The construction corner was a maze of bars at strange angles
that was the basis for zero-gee gymnastics. Not quite as required
as the pressure wheel and other resistance to keep muscle tone
intact, but very useful in learning to maneuver through the
Constanza with reasonable aptitude.

"Just tell me the names and we're even," the informer said
soullessly.

"Right," Émile said. Then he twisted around the bars, using
the push for momentum and launched himself at the heavily
muscled older man. The narc tumbled in an inelegant somer-

sault but managed to elude Émile. And Saint-Just floated past, overshot, and had lost too much energy to double back.

Good enough, Émile thought, letting himself drift. He relaxed and let the atmospheric resistance do the rest. The informer came after him, spewing sweat, but his punch only served to propel Émile further back, and the new prisoner himself reacted by being pushed in the opposite direction. Émile used the extra energy to hit the wall and spring forward, diving straight for his adversary.

Obviously his opponent, while stronger and larger than Émile, was far less comfortable in zero-gee. And as Émile realized this, he started to change his strategy. Not the kind of fight he'd seen a few times in the gym where the antagonists were both completely mobile and free. This person was going to try and use his mass to hammer at Émile the way he would in a gravity well. And all that was going to do was spin him around harder.

This time Émile took the time to get ready. He braced on a grip, coiled against the inner mat and judged the distance. Then he launched on a diagonal, giving a half-twist as he passed the bulkier man. Suddenly the softknife was in his hand, held out in front of him, glittering wickedly violet and shivering with power held in tension.

The informer eyed the knife greedily and thrashed around trying to get to Saint-Just. Émile pulled himself into a ball and rotated rapidly, the softknife filaments flaring behind him like a tail. The passing fiber barely kissed the hair on the other man's hand and a brilliant purple light arced and died.

The narc screamed. Émile used the power of the roll to lash out again with more force and precision. This time he got his enemy across the face, but he didn't see the damage immediately. He was too busy getting over to the far mat for a new push.

When he got hold of the mat grip and turned, the first thing he noticed was that he wasn't alone. Gorvitz and Shadow were both near the door, watching. The second thing Saint-Just saw was that his opponent was blind. His last lash across the face had swept across the man's eyes, a hideous smoking trail only partly covered by the man's beefy hands and climbing howl.

"Do it," Gorvitz said. "You owe me."

Émile looked at his supervisor in horror. He had beaten the
narc; neutralized him, just as he'd promised. Taken him out
of the action. There was no possibility that he was going to
kill anyone, let alone someone already fairly beaten and un-
defended. Maybe if he had to save his own life, maybe. But
there was no reason and he refused.

He made it quite clear to Gorvitz. The older man looked
sorrowful. "Some day you're going to have to give up this
impossible innocence of yours," he said. "Don't you know
that if you let him live, he'll give you to *them*?"

"We'll take care of it," Shadow said. Fox and Chicken
came in as if they had been waiting in the maze and started to
bind the narc.

Gorvitz shook his head. "His blood isn't their responsibil-
ity," he said, looking over to the Hounds, now dragging the
blinded narc through the hatch. "You're willing enough to
play, but not to take care of your own dirt. You're not worth
anything, not as long as you're too fastidious to do it yourself."

Émile squeezed his eyes shut, trying to will the situation
away. Bile rose in his throat and he could feel the sweat rising
to break on his skin. He wanted to not exist, to dissolve utterly
and be free of these men and this place, and most of all what
they insisted that he do.

"Ready," someone said. Émile thought it was Chicken. He
opened his eyes and saw the narc trussed and helpless, held
floating by the white rope like a meal ready for a spider. The
narc's eyes were wide with terror and disbelief. Chicken smiled
thinly and passed the rope over to Émile.

Émile held the end of the rope. Gorvitz and Shadow took
him by the shoulders and propelled him out of the gym, down
the main shaft to the hull exit, and opened the first double lock.
Chicken placed the trussed body in the enclosed space while
Émile looked on, paralyzed. Gorvitz slammed the hatch shut
and sealed it with a twist.

"Now," Gorvitz said to Émile, and pushed him until his
nose hit the controls. "Do it."

Saint-Just stared at the buttons. He had never really noticed
them before, a combination that he played at least weekly to
get out to check the ceramic lacing. If he didn't *think* about it
. . . He willed his fingers up to the pad, but his hand was

trembling so hard that he couldn't get the right sequence.

He inhaled deeply and thought of Chief David Rimbeau. Rimbeau had been the one who had printed his newly incised cuff into the personality-brain of the *Mary Damned*. There, in that strange perception of space, the gentle mechanic had introduced him to the fire-sprite that was the ship. The AI had closed in on them, flooding him with itself, and his perception had quivered and dissolved. It was Rimbeau who had stayed with him, steadying, soothing the ship's personality and introducing them like a matron at a convent-school dance.

After that, Chief Rimbeau had always been especially good to him, teaching him enough to pass his rating exams, helping out with the late shifts, somehow producing an *éclair* for his birthday. Even encouraging him subtly in the matter of Catherine, although Émile knew it went against both Rimbeau's preferences and personal interest. Émile was not so indifferent that he didn't catch or even appreciate Rimbeau's quiet affection. He was only sorry he could not reciprocate.

This was for Chief Rimbeau, he told himself. This was revenge. This was simply justice. He keyed the airlock faster than he could think the combination.

The warning light went on and the alarm began its count. He could hear thumps from behind the hatch and then he couldn't hear anything more.

"Why don't you go now?" Chicken asked as the light faded back to green. "I'll clean up the rest."

Émile shook his head and waited. The horror of it was too new, too plain. When the door opened and he saw the splattered blood and bits of clinging flesh, the remnants of explosive decompression, he wanted to be sick. He felt dizzy, nauseous, and clung to the nearest strut for support.

Chicken patted his arm awkwardly. "It gets easier after the first time."

chapter
three

After that he lost track of time and nurtured his fury at the Justica until it became something refined and rare. He could see through them now, and that comprehension changed the bitterness to ideology and theory into compassion. The Justica used them. Not because they were criminals and had to be punished or removed from society, but because no sane person would choose to leave time. This had nothing at all to do with justice and everything to do with economics. It was not a thing that Shadow or Fox would understand at all.

The Justica couldn't run without their fleet, without the ice miners and the slow scows and the resupply ships. Unlike the Syndicat, there were many of them in the logistics side without enough wealth to tempt newcomers to sign on and eventually move up. In the Syndicat Émile had every intention of becoming a trader himself with a stake in the ship and a future in the Syndicat. Which meant a future on Beau Soleil. No matter how time dilated around him, there was always the home structure of the Palais to return to. And there were always those who wanted to join the Free Traders, some for the adventure and some for the profits and some to erase their past. The Syndicat didn't care who you had been before, and once out on the lanes time would take care of the rest. All you had to do was qualify and come up with money for a stake.

Not that he had a real history when he had joined the Syndicat. Not like Jacques Cher, his first instructor when he had come to the Palais. Even Jacques Cher's name wasn't the original, although his class could well understand why he'd want to change it. It hadn't been French to start with, after all.

No, Jacques Cher had come from one of the Justica worlds,

one of the would-be artists drawn by Beau Soliel's hypnotic violet sky, artistic community and reputation. The apprentice Free Traders under him speculated differently. There were several failed artists in the Syndicat, but Jacques Cher alone no longer drew or went to galleries or followed the scene down in the Quartier du Paris.

Émile thought he knew who Jacques Cher really was and how he had gotten his stake to join the Syndicat. There was a story some of the artists told down in Lola's, the local chess parlor. A very long time ago, maybe fifty or sixty years before anyone in Lola's had been born, there had been an amazing heist. Two Klees brought from Earth had been cut from their frames at the Musée Roche and never recovered. The Roche trustees had put up a reward that had sat collecting interest for more than half a century and was rumored to be in the neighborhood of two million. The paintings had been the only example of Klee's work on Beau Soliel, and even the Swiss-backed Ariane colony had only one.

There was an original Klee hanging in the Palais. Émile recognized it not because he knew so much about art but because he had seen the other.

At fourteen, the Klee hadn't made much of an impression. His parents had been invited to the section head's home for dinner, one of those average business things that were necessary in life. His father had been a mid-level officer in the Banc and had always seemed a little embarrassed by the fact they lived in the Quartier. That was Maman's one absolute. She had given up being the model and muse for half the Institute of Painting to marry, but she categorically refused to leave the Quartier, where she had once been a minor celebrity in the *café* world.

And, for all her appearances, Maman had never become quite respectable. So Émile thought it was quite normal that, during this miserably stuffy party with the entire Mergers Division, she smiled and invited him in a whisper to explore the rest of the house. Maman always explored people's houses, their most private spaces, and then when they got home would tell Papa all the dirt. Not that it was really dangerous. Papa was too respectable for blackmail and Maman wasn't greedy enough to bother.

Maman didn't merely go through the rooms, she went into

the cabinets and the closets, commenting the whole time. "Look at this," she'd say, pulling underwear out of a drawer. "This is the Director with a salary of over three hundred thousand francs a year and he buys irregulars. No silk at all. Hmmm. And just look at the holes in these socks!" Having been an artists' model, Maman set great store by underwear.

They found the painting in a locked study behind a drape. Locks didn't bother Maman any more than drawers did. She always said that she wore hairpins for more than one reason. So they got through the door and into the plain room with a single draped wall, and Maman pulled back the heavy brown curtain and there was the Klee, too insouciant by far for that place.

For the first time ever Émile saw his mother stunned beyond words. When she did finally speak, her voice was only a whisper. "One of the Klees," she murmured, as if in prayer.

Thoughts of the reward haunted his sleep for weeks. Émile resisted. He was first and forever Quartier, and he didn't narc, and besides there was his father's position at the bank.

Two years later his father was passed over for another promotion, got drunk and tripped on the railing in the *rapide*. The police and the priests ruled it accidental death due to alcohol rather than suicide, so he was buried from the church. A week later, no names mentioned, the Roche had recovered one of the Klees and a certain Bank Director had resigned under pressure. Mme. Saint-Just bought into a chic gallery and took over a house on the Place Baudelaire. And Émile had the thirty-five-thousand-franc stake to escrow along with the ten thousand (nonrefundable) for Syndicat selection.

"If you really want to hurt the Justica," Gorvitz said when they were working on the hull, "you could help out on the next fly-by. When we make the ice delivery to the *Blue Nile*. You're on the transfer crew."

Émile's eyes grew wide. Of course he was on the crew; as a low security risk with a good record on board he was given a few freedoms. He had never considered striking a real blow against the *flics*, something that could do more damage than symbolic action. The possibility was frightening.

So when the *Blue Nile* came, Émile was on the hull, tethered and wearing fully magnetized boots, with a tiny relay in his hand. As he worked unhooking the chunks of ice from the trailer rings he attached the relay pins, one at a time, to the cables as the haulers came to take them away. Right at the nub of the ring, where Gorvitz had said their contact on the *Blue Nile* would find them.

Émile never knew what those relays were, but he suspected they were parts in weapons, some of them, and that the flat ones held data that was damaging in some way to the Justica. He knew better than to ask. What shocked him was that it was so easy, that no one suspected him at all. Perhaps it was because he was from an Ariane colony, with decidedly few attachments to the Justica planets. The European Community always had a vague distrust for the two sponsoring superpowers of the Justica. One was too brash and headstrong, the other was paranoid and headstrong.

Or maybe they just let him on the job because his record was clean. Gorvitz had done a good job of covering up the death of the narc.

And then the *Blue Nile* went on, leaving silently with its ice supply. There was no word at all.

He was becoming truly expert on outsystems superconductors. And he was young enough to think of everything in terms of change. A year was still a long time, a large fraction of life. Ten or twenty years of subjective time was beyond his imagination.

One time a new prisoner came aboard who had heard about the *Mary Damned*. This was the real thing; she didn't know that he owed her for the information and she gave it readily.

Well, perhaps not readily. Her face went white at the mention of the ship and she swallowed hard. "It's just a story," she protested. "I mean, you know how some people are. But I don't believe that. I mean, ghost ships and all. That's like, there were stories about that forever, and who knew what. No, I think that maybe it's just another spacer story."

"Tell it to me anyway," he said softly, encouraging her the way Gorvitz would have so that she would talk. And she did.

"There's a song about it, the *Mary Damned*," the woman began dreamily. "That's about all. That there's this legend that the ship was filled with treasure, and suddenly disappeared.

And when it was found far from the normal lanes the crew was gone and the cargo hold was full. But that's obviously inaccurate because if the hold had been full, why hasn't this treasure shown up anywhere? But that's the story. And she's considered bad luck. My sister said that whoever saw the *Mary Damned* knew they were going to die within a day. My sister is not a reliable source of information.''

Émile had nodded graciously and thanked the woman. He even paid her, six Shaawar cigs, for the information. And he told no one, not even Gorvitz, not even Pauli. The idea of a ghost ship was laughable, and yet there was just enough truth in the story that he felt a touch of chill.

That was the first report. Then Axel, destined to become a new Hound and Shadow's strongman, came aboard and brought more stories of sightings by various Zone personnel before a drone had exploded in the lock, killing fifteen people. Axel believed that the ghost ship was absolutely real.

But he wanted to go home, to see Beau Soleil again, to spend the nights under her insane purple sky. Off shift he began to tell Pauli about his dream, about going home where they could relax in the culture and civilization of Huit Fleurs where the Justica could never gain a stranglehold.

''No, you don't want to do that,'' Pauli told him late at night, in private. ''I went home once, after my first term. You don't realize how the time goes. I mean, I was on an inside ship for that one, first offense, no previous record, rehabilitation rating high. Inside even, and when I got home after serving two years subjective I found all my friends were gone or dead and my family didn't know me. It had only been ten years their time. I never did know just how hard it was till then. And we're outbound now. That makes the time dilation worse and worse until there's nothing left at all.''

''That's why we have the Syndicat,'' Émile told her. ''Doesn't matter how out of synch it gets, the Palais doesn't change and our position on Beau Soleil doesn't change. But what I wouldn't give to walk under that crazy sky again, breathe air without a mask, eat fresh good food. No food anywhere is like the food on Beau Soleil. There's this one *café*, Café de la Montagne, that has the best *beignets* in the whole universe. Sometimes, it's really stupid to think this, but sometimes I miss *beignets* more than I miss anything else about freedom.''

Pauli hadn't laughed at him. She nodded. ''It's always the little stuff that's the hardest. The stuff you don't think about. But what are *beignets*?''

His mouth watered as he described the deep-fried dough puffs covered with powdered sugar. About the *café* where all the people of Huit Fleurs gathered at different times of day, the wealthy matrons out shopping with their friends and daughters in the afternoon, the patrons of the clubs and salons and parlors in the early night and the residents of the Quartier itself in the cold dark hours of the morning. Home. Some things even time couldn't erase, time that was the greatest enemy of flesh. Time that the Justica used in its blind cruelty to separate him from his people. Time that passed on the *Constanza* without reference home, unbroken except by the next iceball, the next refueling point, the next set of relays frozen to the cable rings.

''I wish I could do more,'' he said once as they pulled away from a rendezvous with the *Harry Ye*.

''We all do,'' Gorvitz agreed. ''Until we get rid of the Justica leeches there'll always be something for us to do.''

And then the witch doctor called him in.

They called her the witch doctor because of how she looked. Sentenced to life on the *Constanza*, she was already very old and a little crazy. She also prescribed unscientific remedies like brandy and honey tea and everyone aboard was sure she was a boozer. Only Gorvitz had ever shut them up on the subject. So Émile was shocked when he found himself summoned to sick bay.

He hated this part of the ship. It smelled like the blanket in the holding cell had and reminded him of that time. And everything was pale puke green, the color of sickness and mold and decay. But he went because not to go would mean a mark on his record and he wanted out more than he wanted anything. They had said ten years and they owed him, and Émile Saint-Just intended to walk.

Gorvitz was waiting with the witch doctor in her office, which Émile didn't understand at all. ''You're doing well,'' Gorvitz said. ''Keeping out of trouble. Been a long time now. You keep going like this and you're up for parole on the next fly-by.'' Gorvitz smiled at him. "Looks like you're going to walk, Émile. Be happy to get home?''

"Everyone prefers to be home,'' Saint-Just answered cagily.

"True. But since it looks like you're going to make it, which not most of us on this ship can say, would you like to do one last little job to make life for the Justica just a little more exciting?''

Émile hoped he knew what was coming. They were limited as to what they could do on the *Constanza*. Prison, after all, was supposed to be restrictive. But to do something truly daring, something that would make the Justica look like fools while enhancing the honor of Beau Soleil and incidentally Émile Saint-Just—the opportunity to do this was something he had dreamed about. "It would be my pleasure to assist in any small way that might make life for our underappreciated overlords a touch more interesting.''

Gorvitz smiled broadly. "Excellent. Because, you see, we have a little proposition to make that should make life very uncomfortable for our green-robed friends. The doctor here has created a retrovirus. One that becomes part of any person's DNA. It can't be detected by any retina scan or fingerprints since it actually becomes part of your own genetic makeup. I don't pretend to know the biology, but I do know that it won't spread unless someone actually shares blood with a person who's been engineered. We need to get this stuff off the *Constanza* before any of the Justica clowns try to find it. One little injection is all it takes.''

Émile narrowed his eyes. "Why don't you do it, then?'' he asked, miserably disappointed.

"Because we're not leaving,'' the old doctor snapped back. "You know the basics of genetic engineering. Use a perfectly harmless virus and infect you. The virus carries the new DNA to be incorporated. Happens naturally. Virus doesn't hurt you at all. And you can't spread it, not unless you give your blood to someone.''

"And what is this DNA going to do to me?'' Émile asked, bored.

"You just smuggle it out,'' the doctor said brusquely. "Then we recover it and use it against the Justica. A plague.''

Émile glanced at Gorvitz with a silent plea to be rescued. "Great. And what about me?"

"Émile, this is more dangerous than anything a hundred Hounds could come up with. You know enough to understand that the virus won't be active until it's stimulated by a secondary virus, which we'll be smuggling separately," Gorvitz said smoothly. "But getting this technology out is vital to the effort, believe me.

"And getting it out won't hurt your chances at parole. I can't tell you how or where, but we'll send someone after you. You get the stuff out, you get the benefits yourself, and then all you do is donate a few cc's of blood to someone who mentions my name. And then you're in contact with the Party, the underground opposition, yourself, as a loyalist who has risked a great deal for the cause."

Émile's eyes narrowed. "Is this what you meant? Is this your big plan to get us all out?"

The witch doctor cackled. "He's good, Hugo. I told you he was a good one."

"Have I ever told you something was important when it wasn't?" Gorvitz demanded. "Believe me, it is. It's my fault. I keep trying to treat you like a Party member and I keep forgetting you're just a hotheaded kid who doesn't have any discipline. But maybe I should put it like this. What we want you to smuggle out is very dangerous to the Justica. It could be the thing that destroys them."

Something about Gorvitz convinced him. Maybe it was the years of working together, his own assessment of the older man's abilities and character. Maybe it was hypnosis, maybe only the need to make this moment different from the others. Whatever. He nodded his head.

The witch doctor smiled and rolled up her sleeve.

chapter four

The walls shifted slightly, darkened and then returned to the miserably familiar pale green. He was still in the sick bay and his throat was miserably dry. Someone put a straw in his mouth. The tepid water tasted good.

"You've been out for two days," Pauli said in a hoarse whisper. "How do you feel?"

Émile groaned, clenched his fists and wiggled his toes. Everything was in working order. He blinked and tried to sit up too fast, got dizzy and had to lean back before making another attempt.

"Where's doctor?" he asked. Talking made him breathe hard and he didn't; understand at first why. He was fine. He knew he was fine, the newly integrated neural links assured him of that as his mind raced and rebelled against the slow procedure of speech.

"She's off duty," Pauli said. "I'll get her. She wanted to know when you were awake."

Pauli left. That made Émile sad. Maybe she was upset that he had asked for the doctor, but Pauli couldn't reassure him that his strange new wiring was not about to break his body. No, Pauli was fine, he told himself. She was, and so was he.

The doctor arrived, her wiry steel-wool hair making a halo. *A slightly crazed Angel of the Annunciation,* he thought. Then she leaned over him, plucked his wrist from the sheets and squeezed. He yelped.

"What took you so long?" the doctor groused. "Goldbricking?"

Saint-Just got up very slowly this time. "Just trying to get my full quota of sick leave before I quit," he joked. The doctor snorted and pointed to his clothes. Then she left abruptly, Pauli in tow.

He pulled on the uniform green coveralls and mocs and left in search of food. If he had been down for two days, no wonder he wasn't good for much. He headed to the galley.

There was no proper cook aboard a prison ship. Instead the galley consisted of stacked prepared meals. Heat 'em and eat 'em, so the drill went. Émile searched through the recently restocked bins until he found something that read "Chicken Dijon with rice and carrots." Not that it would bear the slightest similarity to real chicken dijon, but it was infinitely superior to the prepackaged "Curry and rice," or the absolutely flavorless "Coq au Vin."

Eating helped. Lightheaded and dizzy no more, Émile found himself more connected to the real world. And much more aware. The food seemed to dampen the drug's effects, although he was conscious that he could call up the new memory and strange hearing should he wish. Only now it was under control rather than controlling him. Better and better.

Then he heard the pager, went over to the corner and slapped it for the message. "Prisoner 55129-CSZ, Saint-Just, report to location A." He slapped the depression again to shut it up. He didn't need to hear the thing twice over.

Location A. That was where he had been brought in, his security patterns taken, his file input into the *Constanza*. It was officer territory, and the crew avoided the officers as much as possible. Turncoats, the lot of them. But there was no reprieve from a direct summons. And the heat readers wouldn't let him get away.

He floated from the galley through the rec chambers and the gym to the barricade that shut the officers off from threats. He waited while the energy field double-checked against his file and verified his summons. The red light clicked and went blue as the hatch opened.

On the other side of the barrier, officer country wasn't different from the rest of the *Constanza*. The same grating and grips on all four surfaces, the same miserable pale green color on the bulkheads. Saint-Just remembered how, when he had first arrived, he had held on to the grips until his knuckles turned white. After long familiarity all he needed to do now was hook his foot through the soft loop.

The officer who came in was a stranger. Émile didn't care.

"Saint-Just?" the officer read perfunctorily.

Émile shrugged. There was no point in an answer. If he hadn't been the right person, the barricade wouldn't have opened in the first place.

"Émile Saint-Just of Beau Soleil under jurisdiction of Zone 7–3A administration Justica sector, you are being called for parole hearing at seven hundred hours tomorrow." Then the man stopped reading and looked Saint-Just in the eye. "They waited until you had recovered from your sniffles. You're fortunate. There isn't going to be another fly-by until you'd served your term plus, and they didn't have to wait. We told them that you'd been exceptional, smart, hard-working, didn't give anyone any trouble. You'd better act it when you go in there."

Émile knew better than to smile.

"Hugo, what was that thing you said about a second virus?" the doctor asked, wrinkling her nose. "I explained that very clearly. If this thing works, and it should, then we've got the perfect killer. Oncological retrovirus, incurable, unstoppable and untraceable. There isn't any second virus."

Gorvitz kept all expression off his face. He still had pangs of conscience about that one lie. Saint-Just had deserved better. But one life against many, Saint-Just against the destruction of the Justica, the ends justified the means. He had always believed that and lived that way. He would have carried the virus himself in Saint-Just's position. At least he thought he would.

But Émile still had illusions about life, about a future. And in two years or so he would go to a doctor and find an inoperable tumor in his stomach or spleen. Or his brain. There hadn't been any clinical trials yet.

Hugo Gorvitz looked at himself head-on and knew that the person who had become a revolutionary would be disgusted by what he had just done. Condemning one of his own comrades to death without even giving him enough data to make a decent choice. Who knew, Saint-Just might have been willing.

Orders, however, were orders. These had come in the usual route, slipped in with medical supplies in the delivery drone.

His reports went out in the ice pick-ups, disguised and coded so that no one would trace them. Every time he did it he worried about discovery, but the Steering Committee was good.

If they weren't, if they hadn't already started setting up a contact network to recover the doctor's microscopic weapon, Gorvitz thought he might have disobeyed. The idealist he once was was horrified at what he had done. His mother's son recognized cold pragmatism for what it was.

But Hugo Gorvitz was not the same person who had become a revolutionary, and he wasn't willing to bet on Émile Saint-Just choosing to smuggle out a retrovirus that would cause his death long before it contributed to the Justica's downfall. Gorvitz recognized the small twinge of guilt, and then banished it. He thought about the important things instead. Like how to incorporate the retrovirus into some Justica program. Maybe in the blood supply in the Star Medical Center where all the major officials had minor surgery. That was the best idea he'd come up with so far.

"Hugo?" the doctor interrupted his thoughts. "Why didn't you tell him? Why did you let him think that I couldn't make something simple and elegant, that I made something useless? You don't think my work is good enough for your precious revolution, do you?"

It took a good bit of patience not to strangle her. "If we'd told him the truth he wouldn't have done it," Gorvitz said.

The doctor snorted in disgust.

At twenty-two hundred hours the sick bay lit up. Officially it was closed unless there was an emergency, which made it a great place to hold a party. The doctor herself had made chemical champagne, and Shadow brought a few liters of his own patent gin. Even Gorvitz opened up a little and gave out Shaawar cigs like candy.

"Ya know, I remember when you first came aboard," Ice said, his head bobbing around his glass, cig firmly chomped between his teeth. "You was one green kid, I'll tell you. Never woulda took you for street. Now, of course, that's all fixed." He leered over at Pauli.

"Which reminds me, Pauli's gonna be pretty lonesome,"

Fox said meaningfully. "Think you could use some company?"

Usually that would have made Pauli angry. Tonight she was drunk enough that she passed it off with a solemn shake of her head. "But I am going to miss you," she said to Saint-Just softly. "Maybe I'll go to Beau Soliel if I ever get out. Crazy purple sky and all."

"Don't do it, Pauli," the doctor said. "He'll be an old, old man by the time you get there."

"Good," Pauli laughed. "He'll be old and rich and set me up and I'll take a bunch of young and handsome lovers. How's that? From what I've heard that's pretty normal on Beau Soliel."

Émile shook his head and colored slightly, more from the drink than from the question. "Don't, Pauli," he said softly. They'd already said good-by and he hated to admit how much he was going to miss her. But he wasn't ready to stay on the *Constanza* for her, and the Justica wasn't about to let her go.

And it seemed like everybody there knew it, too. He could feel Fox and Shadow and the doctor all staring at him, wondering how he was going to react. There wasn't any choice, he had to break the tension. He cleared his throat and made an announcement. "The one thing I'd really like to know is what happened to everyone else from the *Mary Damned*," he told the group. "I'm going to have to report in to the Syndicat and they're going to want to know. Anybody have anything? Gossip, rumors, made-up stories?"

He turned to look not only at Gorvitz, but at a couple of the newer prisoners, both of whom sat with the Hounds. They weren't listening, though. At least they'd lost interest in his personal life. He shrugged and got up to refill his glass.

Shadow was right. The champagne was awful. The bathtub gin the Hounds had contributed wasn't much better, but at least it was mixed with ersatz orange drink which made it almost palatable. The only word he could associate with the pleasure he felt at the thought of leaving was sin.

It was a word he hadn't used since he had graduated from the pro forma catechism class all the children took until they were twelve. The only reason he hadn't skipped it was because Marie-Claire Guidray had been there, and even at twelve she had been beautiful. In his softly sodden musing he realized that she was most likely a grandmother now. If not dead.

In a corner he saw Pauli with one of the new Hounds. They'd called him Axel, he thought. Not that it mattered. Axel's hand was on Pauli's thigh and she wasn't pushing him away. That, too, made him only sad. It didn't matter any more; he couldn't permit it to matter any more, just as he and Pauli agreed. He should be glad that Pauli wasn't going to be alone, but he could only feel jealous and hope that Pauli was simply being polite. Jealousy was not considered good manners on the *Constanza*. He was glad he was going home to a place where jealousy was an acceptable emotion.

Pauli giggled. Émile turned away. He could hear somebody singing in the lab. He didn't like the lab, could still feel the long icy needle sliding into the soft fold of skin inside his elbow. And then had come the craziness and then the changes that made him uneasy. The changes that were somehow part of Gorvitz's plan to get free.

He wandered toward the singing. The music was familiar but the words were different. It was the newest Hound singing. His alcohol fuzzed brain refused to access the name. Glass, that was what they'd called him. In for manslaughter, got a little too drunk one night at a Zone bar and got into a fight with his best friend. Hit the friend with a full bottle of Chantilly d'Or, all cut crystal facets. It doesn't take much pressure to crack a human skull.

He had a good voice, Émile had to give him that. He began to listen to the lament, get caught up in the melody and the narrative.

"The *Mary Damned* went into Hell with her Captain and her crew, but she comes back where the Void is black to catch the likes of you."

"What about the *Mary Damned*?" Émile shouted, bursting into the small office.

Glass shrugged. "It's just an old song. A story, really. I mean, I learned it from my aunt and she said that it wasn't true or anything like that. Just a story. But I'll tell you something. I mean, you all may think I'm crazy or something, but I'll tell you." He paused to gulp at the air and then lowered his voice. "I mean, I'd never been in space. Except for the

Zone, of course, but it doesn't really count. Anyway, I just thought, you know, that these spacers are really nuts. Got all kinds of little rituals and beliefs and stuff that doesn't have anything to do with the real world. But if you think it does, it does. So I thought the whole thing with the *Mary Damned* was one of those, you know.

"But when they were bringing me out on the transport, well, you know how they don't talk to you then. I mean, you're just cargo. But they also don't notice enough not to talk when you are around, and so they say lots of things they shouldn't. I mean, maybe you didn't notice anything like that."

"Yeah, we know what you're talking about, kid," Gorvitz said. "On my transport they let on that the *Justica* was having problems with the Arcasi region. Being from there myself, I was kind of proud. But what about the *Mary Damned*?"

"They sighted her," Glass said. "Just outside the Gordon sling. At least, I figure that was where it was, because we were strapped down with a lot of gravity for a lot of hours afterward."

"What was she doing?" Saint-Just asked, barely able to contain his curiosity.

Glass blinked at him. "Well, she wasn't doing anything. I mean, she's the *Mary Damned*. You know. No Captain, no crew, no sign of struggle found aboard. The holds all full. You know."

"Yes," Émile said slowly. "Yes, I know." The name of the ship, the place it had been sighted and the place where he had left all raced through his mind, tumbling together in a pattern that almost came into focus and then recombined into something else.

Glass hissed through his teeth. "Well, she's a ghost ship. That's why my aunt said that it was all just garbage. There've always been stories about ghost ships. But anyway, the *Mary Damned* was supposed to have been this real rich Trader and was abandoned for some reason. Only no one knows why, and so she drifts dead in space. And the legend goes that any ship that sights her is doomed to die in space. Now is that a crock, or what? But if they really did see her, well, then, at least part of the thing is true, right? Besides, I told you all about it when

I came aboard. You didn't seem so taken up then. Or you're a soggy drunk.''

Émile swallowed hard. How much could they have covered up? he wondered. How could they get away with it? But he knew the answer to that entirely too well.

And then all together the answer came in a single brilliant flash. No one else had sufficient data on the ghost ship or its position. He did. And he went to pull Gorvitz away from the knot of hopeful hangers-on.

"I have a gift for you," Émile muttered under his breath. "You once said there was no place you could run to with this old bucket. But according to the drift pattern, speed and mass, the *Mary Damned* should be close to here. Very soon."

Gorvitz blinked and paled as Émile gave him the hard data along with the original coordinates and figures. "You'll have to do the calculations, but you've got all the numbers," he told Gorvitz.

"Are we even now?" he asked when he had finished.

Hugo Gorvitz nodded once, firmly. "For everything."

chapter
five

The parole hearing took longer than his trial by all of ten minutes. Three women and two men sat behind a table that Émile supposed was there to be impressive. They asked where he would go and what work he would do. Stupid simple questions.

Home to Beau Soliel, he told them. And his job training aboard the *Constanza* should qualify him to work on the *rapide*. He had thought of those answers long ago, knowing full well that a return to the Syndicat was not exactly what the Justica considered proper employment.

Parole granted, he did not return to the *Constanza*. He remained aboard the fly-by in solitary custody for nearly a week. The parole board was obviously not taking chances. Then he was transferred to the *Adria*, a Trader with an appointment on Zone 6. From there he could catch transport all the way home, or so he was told.

They gave him a fresh coverall, stiff and too large; an ID with his complete record; and a packet with three hundred current francs Beau Soliel currency, his belt and his sapphire earring. The money, belt and earring had been on him when he was captured. So had the Syndicat cuff and an expensive watch, neither of which had been returned. Or compensated.

He told himself to stay calm. He knew they wouldn't return all his goods; he should be glad that he had the cash and the sapphire. The belt was worthless.

But the cuff was priceless. It was his identity in the Palais, his passage through the Zone, meals and a place to stay. It was everything home was about and he wasn't about to lose it without a fight. He refused to sign the release without it.

The officer in Justica green stood his ground. "That was contraband," he said without inflection. "The Syndicat of Free Traders is an unofficial organization under investigation of the Justica Court of Inquiry. I would suggest that you withdraw your request."

Émile wanted to shout that he would never withdraw, that they had no right to take away his place in his own world. But he also knew that not withdrawing the request would mean that perhaps parole would be withdrawn, that he could be sent to a destination even worse than the *Constanza*, that he would never see Beau Soliel again.

It hurt, but he withdrew. Gorvitz had taught him well. Better to consider the alternatives than stand on a point of honor. Although giving the point hurt like drawn blood. And then Émile faced the officer and knew that he would not give again. He had given enough. Next time it would be their turn.

There weren't many merchant ships with free crews, so Émile had to sign on for short hops. His work record on the hull conductors was superior, and he had passed the rating test for first mate. He did his work and kept to himself, and generally Émile was left alone. When one of the crew of the Zone transport did ask, he said that he was bound for Beau Soliel. That was enough of an answer. Of all the planets in the known worlds, Beau Soliel was still the destination of artists, poets, lovers of music and culture and sadece senin. Beau Soliel with its violet sky and glittering cities was still a destination for those who had something to gain or nothing to lose.

By the time he disembarked at the local Zone he no longer looked like a prisoner. His hair had grown out from the close cut on the *Constanza* and now nearly covered his ears. It would take a few months more subjective to look proper in the Quartier again, as he remembered the Quartier, but at least no one would stare. And among the locals he again stood out for being just a shade more blond than the norm, and maybe a touch taller. He hadn't reached his full height when he had left Beau Soliel, so this surprised him. A little skewed to one side but still well in the normal range. After all, his wasn't the only family in the entire colony that had Alsatian blood.

Now there was nothing remarkable about him at all. Except for his Justica green overalls, and there was nothing he could do about that. With only three hundred francs cash he couldn't afford new clothes, not until he had a place to eat and sleep and a berth on an outgoing Trader. At least now he should qualify as a specialist with a cut of the profits.

So thinking, he found a cheap bistro in the Zone and decided not to bother with a room. His shuttle left for Huit Fleurs at fourteen hundred hours the next day, and he was anxious to be home. All he could think was that he would go directly to the Palais Syndicat and demand to be reinstated, and test for his rating on conductor ceramics. His wrist itched for the cuff he needed, and he was restless with apprehension. Still, there was a long wait before he would be under his beloved violet sky again.

It was not only his first time aboard a Zone, it was his first experience with persistent gravity in eight years subjective. The Zones were oversized space stations, nearly large enough to house early colonies if they had been built for that purpose. They hadn't been. They had been built jointly by the colonial authorities and the Justica as trade and transport stations and were technically under joint control.

Which meant that Saint-Just had to check through the Justica points and report his arrival. Then and only then could he fade into the Zone itself, abandoning himself to the travellers' rest area between the two control ports—the one uniformed and controlled and Justica and the other the downstation to Beau Soliel.

The first thing he noticed was the language. It had been so long, so very long, that he had forgotten how beautiful his own language sounded. Especially when spoken with the soft accent of Huit Fleurs, the largest city on the planet and his home. He picked up a copy of *L'Ami du Peuple* for two francs and checked the date.

Fifty-seven years had passed on Beau Soliel since he had left on the *Mary Damned*. Eight years for him and more than two generations for his home. He fought the fear, the anxiety. At least *L'Ami du Peuple* was still being published, and from its editorials he thought that it retained its Quartier du Paris slant.

He held on to the paper like a life rope on EVA as he wandered through the Zone. Two francs for the paper. He bought his downshuttle ticket before he spent any more money. At least there were public ticket facilities at the Public Information Center where he'd found the paper. Another two hundred twenty francs gone for a reserved seat on the next downbound. It was then Émile began to worry seriously about money.

He touched the screen on the Public Information Center, but without half a franc it was perfectly dead. And the paper, instead of remaining where he left it, responded to the false spin gravity of the station and had the indignity to fall all over his feet. He cursed. With his cuff, the Zone would have been so much friendlier. He could have stayed at one of the Syndicat homes, eaten at their table as a member of the family. He could have walked into any of the bars or entertainment establishments and charged against Syndicat credit if he didn't have the money. Now, however, all he could do was turn and see the brilliantly lit glass facades promising food and drink, gaming and sex and dreams.

Like a series of posters on the wide white-tiled corridor they offered their promises, the colored lights reflecting off the slick white glaze and staining the whole with emotionally vague recollections of parties and good times. They weren't places Émile could afford. Reluctantly he turned off the main hall down one of the side alleys.

The tile work here was not white or gleaming between the buildings. The ceiling was painted out matte black and the deck was a worn steel grate. He found a bistro with the menu posted in the window and the prices displayed prominently. He could afford a *cassoulet* and a glass of wine. Besides, he was tired. His legs were on the edge of cramp and his back was sore. He had forgotten how much work walking was.

The food in the bistro smelled good. For the first time in eight years he ate with pleasure, the thick white bean stew heavily laced with basil and carrots and tarragon and wine, the bread soft in the center with a crust that crumbled on the uncovered marble table. Once he forgot and left the wine glass suspended in midair. It fell and crashed and Émile flinched. At least it had been empty.

He sat a long time savoring every mouthful, until he attracted the attention of the proprietor.

"Is there anywhere I can just go and sit?" he asked. "Where I won't have to pay?"

The round-faced woman studied him carefully. "Well," she said finally, "there's always the Parc Floral. Around the center rim, half gravity. That's free."

She looked at him as if she knew. Émile was grateful that she didn't mention the fact he was just out of prison.

Émile counted out the eight francs for dinner plus two for the broken glass and headed out the door. The park had not been exactly what he'd hoped for his first night in the Zone. Disappointment threatened to overcome him as he followed the lines of Parc Floral pink lights into the inner spokes. But when he arrived he had to admit that he was glad he had come. In the years aboard the *Constanza* he had forgotten the joy of open space, the lure of growing things, the impossible beauty of sheer life.

The Parc was large and open across the central hub, and all around, overhead and underfoot were profusions of flowers and trees that he had never seen. Colors of blossoms he had not even imagined, violets and honey-tangerine mixed in with more familiar species. And the scent was overwhelming joy.

He had to stifle an impulse to run through the carefully manicured grass, to stretch out on the picturesque iron-and-wood benches and just glory in being here. Close enough to home that he could taste it, smell it.

But none of the flowers was sadece, and the underscent sadece left was missing. Sadece, the most beautiful flowers of all, were banished from the official Parc Floral.

Suddenly the Zone was no longer enough and he felt insatiably homesick for the ground, the canals of stagnant water choked with the large pink and purple and blood-red flowers. He remembered as a child going down to watch the less respectable denizens of Huit Fleurs dropping warm little bodies into the gaping petals. It was a good and traditional way for a child to eliminate the body of a dead pet. A gerbil or mouse or fish offered to the flowers prompted them to puff out a whiff of intoxicating gas.

He stood at the edge of a white gravel path, looking out and across at the bowers and arbors and fruit dripping from the trees and was still not satisfied.

"Émile Saint-Just?"

Émile started violently and swung around. The speaker was a woman, young and soft-seeming in her light print dress. She didn't strike him as threatening at all, and so he identified himself. She smiled and her face was as pink and open as the beds of roses.

"Bessanti contacted me," she said.

"Bessanti? I don't know any Bessanti."

She lifted an eyebrow, then laughed. Her laughter was as light as her summer dress. "I'm sorry. You know him as Hugo Gorvitz. He told you we would be in contact. You have what we were promised?"

Saint-Just nodded wearily. He hadn't expected his freedom to be curtailed so soon. Just a blood sample, Gorvitz had said. Only he hadn't said his name was Bessanti. And the girl seemed to be waiting, expecting something more. "Now?" he asked heavily.

She touched one perfectly pink nail to his hand. "No. We'll be expecting you at home. Huit Fleurs. You know the Café de la Montagne? At two in the morning, Thursday. You will be there?"

"Of course," he agreed. What else was there to do? "But just one thing," he interjected. "You know who I am. Who are you?"

She laughed again and a wisp of auburn hair clung to her cheek as she turned. "Anne-Sylvie Corday," she answered. "But don't think of it. We will meet again. Soon."

chapter
six

Stepping out under Beau Soliel's insane sky was a culmi-
nation of faith. Émile Saint-Just looked up at the violet haze
of the reflection nebula around a white dwarf that had given
the colony its name. No other place where humans lived was
anything like it, and Émile could hardly resist the tears that
came with the nostalgia that welcomed him home.

Home had changed in fifty-seven years. The Quartier du
Paris was perhaps more picturesque than ever now that the
streets were flooded, and the sadece flowers grew thick under
rust-iron balconies. Sadece might feed the Quartier, but Émile
remembered a time when there had been respectable trade as
well, the streets full of tourists and shops and sidewalk artists.
Artists were still willing to leave the rest of the universe behind
for the unparalleled light of Beau Soliel, but now, according
to the city tourist briefing, they plied their trade on the fashionable Boulevard Lafitte. At least the Café de la Montagne
was still at its old location in Place Baudelaire in the Quartier,
terraced above the seeping waters that covered the center of
the square.

Indeed, for all the damage done by the sadece trade, the
Quartier retained its bohemian charm. Perhaps the drowning
even added to the ambience for those who slummed down to
the avant-garde galleries, and performance lofts and clubs.
Émile Saint-Just found the new atmosphere enticing and un-
trustworthy. The scent of the sadece alone was mildly disori-
enting and vaguely corrupt, and he was certain that it had to
hide the stench of rotting upholstery and mildewed doorframes
from those underpinnings that had once been the ground floor.

Nor did he care. He was home. The smell of good bread

mixed with the stench of standing water, traces of sadece gas and the expensive perfumes of the well-to-do who came down to catch the local color, the air of Beau Soliel itself embraced him.

He ducked in the *café*, in the back section where the *pâtisserie* still operated out of a single glass counter. He wanted to sit here, to drink coffee and listen to the soft, slow accents of Beau Soliel, of *la belle langue* spoken even by the uneducated with the undeniable history of civilization in every word. But to stay would be to linger and to remember a time in the *café*'s past that was now beyond the living memory of most of its patrons. There was little chance that he would ever meet any of his old friends down here again for a glass of wine in the evening, discussing the editorials in *L'Ami du Peuple*.

He had to come back later anyway, he reminded himself. To meet Anne-Sylvie. There would be plenty of time then to drink *café au lait* and talk about affairs of importance. Later. After he reported to the Syndicat.

He bought two deep-fried pastries thickly dusted with powdered sugar for a franc apiece and ate them as he walked. A fine white mist settled over his dark green work clothes. At the Palais Syndicat he could tell them what really happened to the *Mary Damned*. And change from these chain-gang garments into something a Free Trader would wear. Something that fit properly and was made of soft fabric and, above all, was not Justica green.

He walked across the rooftop latticeways of the Quartier until he reached Avenue de Sorbonne where the old university had been. There he crossed over the delicate sky bridges, their ceramic scaffolding unaffected by time or sadece. The bridges brought him through another maze and down until he was overlooking Avenue Marat. This was well out of the Quartier. From here, for a fee, he could hire a cab or take the *rapide* to the Palais Syndicat on the very fashionable Boulevard Lafitte.

Urgency pressed on him, although perhaps ten minutes in the effort of years was no great thing. But the walk would be good, would orient him in time, tell him where to find *crêpes* and smokes and the latest theatrical postings. More important, it would give him time to think about exactly what to say, how to explain it. Besides which, he only had six francs left.

Maybe he wasn't the first, he told himself again as he started to walk up the wide boulevard. Someone else might have gotten time off, too. Someone else might have been on a faster ship, or had served out their time closer to home. With all the time shifting there was no reason to suppose that the Syndicat hadn't heard.

The Boulevard Lafitte was wide and clean. Red and yellow awnings shaded the painted furniture of the *cafés*, tables and chairs green and blue and white, mostly abandoned now in the afternoon. A few older gentlemen, wearing caps and smoking, were gathered over coffee cups, playing checkers. Further down a pair of chic women sipped wine and leaned their heads close as they spoke. Waiters in white coats socialized across the color barriers, eyes constantly on their tables, and ashes invariably dropping from their cigarettes.

The shops were still expensive, Émile saw. And although he didn't know what things ought to cost any more, he could easily identify the jeweler's display as real and tasteful, and the leather shop as the same elegant establishment he had passed a thousand times in a bygone era.

Uncomfortable familiarity assailed him in this district. His favorite bookseller was gone, the stall now given over to a tempting display of apples and tangerines and bright yellow guava. The trees had grown and the monumental structure of Hôtel de Ville had darkened over the years. The Palais Syndicat was on a block by itself, still surrounded by the luxurious gardens of the Nouvelles Tuileries, where ice-cream stalls still served children in school uniforms. Those hadn't changed, the boys in their short pants, the girls in their ribboned hats racing through the flower beds with complete disregard for the property. Nothing had changed. Nothing important except Émile himself.

There were more people wearing cuffs now, some of them shiny and others dull with the patina of service. He rubbed his own left wrist, the place that had felt empty for so long. Funny that he had never adjusted to the loss of that weight.

He walked up the front steps to the massive door, aware of the children watching him quietly.

"He doesn't have a cuff," he heard one high-pitched voice explain.

"That's the Syndicat," another youngster, bolder, shouted.

Émile turned and smiled at them, standing tall and insolent as only a Free Trader could. "Have you ever heard of the *Mary Damned*?" he asked them.

The children had the grace to looked frightened before they ran back to their games. Saint-Just turned back to the door and rang again. Without the cuff he couldn't pass the locks unescorted. He waited impatiently, knowing that they must have heard what he had said to the youngsters. Or had someone else from the *Mary Damned* come in before him and established their rights as a crew?

The heavy brushed steel doors embellished with scenes from trader life opened into the dark. The last time he had been admitted was the day he had been received as a member. Now he slipped into the gloom away from the street and the door shut behind him.

It took a moment for his eyes to adjust to the dark. Then he saw that nothing had changed, that the cherry and white striped satin sofas were still in place against the wall under large impressionistic portraits of various famous Traders. Émile wandered down the line, wondering if the *Mary Damned* had made it to the gallery. Certainly she deserved to. More than any other ship he had ever known, the *Mary Damned* had been Free Trader to the last and had died for her sins.

"You claim to have information on the *Mary Damned*," a young woman greeted him without an introduction. "Come, Captain Dumouriez wishes to see you."

The third-floor corner office was not exactly the same as it had been under Henri Plessey. The celadon walls were hung with oversized abstracts, and the elegantly curved sofas around the watered green art-table were unfamiliar. At least, for all the green, none was the dull dark color the Justica used so freely.

Captain Dumouriez himself was grey-haired and stone-faced. Crags and fissures were carved in his flesh so that he appeared inhumanly severe. He did not smile at Saint-Just, did not offer his hand in greeting, did not gesture away from the stiff desk and visitors' chairs to the friendlier informal arrangement. Instead he sat behind his desk and studied Émile in silence.

The gesture did not disturb Saint-Just. He had experienced

it many times in the Justica prison. He stared back, challenging the Captain to begin as if the estimable Dumouriez were the lowest Hound.

"You claim to have knowledge of the *Mary Damned*," Dumouriez said. His voice was well modulated and cultured without any trace of emotion. "A number of people have claimed such in the past and we have always heard them out. Some of the theories have been very interesting. However, nothing has been verified. Some traders have insisted they have sighted the vessel but nothing has shown on ship's records. The Syndicat has published our collective opinion that the *Mary Damned* was destroyed by a drive accident. If you wish to report another sighting, I would suggest that you approach the university faculty of psychology."

CHAPTER
SEVEN

Émile sat without invitation and told Dumouriez in unvarnished detail exactly what had happened, about running senin through the Dark and how they had been caught. Bad luck, he said, shrugging. The Syndicat knew there had been a chance and the *Mary Damned* had been pleased to take it.

"And you have no more information as to what became of the others?"

Saint-Just shook his head. "I had hoped that you would, that the Justica would have contacted the Syndicat. They took our cuffs, you know."

"No, they have given us no information of the sort," Dumouriez replied evenly. "They have never reported the *Mary Damned*, either as captured or as landed, nor do their records show any of the names you listed. In fact, I do not have a complete manifest from that journey. I requested the data when you arrived and there is no record available."

The Syndicat section head seemed reasonable, his tone even and his eyes calm. Saint-Just had seen that look before, on Justica programmers whose professional patience had been no match for his stubborn defiance. The more coldly rational they became, the worse his case was. Now he knew it was very bad. Dumouriez did not believe him at all. Or worse, thought him one more of the nut cases that showed up every year or so to get publicity.

"We will, naturally, add this to our file on the *Mary Damned*," Dumouriez said carefully. "And we are certainly glad to have the information. However, grateful as I am, I can't believe we have any more business."

The concierge appeared, slipping through the crack in the

door like a ghost. "M. Saint-Just is ready to leave," the old
Captain told her.

Émile hesitated. His cuff. He had come back for it, to be
readmitted to his place in the Syndicat. It was his right. He
had paid his stake and he had paid again on the *Constanza*.
The Syndicat was for life, was the complete and utterly trustworthy family of all Free Traders. Otherwise what did they
have? Without its unchanging aspect and perfect record there
was nothing at all in the shifting mire of time to anchor them.
There was no reality at all then. Just constant relativities grating
one on the other around their edges, setting off a spark or two
that died in the Void.

Besides, there had to be a record of him. He had gone down
to the main system and been directly connected to the fiber-
optic filaments, attached at each sense nexus to the organic
composite compound that was the memory and internal core
of the Syndicat. There the system had printed him, charted
everything from retinal patterns to brainwaves, so that it could
not only recognize him but knew more about him than he would
want anyone to know.

At the time it had been part of the ritual necessary to get his
cuff, to install him as a full member of the Syndicat. Once he
was printed in the system he could never be lost, he always
had a home. Or so he had believed. He decided to maintain
his faith.

"Excuse me, but I also came to check the crew manifests
and see if anyone needs environmental crew. My rating, now."

Dumouriez looked like he wanted to kill. It was his first
human expression in the interview. The captain brought his
features under control. "I'm afraid that will not be possible,"
he said in a voice that would freeze hydrogen. "Those requests
are available only to Syndicat members."

"But I am Syndicat," Émile protested.

"I am sorry, but there is no Émile Saint-Just in our database.
No records at all. If I were able to pull your file there would
be no problem, naturally, but without documentation and without the cuff that is just not possible," Dumouriez said evenly.

"Then check the print core," Saint-Just suggested icily.

"That is no longer policy," Dumouriez answered.

Saint-Just did not put the old man out of his obviously miserable existence, for which he deserved a medal for self-control. No longer policy? That was absurd.

And yet he knew that once the cuff was welded on it was intended to remain for life. Just in case of such a problem, in the event that anyone questioned. One joined forever and there was no getting out, no hiding the mark of membership. But nothing had ever been said the other way. To Émile's knowledge no one ever had had the cuff cut off before.

But there were other things that he could tell Dumouriez, things that only a Syndicat member would know. The shipping lanes from Zone 6 to the Clusters, Captain Plessey's record as Chief of the Syndicat, the cargos carried by half a dozen ships and their manifests. And it meant nothing. Dumouriez did not want to know, did not want to have to accept this ex-convict as a brother, did not want to be responsible to the Syndicat if he admitted the wrong person by mistake. Was willing to risk injustice and ignore the truth for his own miserable career.

He recognized it, though. It was Gorvitz and the Hounds, and the Justica too. Protecting their turf no matter what it cost, they called themselves pragmatists. He had always thought that self-interest unenlightened with ethics was as alien to the Syndicat as to the people of Beau Soliel themselves.

Émile wondered just who Dumouriez was and how he had risen as high as he had. No one with that attitude would have lasted under Plessey for fifteen minutes. He would have been shipped out, a Zone drone for the rest of his career with a black mark on his cuff and no captain willing to sign him on the manifest.

But Plessey was in charge fifty-seven years ago. Saint-Just wondered idly what had become of him, if he had shipped out again or if he had died. The image of Plessey coming back and giving Dumouriez his just reward was all that stood between Émile and a serious fight. Which would not help at all. No matter how richly the old man deserved it, Émile knew that enraging him more would only make other avenues harder to pursue.

And there were other avenues, other ways into the Syndicat and to its records. Not that he knew them. That was another problem. But they had to exist because by all the laws of the known universe no human ever built a system without leaving

some flaw somewhere. And Émile Saint-Just knew that he
would have to find a way of slipping through the flaws, out of
the Justica and back home.

He didn't notice the concierge as he was ushered out of the
building, but he did peer through one door that had been left
casually ajar. In it, hung on the ice-grey wall, was a large
painting that looked strangely like the work of a small child.
And, even more strangely, the Klee disturbed him subtly in a
way a child's drawing wouldn't.

He didn't watch the street as he made his way back to the
Quartier. Though the day was brilliant and the Boulevard Lafitte
picturesque, he paid it no attention. Hands clenched at his sides,
Émile Saint-Just walked simply to bleed off the energy of his
fury. And to plan.

The rhythm of motion began to calm him enough to actually
think rather than react. It was something he had learned in his
first days in zero-gee. Never react, move. Motion always
brought some semblance of rationality. Reactions were almost
always useless and usually led to painful ends.

So he walked further, heading for the Quartier by instinct
and not design. He didn't even realize where he had been
heading until he crossed the university district and entered the
Quartier proper, climbing the pastel skyways above the flooded
streets.

Below him the sadece bloomed in stagnant water. Violet and
pink and faded black, the long-stemmed and those that grew
directly on the lazy floating pads in the water, they almost
choked the patches under low-hung rust iron balconies. Feeding
platforms, Émile thought.

If only the Justica could see them, clustered on the street,
ripening their gas and juices. He could smell the residual gas
that the flowers released, the mild euphoric that made the Quartier so very pleasant for those who spent little time there. For
residents the happy infusion simply helped them survive the
necessities of Beau Soliel. For the artists who didn't make
enough money on the broad avenues it muffled the hunger
pangs; for the students it hid their mediocrity, and for the rest,
it made their poverty bearable and bohemian instead of merely
grim.

As he approached Place Baudelaire it grew dark and the crowd changed. The solid bourgeois daytimers who had come to shop and stare at the locals drifted away. Richer and more daring interlopers invaded the Quartier in glowing violet dusk, going to the famous restaurants and clubs, listening to the music of the night and drifting on the sadece-scented *bonhomie*. They reveled in sharing a table perhaps, or a vanity shelf, with the demimonde.

The rich who came down dressed vaguely like the inhabitants, but they reeked of money. Émile could tell from the way they looked at real residents and then turned away. They were far too worldly to have to look, after all. And their tones were soft and cutting at the same time, wondering if that table over there were just bums or professors or maybe chess masters negotiating an informal game. And if the younger people were maybe artists and musicians or just shop clerks.

Saint-Just smiled evilly to himself. If they didn't realize that the shop clerks and waiters were the artists, the painters and musicians and poets and actors and columnists for *L'Ami du Peuple*, they didn't understand the world at all. They waded into the low flood of the Quartier but it never touched them because they could not see that it had nothing at all to do with their society of categories and social distinctions.

Then he caught drift of a conversation that enticed his attention.

"If Madame Georges is having an affair with a Neferasian, then exactly how do they do it? Neferasians don't have any, well, their sexuality is primarily oral."

Laughter, high and silver and feminine. "And you have to ask how?" The laughter came again. "But at least they speak good French."

"Unlike the Justica *flics*," the first voice said again.

Émile turned and saw the group as they drifted out of his immediate vicinity. They were residents, all right. Two women and three men, all moving confidently through the press in the open square. One of the women turned back and he caught her eye, and her look went through him. She rejected him as a stranger but didn't seem able to assign him a category in the inventory of the Quartier.

Saint-Just turned and went on. He had little enough money

in his pocket and nowhere to spend the night. He headed up
to the roofways, a crazy patchwork paving that wound over
the ancient buildings that made up the Quartier. Each one was
an individual discovery. On some there were stalls and even
semi-built shops that no doubt the landlords had never seen.
Some were feeble attempts at gardens with scrawny plants in
neat boxes, while others were splattered with the materials of
ateliers. On three so far he had encountered old greasy-fat
women sitting at tables offering to tell fortunes for ten francs
each, and he had even run into one three-card monte game, all
highly illegal.

He found it hard to find his way. What had once been familiar
territory had become a maze of high structures and a glittering
reflection of the nebula that still covered half the sky with
lavender phosphorescence. From here, he finally concluded,
he wouldn't be able to find Lola's anyway.

He had to get help. Café de la Montagne, at least, had not
changed. Émile doubted seriously that it had become so fashionable that the locals were no longer a major part of the
clientele. So he would have to wait just a little longer now,
until the third shift took its place and it was time for his rendezvous with Anne-Sylvie. Then the rich patrons of the Quartier's various and sophisticated amusements would find their
way back uptown to the security of their locked buildings and
cleaning services. Then it would be time for the locals to take
over the neighborhood, when the real flavor and edge surfaced,
violence and poverty and pain all washed up together into a
single texture that was the Quartier du Paris.

Saint-Just sat on a roofdeck off the structured maze and
waited. Overhead the nebula swung lazily through half the sky,
its internal floes sparkling in hallucinogenic patterns reflected
from the now-invisible sun. Not that the star itself was ever
truly visible. Too brilliant and white to look at directly, only
the presence of the nebula made Beau Soleil bearable at all.

With all of space to choose from, Saint-Just understood that
his people had taken the most beautiful. Not necessarily the
easiest or the most useful, but without a doubt the single rarest
gem in all creation.

The night was not cold, not what he had remembered about
nights past. The layer of water flooding the streets must have

something to do with that, he decided, the heavy humidity holding the daytime heat. And the stench grew heavier, bloody and thick. Émile went to the edge of the roof and looked down. Yes, there was a patch of sadece directly below a rusted iron balcony across the street that had once been covered with fancy work. Even in the near dark he could make out the glow of yellow hair as someone bent a head and fed things to the sadece. Wriggling things that squealed as if they knew their fate.

Émile looked away. He knew about sadece. Everyone on Beau Soliel did. But fifty-seven years ago they had been cultivated on plantations far from the city and the sidewalks had been dry and dotted with white metal tables for a hundred *cafés*. It was a foreign world he had come home to, changed beyond mere acceptance. Slow leeching of its economy by the Justica had effected something akin to the mildew that clung stubbornly to the rotting wallpaper in the ground-floor apartments in the Quartier.

He turned away. He had more urgent things to think about: shelter, money, a way to win back his status in the Syndicat or at least a way to make someone in authority listen about the Justica. And the only way he thought he could do it was through Lola's connection. If the connection was still good, if the Hôtel de Ville hadn't changed the way the Syndicat had, if the chess-players were still a power on the streets and Lola herself would admit him into her net.

Too many ifs. If he thought too much, Émile realized, he would end up feeding himself to the flowers. No, he had to wait. Go to Lola's. If Lola's didn't exist any more, then he would have to find a squat for the night, maybe for a few nights. Maybe forever. But that was not a problem yet. Only one thing at a time. Only one moment, this moment.

How deeply he hated Dumouriez had not fully penetrated until that moment. It was rich and personal, unlike his hatred of the Justica. The Justica was a thing and it behaved like all things, without passion. And so he hated it coldly and without passion.

But Dumouriez, that was different. That was a single man who had slapped his face. Émile was glad that he had walked away when he did, without an outburst of the violence that had become habit on the *Constanza*. His revenge on Dumouriez had to be more complete, more exacting, than an ordinary fistfight.

The hate kept him warm as he waited for the streetlights to dim and the uptowners to go home. Until it was time to go to the Café de la Montagne and eat *beignets* like in the old days, in the one place Émile thought might not have changed.

chapter eight

The Café de la Montagne, at least, showed no signs that fifty-seven years had passed. The inside was still gloomy, with the *pâtisserie* shut down and the lights off. The tables were still set a little too close together and the people at them still talked too loud.

He took his time in the dark looking for Anne-Sylvie, although he knew it was too early. Some of the chatter was still too cultured. Uptowners, he thought, stretching out the evening, soaking up one last measure of dirt and glamour before returning to their real lives. Snatches of conversation cut through the din and Émile listened, unashamed. Eavesdropping was not simply habit, it was survival.

"But why would a Neferasian have an affair with *her*?"

The voice was strangely familiar. Saint-Just turned to the sound. Five people sat around a table. He could not make out the face of the speaker, but he knew immediately that he had seen them earlier in the evening.

"Leave it, Daniel," a girl said. Her voice was low and weary. "I don't care about Madame Duplay and I don't care if she has fifty affairs. What news from the Académie?"

A hard, staccato laugh answered her. "That's less important than the concierge," one of the men, not Daniel, said. "It's thirty years out of date even if they did say anything."

The woman who had not spoken before shrugged coolly. " 'Republics might come and go but the Académie is forever,' they say. And if they make some ruling then it will stand for at least thirty years. Maybe three hundred. Most likely. So even if the news is old it's still accurate. Better than any of the other news imported from Earth."

This time he did more than recognize the voice. There was a face to go with it. He did not know how he could have missed Anne-Sylvie. He was certain he had looked carefully. And then he realized that he assumed she would be alone, they would make their transaction in privacy. He had dismissed the group of five out of hand.

Émile drifted until he was standing nearly behind them. Only the business of the *café* and the smoke of a hundred types of tobacco shielded him. Their voices and accents were more cultured than he had expected. They were most likely part of the university crowd and likely to have more political fervor than the actors and musicians and itinerants who wandered the Quartier.

"Is my poetry in there?" the third man asked. Émile thought he detected a whine and his opinion of the group plummeted.

A girl with a triangular face and large eyes took the paper and flipped through it. "I don't see it, Alain," she told him. "When did they say they'd print it?"

"Stop it, Nathalie," Daniel told her. "It's not in there. It hasn't been in for six months. I wonder if he even wrote anything. Or they rejected it. I'd believe that faster than that it's going to be in today or next week or the week after that. I'm sick of his literary pretentions. Let him feed the flowers; at least that's useful."

Then they noticed him. More specifically, Alain looked up to challenge Daniel and found himself staring directly at Émile. "Who's that?" he asked no one in particular.

"Slummer," Daniel said icily. "Flower food."

It was Anne-Sylvie who turned carefully and stood facing him. She barely came above his shoulder. A smile spread over her lips like seeping blood, terror and pleasure all one thing. Her hand ran down her side, over her ribs, emphasizing her hard, boyish build. Then she teased her skirt up just a hair and caressed her thigh.

Or did not caress. Émile stood transfixed as her hand came away suddenly with a hardknife. She hissed as she held it toward him, blade first, loose and straight up in her hand. Like a pro. And she stalked him between the tables relentlessly, her focus shining in her face.

"What are you doing?" he whispered, shocked.

"What I came to do," she replied, her smile widening.

She thrust forward in a lightning-straight line, her body light on her toes and her shoulders hard back. Émile dodged to his right and caught the back of her arm. She snapped his hold as he suspected she would, using the momentum to balance a kick.

Émile didn't trust her. He dropped and pushed up against her leg just as her knife snaked forward to where he had been standing. She let her lunge overbalance her into the *pâtisserie* case and rolled on the smooth plexi surface until she was upright again.

Saint-Just was impressed. His opinion of her rose considerably. Her knife rose again also.

He could feel the crowd in the Café de la Montagne watching. Heads turning in practiced boredom, they still couldn't ignore the fight. Not when his next move would take him across a patron's lap.

"Slummer," Anne-Sylvie hissed loudly. She stood stock still, waiting. He could feel the tension grow between them, a living energy that was as much sex as anger, a connection in combat that he had felt before and hated and tried to deny. She tossed her head and reveled in it.

Her delicate tongue darted out and touched lips in anticipation. "You're gone," she said softly, like the caress of a lover.

Émile was mesmerized. She walked toward him, one deliberate step at a time, and with each step he fell back. She paid no attention to the tables and chairs and jackets strewn on the floor, to the cups of steaming coffee that could so easily be pulled from the tables. Unconscious of every effort to end the battle that Émile could see, she paced him down the dining room.

He fell back, step by painful step. And he knew he could end it, break the tension, turn, run. She would have made her point. But the energy caught him as much as her, and Émile knew that he was locked into the pattern that she had created. He knew where it was leading and he was both exhilarated and a little frightened.

The fight was ritual, was regulated by the unspoken laws of the Quartier. *Slummer*. So.

His back was against the wall, the dirty cut wood pressing into his back and reinforcing his awareness. How strange the lights seemed, so perfectly aligned and glittering, how uniform the masks of the people who watched, hoping for blood.

Émile smiled. He knew this ritual. He had played it before, but only on the other side. The uptown slummers had devised it for their own amusement, to add to the edge of danger they found attractive down in the Quartier. But slummers ran or fainted before they reached the wall. He had never seen it taken so far, and he was curious to see just how far she would go.

This one was rare. The power in her face was incandescent. Pure awareness tensed every muscle in her. Quavering on the edge of control, she trembled between desire and discipline. The knife danced in the air, sparkled with refracted light, dazzling and lethal and alive.

It danced closer to him. Émile stared deep into her eyes, into the ice-blue anger there and beyond. He met, challenged, resisted only in thought, only in her own knowledge that a fight would be forgotten but an actual killing could not be ignored. Not even in the Quartier du Paris.

Steel rested cool against the base of his throat. He swallowed and felt the point of the knife keenly, pressing, demanding. He met her eyes and saw something new. She had never meant to kill. And, smiling, he was with her. He understood, acquiesced, tilted his head back half a millimeter and met her challenge.

"Do it," he whispered, his voice heavy with anticipation.

Her eyes sparkled and he could feel the desire quivering between them, a physical thing as sharp as the knife and as cold. The urgency of it mounted, ate at him, burned, until he was aware of nothing but the desperate need for release.

He did not feel the cut until it was over, a warm dribble running down his chest and a burning sensation where she had nicked him ever so delicately. Her sample, taken in public, in a way no one could ever trace.

The knife was withdrawn and became lifeless again, only a tool. She turned away, rested her foot on the rung of a chair and slipped the weapon into a thigh sheath, locking it into place for everyone to see.

A residual energy still crackled but it was fast becoming

pallid. Émile had to know this woman. The way she fought, the shimmering purity of purpose in her, these were things he respected.

Passion. Passion outside Beau Soliel was dead. Saint-Just had been to nearly a dozen worlds in his servitude and had known the inhabitants of nearly a dozen more. And all of them had had the juice of living squeezed out by the dry pragmatism of the Justica. Even Gorvitz was less fully alive, less vital, than this woman.

She was already on her way back to the table. Émile picked up a *beignet* from a convenient plate and blew a cloud of powdered sugar at her back. She wheeled around, startled, and then laughed. Grabbing another pastry, she blew sugar all over his face and shoulders.

"Sugar fight," someone screamed from a perch on a chair, and suddenly the air was full of sweet detritus. It swirled and eddied like a demon blizzard so that Émile was lost in the flurries.

Someone grabbed his arm. "Come on."

He was propelled around obstacles and pushed into clear night air that he gulped deep into his lungs. The sugar lined his nose and throat and made the rancid air smell sickly sweet.

"Damn, I hope no one torches the place," his rescuer said. He stared at Anne-Sylvie.

Émile blinked in confusion; Anne-Sylvie shrugged as if it were obvious. "Well, you knew once you started a sugar fight I'd know you were really one of us, not one of Gorvitz's uptown cronies. Uptowners wouldn't even think of doing that. It would ruin their pricy clothes."

"That was the idea," Émile acknowledged.

"I just hope there weren't any idiot slummers in there. One match and *va-room*," Anne-Sylvie added.

Saint-Just shrugged. "It's happened before."

"So you actually live here?" Anne-Sylvie kept the intonation just between a question and statement.

Émile nodded. "I used to," he said carefully, not wanting to tell her any more than necessary. "I used to have some friends down here. I don't know if they're still around. They could put me up, maybe put me in line for a job."

Anne-Sylvie studied him in the unlit night. They crossed

Place Baudelaire and climbed the ornate stone steps to the rooftop world. No fire shot out across the square, no explosion rocked them as they strolled above the sadece-filled streets.

"You need a place to stay, come to our squat on Rue Jacques Doré," she said softly. "We've got room. And we could use the help."

Émile raised an eyebrow. "You trust me so quickly? I almost thought you wanted to kill me back there."

Anne-Sylvie's face barely moved. "I might have, if you hadn't caught on. That's the way it is. But you have nerve. That's the most important thing. We need someone with nerve. Nathalie is over the edge and Alain is cracking."

Émile stiffened. "I'm sorry. It sounds interesting, but I have some rather pressing business. I'm afraid I can't accept your invitation." One of the old phrases he had heard traders use in satire came out in earnest.

"And what business could that be?" Anne-Sylvie asked, taunting.

"You won't believe me," he said bitterly. "No one does."

"Then it couldn't hurt to tell me," she countered.

Émile smiled bitterly at the logic. She sat down on the roof, her legs dangling over the flat edge. No vertigo, he thought, as he sat down beside her. He let his legs dangle over the edge, too, but then moved back and crossed them. The water lay like black ink below, tempting and repulsive at the same time. Like Anne-Sylvie and her little show at the *café*.

He needed to talk. For years he had thought of nothing else. Now he had come home and been rejected by the Syndicat. All of it in just a few hours fifty-seven years too late. The disassociation hit and spun his mind like a filament of shame.

"Just because you're one of Gorvitz's contacts doesn't mean that you know the Justica," he started slowly, not sure just where to begin or if it even mattered. Only the sound of the words calmed him, reassured him of his own reality and of the truth of the years he had lived so recently. Here on the roof that life was unreal, a fiction he had invented and was no part of himself. Eight years in his life, the time between apprentice and journeyman and assistant trader, had never existed from the moment he had returned home.

But they had existed and they had been real and he had the

scars to prove it. The words, the memories, knit it into a cohesive shell under which he could hide the naked virgin years.

"Or hate them. The Justica has become something more, in their own vision of humankind. They think of themselves as Rome, I think, or maybe France under Napoleon. They have the right and the law and the good of every individual in their care. Not that the individual's desire to have that care is ever taken into account. They are the law, by right of force if nothing else, and they enforce their own code on the galaxy.

"And by their code the sadece senin trade is illegal, which makes every trader from the Beau Soliel Syndicat a pirate and every ship a boardable prize. And when they capture pirates they consider themselves humane. We were pressed into service on the Justica long hauls without reprieve. After a trial, of course. They wouldn't do anything without a trial.

"But the sentences they hand out on the long hauls are for life, no matter how little time you serve. Because time goes on at its varied rates. Time is the enemy, always the enemy. But time is not malicious in itself. It gains nothing from a human's pain and it loses nothing at all. It only goes at all its varied rates of speed until it all curves to the end. The geometry of hell, someone called it once.

"Anyway, I was an apprentice. I was sentenced to ten years. They train their workers, and you don't rebel because space is more cruel than the Justica and less forgiving. At the end of your sentence you can join voluntarily and become an officer. An Outtimer. Who else would leave humanity forever except someone who had already left? And besides, no one would miss us when we were gone. It was the one sure job an ex-convict had.

"Anyway, when Beau Soliel signed the Compact, the Justica was just a regulatory trade agency. To insure fair and uniform currency exchanges, list markets and enforce basic uniform safety regulations. I guess you know all that. But they have a different vision of themselves. Too much power too easily for too long, I guess. I don't know. I don't pretend to know. But they thought they would be better at running our homes than we were. For the good of all and all that. The white man's burden, civilize the natives."

"They don't even speak French," Anne-Sylvie pointed out reasonably.

"I thought you were one of Gorvitz's people. I thought you were one of *us*. Or are old pronouncements from the Académie and affairs with Neferasians the only things anyone here cares about? And all you're doing is playing games for the adventure of it. They want to stop the senin trade and they're willing to destroy Beau Soleil to do it. They aren't far away, some distant threat that we can ignore for another generation or two. Gorvitz showed me what happens, how they plan. And we're on the list. Do you understand? If we aren't ready, then the Justica will march in here with their laws and their regulations and their bloodless, lifeless imperial fist."

When he looked up he found Anne-Sylvie staring in his eyes, a hard and lost stare that held too much pity and not a little contempt. "You're too late," she said softly. "Eighteen months old-style too late."

CHAPTER
NINE

"I'm surprised the Syndicat didn't give you a cuff," Daniel said. "Easy way to plant a tracer."

Saint-Just blinked. Obviously Daniel didn't understand what the cuff meant, didn't know the first thing about the Syndicat. Émile had just assumed that everyone of Beau Soliel knew what went on in the Palais on Boulevard Lafitte. Obviously he was wrong.

"If I had a cuff there would be nothing to trace," Émile said slowly, judging how much Daniel would accept. "I would have a room in the compound behind the Palais, eat in the general mess, report to the manifest hall to sign on a Trader. Is that why Anne-Sylvie went through that elaborate set-up? To make sure we weren't traced?"

Daniel shrugged. "Perhaps." Then he frowned, shook his head and sighed. "You still look like a tourist. It's not just your hair. You don't walk right."

There was nothing Émile could say. Eight years of zero-gee had changed his movement habits and the constant gravity tired him more than he wanted to admit. Even sitting upright was a strain.

He'd been led to an old-fashioned tub full of steaming water as soon as he'd arrived with Anne-Sylvie, and when he emerged he found that his clothes had been replaced. Not that he minded; the Justica prison worksuit was not exactly how he wanted to appear. But the group did seem to assume a very great deal.

The new clothes fit well. Alain's, so he was told, a heavy, soft, grey shirt and faded black workpants with extra pockets. Shoes had been harder. Finally some had been found in one of the abandoned rooms, very worn with laces knotted over twice, but he could walk in them.

Anne-Sylvie's apartment was lovely, very large, with two walls of windows and a long balcony covered with vines. It should have cost a fortune, except that this was a squat, its foundations sunk deep into the sadece-infested mud. Sadece roots already had begun to bore into what was the ground floor, snaking tendrils under the doorstop and entering the dark cavity of the downstairs lobby itself.

No one knew how the lobby plants ate. Wild, he supposed. There must be insects and water young floating there to make the ugly stench that overcame even the sadece gas. Besides, what did the sadece do before humans had come to Beau Soliel and begun to cultivate them?

Émile did not see the lobby. "No one goes down there," Anne-Sylvie told him carefully, setting out coffee in mismatched porcelain cups, and a bowl of fruit arranged to hide the bruises.

"Where're the others?" he asked as soon as he emerged, dressed and de-bugged.

Anne-Sylvie ignored his question. Daniel picked up the delicate cup carefully in his wide hands. There was something laughably elegant about it all, decaying and sinking in the mud as they drank from heirloom Limoges. When Émile had lived here before, when there had been gangs and Lola's and busses fired on the street corners and the Café de la Montagne never closed its doors, even then there had been the elegant pretense that he saw immediately in this place. A kind of Quartier tradition, perhaps. His mother had always been so proud of her matching Lalique wine glasses brought all the way from Earth. They had been chipped and passed around a good deal. His mother had gotten them from some obscure sculptor who had been courting her. Or maybe who was paying her for modeling for him; little enough difference.

Twenty-six Rue Jacques Doré had always been an apartment building. It had once been very fine; there were fat gilded cherubs on the ceilings in the hallway and molded garlands and rondeles on the walls. These had been painted in delicate pink and green and gold to match Anne-Sylvie's inherited china. Obviously it had been recently done and Saint-Just thought it was hideous.

"Nathalie," Daniel had said when Émile stared at the ornate walls. "It keeps her busy. Alain might be crazy but Nathalie, well, no one knows if she's even aware of us any more. She hears voices, tells stories, sees ghosts. All very operatic. But she was here first."

Émile nodded comprehension. By common agreement, no one could kick a current resident out of a squat. Good enough; he had no money for rent anyway. Which made him wonder exactly what these people were going to ask him to pay.

Anne-Sylvie brought the coffee pot over to the table. Émile noticed that it was the portable kind with its own power system. Then he realized that the lights were all on remotes and even the ancient heater ran on its own supplies. Not connected to the power grid, at any rate. Now that he thought of it, there wasn't any sign of an entertainment center or even a hookup. It looked too rich for their circumstances. It made him wonder what terror they were hiding. He shuddered slightly and remembered horror stories from prison.

There had been the one woman from Kelemis with Ann-Sylvie's wet lips and smile, a refugee from the famine, or so she said. She had looked too sleek for one of the hungry fleeing that place, and he had heard the rumors from others. That when she and her brother had been caught the Justica troops who apprehended them had found severed hands and forearms, legs and thighs, all carefully butchered, dangling from the ceiling. Two months later the woman was found dead in a faulty airlock. Nothing was ever proved, but most of the prisoners were relieved. Respectable pirates and thieves and killers for hire, they had found the presence of the cannibal unbearable. Lower even than a spy or child molester, most of them agreed. Not proper company for decent criminals.

Anne-Sylvie laughed at his obvious discomfort. "We're not on the power grid," she told him. "When the streets were flooded even the fiber optics went. The filaments got coated with sadece roots and slime and rotted and went brittle. The microwave energy link's too far not to hit the water and if that happens, bam."

There was something in her smile Émile distrusted. Once

more he thought of the cannibal, then pushed the image from his mind. It was just a chance resemblance, no more. There were no bloody bones here, no smell of aging meat.

And besides, it would all be fed to the flowers.

He locked that thought firmly away as well. Sadece was just one more crop, and a lucrative one. One that gave Beau Soliel some power in the Zones, especially since the flowers couldn't be transported. More than one rival Zone leader had tried to steal them. No one knew whether sadece could grow under any but the strange white-violet light, because none of the flowers or their spores had survived the passage. So very fragile and sensitive to light they were it was a wonder they had evolved at all. But before the coming of humanity the sadece and the native insects and the kilometers of algae sheets had done very well. Corals and a few simple sea animals had just begun to emerge, paradise for the biologists.

Ninety-six percent of Beau Soliel's surface was covered with water. The rich primordial water that was the invariable cauldron of life everywhere. No place had been so primitive, so aquatic, hovering at the brink of a living explosion. But the explosion into the millions and millions of forms never came. People came instead.

The sadece had quietly acquired a taste for mammalian flesh. Small rodents were convenient flower-food, but the sadece were not particular.

In the Zones the rumor was that the very highest grade senin came from the human-fed plants. Of course that was absurd. The Syndicat permitted the story to persist only because it brought higher prices, and a sense of awe to the purchaser.

So Anne-Sylvie's explanation of why there was no grid hook in the apartment was perfectly reasonable. She and Alain and Daniel were not involved in some scheme to dismember him and feed him piece by piece to the garden waiting below. He hoped.

"Because of your familiarity with the internal workings of Justica transport, you could be of some help to us," Daniel was saying.

Émile blinked in surprise. "They don't come in from the Zones. And they're armed, most of them anyway. Under programmed command, too, so that even the officers don't have final control. If there are officers. There aren't enough Out-timers to crew all the cans the Justica flies around. You aren't planning to attack them, are you?'' he asked in total shock.

Anne-Sylvie sat and smiled and sipped her coffee. ''That is exactly what we are doing. Why do you think the streets are flooded?''

''I don't know,'' Émile admitted. ''I thought people were cultivating on their own because the franc had dropped and money was tight.''

Anne-Sylvie shrugged. ''No. Times are bad, but not so bad that we need to go that far. When the Justica took jurisdiction over the local Zone they did so in the name of eliminating the drug trade. Naturally they came down and began frying the flower fields.''

Daniel nodded in close sympathy. ''They burned the whole Mariatel plantation. You could smell the stink on the Boulevard Lafitte.''

''All those rich bourgeois, getting their designer clothes sooty from the smoke,'' Anne-Sylvie added. ''There was an ash cloud over Huit Fleurs for days.''

''And the rich girls at Notre Dame de la Paix getting high on the gas and throwing those little uniform hats all over the *rapide*.'' Daniel chuckled at the memory. ''And some of them came down to the Quartier, to the Place Baudelaire, and tried to pick up the residents. That was funny. These little convent-school girls in their very tasteful low shoes and plain gold jewelry throwing themselves at the likes of Alain.''

''The whole city was crazy.'' Anne-Sylvie took over again. ''There was so much sadece in the air that it hurt to breathe. And the very next day the Justica troops burn-sprayed down near the Bois. Which was very stupid and very evil because they got the zoo, too. What did the poor animals do to deserve that?

''But the zoo burned and the animals screamed and tried to escape. Some of them managed. I was sitting in Café Auberge with Nathalie and we saw a burning antelope run down the middle of Rue de la Bois. It screamed and ran and its back was flaming and it smelled like good cooking. It would have been funny if it hadn't been so sad.

''So the flowers are here now,'' she concluded softly. ''All

spread out under different buildings where they can't attack
with spray. They'd have to come in on foot in waders, alley
by alley, to destroy all the flowers. And they know that would
mean open warfare. So." She shrugged and refilled all three
coffee cups automatically.

"And what about in St. Louis? Macon-Grève?" Saint-Just
named off the two closest large cities.

"St. Louis capitulated, what else?" Daniel informed him.
"The idea of flooding the streets actually came from there, but
the mayor was trying to keep the peace and collaborated.
Macon-Grève is under siege. You know them. You remember
their soccer team? You don't play around with Macon-Grève."

"But we're the ones who count," Anne-Sylvie announced,
her voice ringing with pride.

Nor was it false, Émile acknowledged. Huit Fleurs was the
oldest city on Beau Soliel. It was the most cultivated, the
largest, the seat of the Syndicat. Its university was the best in
the colony, its news service the most respected, its restaurants
the most famous and its people the most fashionable. Anyone
who aspired to culture or to power came to Huit Fleurs. Artists,
dancers, musicians, intellectuals were drawn to the Quartier,
which was home to the most famous demimonde in the entire
collection of peopled worlds. On places like Harika and Gel-
misti and New California people knew of the Quartier du Paris
on Beau Soliel.

Huit Fleurs was not only the capital of Beau Soliel, but its
heart as well. Psychologically, as long as Huit Fleurs stood
Beau Soliel was free. Saint-Just felt his throat swell with love
and pride that he belonged here, in this city, in this Quartier.

"It's a delicate balance," Anne-Sylvie said. "A temporary
solution."

"But what precisely do you want me to do?" Saint-Just
asked.

He heard a door swing on an unoiled hinge. Nathalie leaned
against the doorframe, silhouetted by the cherubs and garlands
in the hall. A faint weary smile played around her features.
Her long dark hair lay unkempt on her breasts and she wore
only an oversized man's white shirt that had been shredded
and stained. Her eyes flitted wildly over Émile, the coffee
service, Anne-Sylvie's face, Daniel's hands.

"Mme. Arcineau is with the puss-balls again," Nathalie said. "She's selling them Alain's flowers again, and this time the price is flesh-fed. No more rats in Alain's box. You or me next, Anne-Sylvie. No more rats. Sweet flesh."

She rose on her bare toes, pivoted and fled. Émile wasn't sure she had really been there at all.

Daniel shrugged. "Nathalie lost it when the Justica came in," he said. The explanation seemed to fill the emptiness that hung in her absence. "You wouldn't believe it, but she was, is, a Thiolet. Old Henri's youngest."

"Who is Henri Thiolet?" Émile asked innocently enough.

Daniel and Anne-Sylvie both looked shocked. "He's only the richest man in Huit Fleurs," Anne-Sylvie answered. "Owns the Banc Thiolet, half the real estate on the Boulevard Lafitte and who knows what else. The only thing he doesn't have a hand in is the Quartier."

"And he's a collaborator," Daniel added heavily. "He supported Justica control, said that it would clean up this mess. He has something against sadece, thinks it makes us look bad or something, I don't know."

"Where's he from?" Émile asked. He had never heard of anyone from Beau Soliel having any trouble with sadece. At least not in his time.

"Oh, he's native." Anne-Sylvie picked up on Émile's confusion. "But a small group of influential men want to extend power beyond Beau Soliel, and to do that they have to be Justica citizens. And to do that..."

"We have to become a Justica planet and toe the line," Émile finished for her.

"Exactly," Daniel agreed, nodding. "So Nathalie being here is perfect cover for us. Old Henri isn't about to do anything to hurt her. He comes around here from time to time to drop off food, clothing, a few books. Seeing him try to take care of Nathalie, you could almost forget that he's the one who invited the *flics* here in the first place."

"Gorvitz doesn't know much about us, I think." Anne-Sylvie answered Émile's unvoiced question. "He does know that Beau Soliel is in the process of becoming a voting member of the Justica but he doesn't know the first thing about local politics."

Émile studied Daniel and Anne-Sylvie carefully. "It's better that way," he said slowly, testing the waters. "Gorvitz has the organization and the overall vision, but we're more capable of making local decisions. Besides, the time lag out to the *Constanza* is what, something like four years? And that's if the organization gets through. Sometimes we don't."

"Something like that," Anne-Sylvie agreed dryly.

The coffee had gone cold. Émile set the cup back in the saucer, the delicate white crackle glaze a reflection of the latticework of softknife scars on the backs of his hands. "What do you want?" he asked.

"If you could rearrange a couple of records for us, with what you learned aboard the *Constanza* . . ." Daniel made the pitch smoothly. "And you're Syndicat. You know about their records, how things are organized, how to find what you need and trace the shipments. And how to make connections with the Zones."

"It's not just the drug," Anne-Sylvie added quietly. "Sadece keeps the balance of trade, that's all we need for now. To pay for other shipments, the ones we need help getting through. A few minor changes in a manifest, a routing, a docking permit. Little things that could mean us getting the supplies we need, or having them confiscated. And getting the funds to pay for them. The Independents don't work cheap.

"Will you do it?" Anne-Sylvie asked.

Émile shook his head, not in negation but to clear it. The thoughts were too jumbled, too much had happened in too short a time. "If I can," he said thickly. "I don't know, I've never tried anything like this. But the *flics* are trained and armed and have all the money and support in the galaxy. We don't really have any hope of winning, do we?"

Anne-Sylvie laughed. "No, we can't win. But we can annoy them to death, which is the same thing. But, really, what is the alternative? If we give up the sadece, the bottom drops out of our economy and we're not only a provincial backwater with a reputation, we're a miserably poor provincial backwater so deep in debt to the Justica Development Fund that we'll mortgage the Syndicat out to the *flics*."

"Well, it's not quite that bad yet," Daniel amended. "Although without the sadece trade, our legal exports are all controlled by only a few families. And there are more and more Justica companies buying in every day. The *flics* own the vineyards out near St. Louis. No more Beaujolais Reynard-Marie. All the profits go to the Justica police.''

Émile looked at them, one at a time, carefully. They were crazy, hopeless, the lot of them. They were just going to get themselves killed or sentenced to life on a long-hauler. Complete, utter romantic imbeciles.

And he was going to join them.

CHAPTER
TEN

The *Mary Damned* lay deep in silence. No living being had
been aboard to mark the passage of time since she had been
abandoned, the power gently severed from her mains. And so
there had been no time at all in the years that had passed and
she had drifted derelict.

"Are you sure you know what you're doing?" a harshly
mechanical voice came through the headset.

The small woman wielding a set of delicate probes in the
all too clumsy vacuum suit grunted and went on. At this stage
of the process she had to concentrate. Besides, Gorvitz hadn't
shut up since they had broken out, and now his voice was just
one more background noise. Pauli Tree plied her trade patiently.

Ten minutes went by. Precious minutes of oxygen. They
didn't have much stored in the suit tanks, supposedly so that
none of the prisoners could get out long enough to jump ship.
She had to admit Gorvitz had planned it well. The two of them,
the doctor, the Hounds and the whole Independent-backed Organization on the outside, and then they were gone.

Pauli hadn't believed that it was going to work. She hadn't
particularly cared. If she served out her sentence there was
nothing left to go back to anyway. This time she had taken it
good, no question about that. This time, time itself had destroyed everything that had ever mattered.

She had sworn again that it wouldn't matter aboard the *Constanza*. Things that mattered hurt too much. She thought a lot
about dying and didn't have the energy or the opportunity. And
then Émile had come along.

And so here she was with Hugo Gorvitz, having committed

mutiny on the *Constanza* and run out to the *Mary Damned*. That had been too easy by half, given Gorvitz's connections and the Hounds' muscle. And only two officers to overcome, along with the ship's programming. The officers were more than willing to cooperate in exchange for their lives. So they had made it, and now all they had to do was spring the lock on the *Mary Damned* and they were almost home. Whatever home meant now. Pauli wasn't sure she knew any more, or cared. Only that she was beyond Justica jurisdiction and ready to act out her anger.

She was also wondering if the legendary shipment of sadece senin was still aboard. They had talked about that last night, in the revolutionary mess. Most likely confiscated, Gorvitz had told them, and resold by the Justica agents on the sly. To finance their own little operations. It seemed reasonable.

Gorvitz cursed softly as Pauli worked and wondered if he should have kept his mouth shut. There had been entirely too much interest in the sadece in that meeting the night before. He should know by now that he couldn't trust the Hounds that far; given enough encouragement they might try the mutiny business again, this time to get rich off the senin. Or to use the fabled drug, which would really prove their stupidity. Gorvitz didn't put it past them to use up their one source of income.

And he had plans for that income. Arms, for one thing, and a portable communications post so that he could broadcast to freedom fighters all over Justica territory using the *flics'* own booster power. That came first. Not that he had decided on a base to start from, but the *Mary Damned* would be an excellent staging platform. It had power, speed, riches, and a rep.

Not that he was certain he could even pilot the damned thing. The kid had been right at least about the location, and the witch had been able to calculate the drift. And here they were. Now, if only the Organization had someone expert in Beau Soliel systems . . . He might as well have asked for half the Justica tax revenues.

Pauli tapped him on the shoulder and pointed at the lock. The red seal around the hand-ring had turned green and yielded to pressure, working on independent batteries. She pulled the heavy ring back and the entrance gave onto thick interior dark.

Gorvitz nodded and they went inside. Cycled the dual hull

controls, waited the requisite time, did not take off their helmets. Gorvitz knew better than to trust a ship left derelict so long. Even if the *Justica* hadn't drained it before it became a ghost, he wouldn't trust it.

There was a hiss of compression before the inner door glowed green. They entered the corridor. Gorvitz checked the pressure. Looked pretty good, but he wasn't about to take the chance. Pauli began to unfasten the helmet clasps and Gorvitz gestured with a finger across his throat. The frail pick-lock looked miserable. The suits were clumsy now that they were in atmosphere. At least the *Mary Damned* had no spin or they would be miserably heavy as well.

His helmet light showed only empty space, clean and well cared for. At least at one time. The dark was scary, reminiscent of ancient human fear. At first he wondered why the lights didn't automatically come on when they arrived, and then he realized that all the fiber-optic cables had been cut and the ship was energy-dead.

"There is nothing here," he told himself over and over like a mantra. "There is nothing at all. Just space, just space."

Like the times when he was little and he'd been so frightened of a pile of clothes on the rocker, a disordered heap of toys in the dark. The shadow-monsters never really had died. They had just been banished to the irrational, the ancient mind that survived only to plague the descendants of the Neanderthal.

Nothing moved at all. Nothing breathed the dark wisps of air still remaining, nothing lurked in the shadows. And yet, from Saint-Just's descriptions, he could imagine what it had been like when the *Justica* interrupted the trader flight. A drug raid, so it had been reported. An anonymous tip. Just the way the *Justica* liked to do things, all neat and legal.

Pauli made a funny humming sound that came through the suit speaker and stopped at a closed door. She hummed some more, something Gorvitz assumed was music, and then the door pulled back to reveal the heart of the *Mary Damned*.

In the dark there wasn't much to see. Only a few dead screens, earphones, and three dustless seats. Right. According to Saint-Just there had been a Captain, a mate and a navigator in central control.

"They just cut it," Pauli said angrily. "No elegance, no

sense of the moment, nothing. A straight cut. A newborn baby
could put this back.''

She picked several tools off her utility belt and launched into
the dark. Her helmet light glowed across the small chamber
but Gorvitz couldn't tell what she was doing. A sudden burst
of white brilliance blinded him, and he blinked as his eyes
readjusted to the dark.

There were moments of silence, the thick silence of concentration. And then the *Mary Damned* came to life again.

CHAPTER
ELEVEN

Hugo Gorvitz sat at the unfamiliar station and stared down Fox. "No," he said patiently. "We are not going back on our word and offing the *flics*. We may need them later. They may come over to our side. They aren't much different from us, okay? Besides, they're taking care of *Constanza* while we tow her."

Fox, disappointed, nodded. "But boss, when are we going?" he asked, whining.

If there was anything Gorvitz hated, it was a whiner. He didn't know how Fox had managed to get into the Hounds and he supposed he didn't want to know. He knew of the more vicious practices aboard the *Constanza*, although he himself had never practiced them.

"We'll go when I decide where we're going," Gorvitz said reasonably. There was no reason to let the Hound know just how unfamiliar the controls of the *Mary Damned* were. Although they had to move soon. The Justica would trace the *Constanza* down once it missed a rendezvous, and although he had timed the take-over and the beginning of the maximum interval, he had never figured out the relative timing and so he didn't know when they'd be missed. Maybe there was already a Justica group heading down on them.

He didn't want to think about that. Just figure out the idiot controls. That couldn't be so esoteric. For a moment he considered asking for the officers off the *Constanza* to brief him, but discarded that idea as useless. The Syndicat ship should be as alien to them as to him.

But he couldn't even ask the computer for help or read the most basic signs. This was bad. Worse than bad. And he didn't have the time to learn a new language. It hadn't occurred to him to learn any French while Saint-Just was around, and now there was no one to translate. The entire set-up stank.

"Yo, boss," Pauli Tree said from the hatch. "Good news."

"Yeah, I could use some," he replied.

Pauli smiled and she looked about a million miles away. Really too thin, he thought; she looked like she would break in a high wind. And her skin was a translucent white, almost glazed and so taut that it, too, looked brittle. And yet she seemed more relaxed than he had ever seen her before.

"We found the senin," she said, smiling dreamily. "Liters and liters of it. A fortune, all stowed in cargo. Looks like the Justica didn't even bother doing a once-over."

Hugo shook his head sadly. He understood the faraway look now, although he had thought Pauli too smart to fall for the trap. "You're high," he said with contempt.

"Well, you don't need me for anything else," Pauli pouted. "I brought you some. And in case you're worried, there's still more than enough to buy an entire fleet, let alone a few rounds of smart-shells and suckers and enough batwipes for the entire Eglentine legion." She giggled and held out an elegant flask.

He handled the vial gingerly. "For the price they give you the package," he grunted. And the bottle itself was unquestionably a work of art in its own right, blue glass richly veined, with fluid silver and red running under the surface. It responded to the warmth of his hand like something alive, the colors swirling into new patterns and separating again.

He opened the flask and sniffed at it.

"Not like that," Pauli instructed. "The stopper should have a dipper at the end. Just touch it to your skin, anywhere. Although the stories say it's better if you rub it inside your cheek or nose, or over your eyelids. I heard some of the artists, not the ones from Beau Soliel, but others, dropped it in their eyes. That's how Jannde Tal-Wing did *The Ascension of the Millions*."

Gorvitz held the bottle away from himself. "How the hell did you know a thing like that?" he asked, more reflectively than making actual inquiry.

Pauli smiled through the senin haze. "I worked rich people's houses," she said softly. "Once I almost did a museum job, only the collector backing our acquisition died before we were ready. Would have been a good haul, too. Collector was high up in the Justica. Very high up. Was going to pay us plenty and keep us out of trouble on top of it. Was going to set us up in a villa on Segunda for two subjective years.''

Gorvitz stopped listening. The drug was making her ramble, and he didn't trust half of what she said. Under the influence, fantasy and reality became interchangeable as pleasure dictated. He turned his attention back to the controls, or lack thereof.

There were words written over blank grey glass panels. He supposed the words indicated functions, and that somehow the panels were screens that needed only to be activated, but there was no indication of how to make that happen. He cursed himself again for not anticipating a foreign technology. He had believed the propaganda of his enemies, that the Justica had the only real viable interactive tech going. No one else had the resources to duplicate their equipment, let alone the research facilities to design anything so complete in the first place.

For the first time in his life, Hugo Gorvitz was stymied by a Justica lie. Because whatever designed the *Mary Damned* had nothing to do with the Justica at all. No wonder they had simply cut the power connections and left without searching the whole ship. Gorvitz thought he knew Justica functionaries well enough to believe that they had been shocked and horrified by systems they couldn't control. Better just to let it alone, pretend that it didn't exist, that they hadn't seen it. Better to blot out the whole past and make believe that memory was at fault.

It made sense, it was Justica thinking, but it didn't help Gorvitz at all.

In the background he heard Pauli still talking. He ignored her, returned his attention to his own misery. And so he missed her movement, her sudden lurch forward and grab at the open bottle. "If you're not going to use it . . ." she said, and jerked the vial from his hand.

The sudden, hard action in zero-gee scattered drops of sadece senin floating around Gorvitz's face. He closed his eyes and flinched. Pauli took the bottle and tried to recapture the opalescent drops that drifted like weightless multicolored pearls in the cabin.

He barely felt the damp as globular drops of senin landed on his lips, his eyelid, his nose, his neck. He could feel a mild warmth spreading through his limbs, his arteries almost illuminated by the drug. The soft distance was comforting. In his mind he knew that it was all over. He was doomed and his revolution was destroyed, vanquished by the *Mary Damned*. He couldn't fly the ship, he couldn't outrun the Justica. They had to be after him by now, or soon. And there was nothing at all he could do but sit here and stare at the blank screens, hoping they would reveal their use through sheer persistence.

They would not, and he knew it. So he only had to wait to be taken, again, to rest in the senin-induced haze until it was finished. At least it wouldn't feel too bad. All of a sudden he understood why some people became addicts. It wasn't because the drug was so pleasant, but because reality was so cruel. Through the creeping sadece he was aware of reality but he no longer cared. About anything.

Hugo Gorvitz lay his head back against the headrest in the control seat (or what he had assumed had to be the control seat) and let the growing warmth and abandon take him. He felt cold against his neck, at the base of his skull. It wasn't entirely comfortable, but buffered by the senin he dismissed the sensation. He could pick and choose his reality, at least for as long as the drug lasted. He hoped it lasted a long time.

Present identification before engaging navigational sequencer.

Gorvitz's eyes flew open but it wasn't the control room he saw. Rather, he was inside a glowing structure, bound by glistening spiderweb threads and only half awake yet. He could see outline of dark blocks in the delicate light, see the darkness gathering and quiver around them as if they were struggling to come back alive after death and regeneration.

Identification. Yes. He remembered something about Saint-Just asking about a cuff, or some piece of jewelry.

Yes, yes, the pulsating web told him as it gathered around him. It was brighter now, he thought, colors rippling through changes from blue to lavender to pink to yellow to ultraviolet. He was aware of its hunger, a loneliness only a purpose and a human could fill. It quivered with recognition, with anticipation so pointed and sexual that he was aroused.

Only a drug-dream, he told himself. Only *sadece senin*. No wonder people were willing to pay outrageous prices for it. And yet this was not the dream he would have chosen, he told the dream quite sternly. He wanted something with a human woman, preferably two of them and neither so small as Pauli Tree. And there would have to be blood and the scent of explosives and the ache of victory.

The setting wavered, dissolved into a chaotic non-space, and resolved into a control room with symbols he could read and a tall, salt-and-pepper haired woman wearing hand-painted silks and a wide silver bracelet that covered her forearm a quarter of the way to her elbow. She turned and he saw a pattern incised in it, two circles with an arrow through them.

She touched the bracelet to a glowing patch on the control board and the net came alive again. Only this time he was seeing it through the screen, and the colors were more brilliant and made less sense.

Is this better? the woman asked.

Gorvitz hesitated. Either he was hallucinating so deeply that he wouldn't notice if they were taken or even if he was dead, or something was going on with the ship.

Laughter came like bells behind him. *You understand*, the voice agreed happily. *You don't have drugware where you come from?*

Drugware? Then it wasn't a hallucination, not entirely. Gorvitz knew that there was no way that idea came from his mind. He had been under hypnosis several times and had done more than one experiment with the doctor. He decided to go along with it. He didn't have a better shot.

But you don't have the key, the computer cooed sadly. *Without the key I can't become fully interactive*.

Gorvitz nodded solemnly. He had expected something like this. No wonder Saint-Just had been so crazy about that cuff. It wasn't just a form of identification in the Syndicat, it was the key to the ship's systems. "We have had some trouble. The cuffs were removed. And we have to get out of here immediately, or the Justica will come again and this time they won't just cut your power lines."

Mary Damned in the form of Elisabeth Sarrault frowned and thought, *How can I trust you?*

"You can't," Gorvitz replied. "But you don't have any choice. We need to get to Herrara. I can give you the relative data."

Elisabeth Sarrault looked distressed. *I cannot accept your data. Without a key I cannot accept your destination nor your commands. My options are limited without proper Syndicat identification.*

"What are your options?" Gorvitz asked.

We can stay here, the ship told him. *Or we can return to the Palais Syndicat, Huit Fleurs, Beau Soliel. I am sorry, those are the only available options unless an authorized key is presented.*

Gorvitz didn't have to think about the options. The fact that he had never considered Beau Soliel at all became incidental. The overriding condition was that the Justica was going to come after them and he didn't want to sit around and wait. He didn't know if the ship could make it home without being spotted and stopped, if they could avoid the Justica for the entire journey, but one thing was certain. There was nothing to be gained by sitting where they were.

The form of Elisabeth Sarrault dissolved into the glowing web. He could read/taste/feel the pleasure in the energy pulsing through the net. *Home, home, home,* it rejoiced, and the colors changed from glistening pastels to strong primaries. Stars wheeled around the dark spaces between the bright structures, flickered and then fixed themselves into intricate patterns.

The joy engulfed him, sang through his nerves, creating a species of pleasure he had never imagined, the single-pointed exultation of a being that was not truly alive but not inanimate, either. Fixed and utterly without need, it had a more than human desire.

Unless this, too, told him something of its makers on Beau Soliel. Because for all the experience he had in the worlds of the Justica, he knew that what the Syndicat had created was anathema. It was an evil greater than the Justica could fathom, and so they had never understood sadece senin and Beau Soliel. In the Justica, machines were machines. But Hugo Gorvitz knew that in some unfathomable way, the *Mary Damned* had a soul and she was going home.

CHAPTER TWELVE

Home. It was a long time since Hugo Gorvitz had thought about home. If he had a home, which he doubted. He had lived aboard the *Constanza* longer than any other fixed place in his adult life. Which left only the home he had repudiated and the family that he refused to acknowledge.

Not that that was solely his choice. His brother Joachann had turned him in, finally. Hugo had known it was going to happen and he hadn't run, hadn't used any of his three false passports to disappear. In those days he still believed that he was invincible, that there was a special magic that protected him from harm. He had believed that it was the magic of righteousness, but over the long years on the *Constanza* he came to realize that it had been the magic of his mother's very important and very wealthy family that had kept him from the arrests and beatings that his friends suffered.

Hugo had been humiliated by his family, by his mother's position in the Justica Assembly, by his brother's screamingly blind ambition and by everyone else's expectations of him. It wasn't his fault that he wasn't like his mother and her siblings, tall and athletic and cheerfully confident of their own rightness. Joachann was exactly the child she deserved. He had not only been the eldest, but the true child of their mother's spirit.

Hugo had been different from the first. He hadn't looked like the rest, not overly tall, not freckled, not fair. His cousins teased him, called him the runt, and the fact that he had asthma didn't help. It was his own fault, they said. Psychological. Obviously bad genes from somewhere, most likely his father. Not that he knew his father. His mother had been very careful on that score. For both Joachann and himself she had made certain that their first and only loyalty was to the Dorn clan. Fathers were superfluous in her scheme. Her brothers served the function as well, and their priority was the propagation of Dorn influence and power.

Hugo had never even tried to play the game. He couldn't compete physically ("It's all in your head, you're doing this because you want to," his mother had said only too often) and while power and its uses fascinated him, he got much more mileage out of goading his cousins and going behind their backs.

Like the incident with Yolonda, the maid, an indentured girl from Cariha who wanted to go to school and maybe learn garmenttech. A reasonable ambition, not beyond her intellectual means and reasonably middle-class. He wondered why he remembered Yolonda so well. There had been other women, both in the household and beyond. But something about the Carihan maid, maybe her anger or just her pride, that made her stand out in his memory. Maybe it was because his cousins thought her unattractive and accused him of accepting charity from a dependent.

But it wasn't charity he recalled. It was the small chapbooks, flimsy paper-printed things that littered the whole of her room. He read them, all of them, the newspapers and political diatribes. And Yolonda, finding him among her readings, had tried to shoo him away.

He asked questions about the stories he read, the romances and confessions and essays that somehow didn't reflect the reality he knew. At fourteen he had been insatiably curious and shopping for a cause. It hadn't been the first time he'd been seduced, but it had been the best. Later she told him that she'd been afraid that he'd tell, and she had tried to distract him.

He had only been fascinated and wanted more. More of her body and more of her rebellion. Looking back he understood that it was simplistic rebellion at best, the straightforward fantasies of the underclass that reduced everything to a good-and-evil formula. But it was his first contact with something he knew in his heart had to exist outside of the compound, a universe where the Justica was not the top prize in a convoluted and all-encompassing game. Secretly he had always reviled the

Justica because it was the goal and source of Dorn power, but he had never before known others who felt the same way. That they wrote these feelings into stories and essays thrilled him.

His favorite stories were a graphic series about a man named Beamer Gorvitz, a drifter and urban guerrilla who organized columns of the underground in various cities. He stood for the rights of the non-incorporated minorities, the "paper citizens" who were subject to Justica law without the privileges of the legal responsibles. Beamer Gorvitz, of course, had been a legal responsible and had repudiated that greatly valued status to fight injustice and economic exploitation.

The best story in the series had Beamer Gorvitz helpless, wounded in a safe house, waiting to be caught for having blown up the power cells of a denser factory. Caught in the back-blast fire, Beamer had risked his life yet again to save a girl who worked the power stocks. As he recovers he teaches her that the central Justica planets are overdeveloped and depleted. They need the resources and the trade of the younger worlds to survive. That their fleet and riches and all the Zones through-out the Justica dominion are financed on the backs of "paper citizens" so that the legal responsibles can live in luxury. And it showed some of Beamer's own background, not terribly different from Hugo's own. Beamer Gorvitz was his role model and the person he fantasized being when he locked the door to his room during the day.

His mother seemed to consider the liaison with Yolonda healthy and did not inquire into what Hugo was learning from the maid outside of bed. He believed that his mother never thought that he bothered talking to Yolonda; certainly she and his uncles didn't worry about conversations with people whose only use was pleasure. They were usually stupid, his mother complained frequently, boring, and they expected you to take their priorities seriously. Which was naturally ridiculous.

One day Yolonda finally asked if he would help her. Only a small task, but important. If he would interface some data into his mother's office equipment. It wasn't very impressive, Yolonda had said shyly, just a little message from the under-ground. But Hugo could get into her Assembly office and Yolonda, as a housemaid, couldn't.

He had agreed eagerly, took the denser and downloaded it

as soon as he could slip into his mother's office. Less than a full day afterward, he had been so pleased with himself that his cousins' jibes barely scratched the surface of his good mood. He went back to Yolonda's room and when she arrived she treated him more like a man in bed than the boy she had once seduced. It was early morning before he made his way from the servants' hall to his mother's bungalow.

They should have been asleep at that hour, but all the lights were on. Joachann greeted him at the door. "You better get your ass inside and upstairs fast, because you don't want to catch what's going on around here."

"Huh?" Hugo had been in another dimension.

"Move," his brother had whispered. "Before she comes down again."

"What happened?" Hugo finally had the presence of mind to ask.

"Some terrorist slipped a virus into the Assembly system. Through her terminal. Chewed up half the memory before Winston nixed it. And now she's under investigation by the Internal Affairs branch, besides being the target of a terrorist attack. Maybe someone wants to kill her or something, and then where would you be, you little worm? In bed with your mulatto whore, like always? Mother's going through Hell and I'm trying to keep things halfway in shape, and you go off screwing the help. You know what I think of you, Hugo? I think she should take her name back and toss you out. And the only reason I haven't suggested it so far is because you're still under age."

Hugo edited out the usual and was left with the new data about the virus. It took more than a moment to realize that he was the terrorist. He was half pleased and half horrified.

When the incident was aired on the public newsnet he was fascinated, glued to the story for days. Both uniformed members of the Assembly Security Force and plainclothes detectives of the Secret Service stayed around the bungalow asking questions and searching for days.

Once an announcement that the perpetrator was known and was going to be apprehended in hours had Hugo terrified. He had sat on his bed with a comforter tucked around his feet and read comic books with the stereo on full blast, waiting for them to come and haul him away. It never happened. Yolonda had planned her action well. She avoided him in the weeks after the virus, and when he went looking months later she was gone.

She had left him a good-by note and a package of old magazines bundled up inside a box. The note was short and sweet, what a maid would say to one of the family she'd been sleeping with. No more than any of the notes his mother or his uncles had gotten. It cut Hugo to the quick. There was nothing at all special, nothing to acknowledge the thing they had done together, the blow they had struck.

From the time Yolonda left until he himself was of age and ready to leave, he became cold and remote to the rest of the family. He didn't go out of his suite except when demanded, and then only did what was absolutely necessary. His brother still taunted him for a while, and then stopped because Hugo didn't react satisfactorily. He no longer turned red and balled his fists and threatened an asthma attack. He just sat on his bed and stared at the offender, Joachann or cousin, playing offensive music as loud as it would go. Eventually they became bored and left.

On his eighteenth birthday he went down to Citizen Registration and became a legal responsible of the Justica, his identification issued under the name Hugo Gorvitz. Then he claimed his legal share and left home for the university. He never returned.

Hugo Gorvitz studied economics, traditional and Justica and revolutionary, and found that it was more complex than he had imagined. In fact, there was no simple and clean-cut flow from the newer worlds to the Justica's ruling families. It was far more convoluted than that. And perhaps in the beginning there had been little bad intent, but only stupidity and laziness and greed and ambitious underlings. Excesses became institutionalized and then traditionalized. The process of becoming Justica property, for example, was considered straightforward. Its one fallacious assumption was that any population would prefer to be Justica than Independent or, evil above all by Justica standards, unaligned.

Being a good student didn't matter. He wasn't contacted by the Organization until well into his second year, and the first contact was very tentative. He was assigned plebe tasks, delivering messages and bail money, mailing newspapers and graphic magazines, supplying money and rides and crash space to comrades who were just passing through. By the time he had graduated he had become the leader of the local cell.

All the Dorn tricks were just as useful in the Organization as they were in the Assembly. The lobbying and gaining consensus, the subtle organizing and arranging for support of a program, all the things the clan despaired of him learning, now came to the front. He was, in fact, as much the son of Alia Dorn's spirit as Joachann had ever been.

And, much as he hated to admit it, Hugo Gorvitz enjoyed what he was doing. Rebel prince, firestarter, zealot. It didn't hurt that it was more than attractive to women. A lot of women. On the Steering Committee, his nom de guerre was merely "Gorvitz." Everyone in the Organization was familiar with the fictional graphic hero. No one had any idea that it was his legal registered name.

He'd been on the Steering Committee for almost a year when he suggested what was later dubbed "Operation Groh" for the Groh Standard Operating Systems Central that was their target. Hugo hated Groh with especial venom, which would have pleased his mother and brother no end. Sebastian Groh was Joachann's most bitter rival on the Expansion and Exploration Committee. Not that Hugo realized that consciously at all. He just knew that the Groh Systems Central was one of the most profitable nets in the Justica, and one of the most respected. The fact that they practiced no more censorship than any other data management bank did not affect him in the least. They were to be made an example, that was all. And in his plan it was an example that every subscriber would know about, and learn the basics of revolutionary philosophy as well.

The plan was perfectly simple. Hugo and his team would go through the standard interface and join together on-line. Then, from six different and widely spread ports, they would set up a sympathetic vibration on-line. One or two lines in wouldn't hurt a net the size of Groh, and no one had ever bothered with the complications of setting up a multiple feedback loop that would actually do real damage. Coordination, calibration, enough backing for the subscriptions and the people to go in and do the job, take the risk. The plan wasn't simply a matter of tearing down the Groh net for a while, it was a way of making the authorities take the Organization seriously. The authorities, and the people the rebels desired to win over.

As long as they were perceived as a band of young malcontents without much serious coordination and financial backing nobody would join them. The urban raids they ran would be meaningless unless there was some hope of popular uprising. No revolution ever succeeded as a top-only movement; those were coups d'etat and were motivated by completely different forces.

The whole plan, from beginning to end, had been Hugo's. He had the people who could do the job, the ports already placed and the subscriptions laundered. The Steering Committee gave varied approval, from "Tania LaLutta" who thought the whole thing elitist grandstanding but was intrigued to try it, to "Lenin" the tech nerd who was utterly entranced and whose only objection was that he wasn't included in the team. Hugo pointed out that it was "Lenin" himself who had proposed the rule that only one member of the Steering Committee should ever be involved in any single operation. For security, and for stability of the committee. Two busted operations with multiple Steering Committee members rounded up and they would be in bad shape.

The set-up had been perfect. As per plan he had been the first on-line. He timed it, watching the tenths of seconds drag by before he put the sequence in the port. Nothing that, by itself, the net would find worth noticing.

Time passed, a tenth of a second at a time, while he was wired to nano. Anticipation tasted metallic, tuned, ready. And the numbers went so slowly, so very slowly.

And then there was only silence.

He awoke in a private cell in Rutland Holding Facility. He never knew how long he had been out. He never knew who had spilled the plans. Or if the net itself had identified the potential danger in the series sequenced by six supposedly unrelated ports.

At his trial he realized that it was something intensely more personal. Groh against Dorn. The fact that he had registered under the name Gorvitz was taken as a political stance to give him the freedom to move against the family's enemies, his actions monitored as a matter of course by the Grohs, who kept tabs out of informed paranoia. This time it had paid off. The one who had betrayed the plan had been Hugo himself, his own bioprint a red flag in the Groh net.

Neither his mother nor his brother attended the trial, which was hot news for at least thirty-seven hours. Nor did any of the Dorns appeal his sentence, fifty years subjective aboard the *Constanza*. His only solace when he was shipped out in chains was a contact from the bonding clerk, who counted up his belongings and marked them for safekeeping. The clerk passed him a message folded in his receipt: the information that his mother had lost her Assembly seat due to his actions, signed "the Steering Committee."

CHAPTER THIRTEEN

Émile Saint-Just lay on his own sofa in his own apartment and tried to ignore the smell of mold coming from the first floor. They had tried to set him up in the building, but the only apartment that was still habitable was only two flights up from standing water, which made it less desirable than those that were already claimed.

With the exception of Alain's apartment, of course. Alain's was on the second floor, his balcony directly over a thick stand of dark purple and green-white sadece. Even from Émile's wrought-iron terrace he could smell the drug-gas so strongly that it masked the odor of the stagnant canal. Only when he went inside and closed the window was he assaulted by the stench of the first floor. That wasn't considered so bad.

The plants were thick-petaled and healthy, well fed. He had watched Alain that morning, dropping small rodents expertly into the waiting cups. Alain had looked up and waved. Émile had managed to keep his features in order and waved back. It would have been very bad manners not to. It would have been very bad politics. But it disgusted Émile all the same.

Just before dawn found Émile sitting over *café au lait* and *beignets* at the Café de la Montagne, waiting for the first edition of *L'Ami du Peuple* to be delivered. Émile needed to find a job, and the advertisements in the Quartier paper promised to be more palatable and more flexible than those from uptown.

Flexibility was important if he was going to work with Daniel and Anne-Sylvie. He had to be master of his time. But he couldn't live off them, either. Any moral lack was more than offset by the fact that they didn't have enough money to keep him in more than a few days worth of bread and coffee. Na-

thalie, of course, had money from her father. Émile had asked
Alain how he managed to keep himself fed and remain free.

"I keep our flowers, which are excellent and highly pro-
ductive. And we have a number of the Green Monsters, which
I process separately."

Émile had nodded. Green Monster senin was one of the most
potent and highly priced. It was also stockpiled by the Syndicat
for navigators and pilots. A mere apprentice trader, he hadn't
been in interface, but he knew that "green senin" was one of
the bridges into the systems.

"And I breed feed," Alain had continued matter-of-factly.
"Mice and gerbils and hamsters. I break their teeth off, of
course, and take out their claws before I feed them to our
plants. We suffer far less damage that way. I don't understand
cultivators who simply can't be bothered. And I don't do rats."

"Oh?" Émile asked weakly. He didn't want to know, didn't
even want the conversation to go on at all. But there was no
polite way to stop Alain. Privately, Émile was of the opinion
that Alain was as crazy as Nathalie.

"No." Alain ignored Émile's disinterest. "They're too
smart. Much too smart. First they get out of the cages, then
they get out of the apartment. And when you build stronger
cages, well, the rats know. They know where they're going
and they protest. They become violent, you can't handle them
at all. And the sadece gas only makes them worse."

Émile nodded. It made him slightly sick, the idea of something intelligent, something knowing that it was going to be
fed to the lustrous beauties that choked the streets. Or maybe
it was only the hour, his long nights and the fact that he only
had three francs left in the world, one of which was already
committed to a copy of the paper. It was a new feeling. On
the *Constanza* he had never had to think about where the next
meal was coming from or if he could afford the microbattery
time to turn on the lights. In the Syndicat and in prison both,
he had never been prepared for everyday life. For money.

"You know, you could run some deliveries for me," Álain
said. "I have a couple of shipments going out in the next few
days, one to your old friends in the Syndicat. I could pay you
maybe ten francs for the job. It's not much, but when it comes
along . . ."

Émile's eyes lit up. Not that he wanted a delivery job. There had to be something he could do, there had to be openings for a ceramic power worker somewhere. And with his skills there should be something for decent money and flexibility. Maybe even enough money to work part-time. That would be perfect.

But no matter what he did, there was still the problem Anne-Sylvie had set him. And although he could jump the interface, he had to get to a Syndicat port to do that. And those were all restricted to Syndicat members only, in areas where outsiders weren't permitted. And without a cuff there was no way Émile could pass for anything but an outsider. The Syndicat was jealous of its privilege and guarded its privacy zealously.

But delivering green senin to the Palais, well, no one would notice him. No one would even see him at all. Pauli Tree had taught him that, one early morning when she grew nostalgic for the tools of her trade, her enzyme picks and magnetic code box. She had been taught how to go in and case a job carefully. Never, never, never start without a good layout of the security system, without a complete schedule of every occupant. Better to have someone on the inside, of course; that was ideal. It didn't always happen, but sometimes it was possible to get on the inside.

Porters, repair techs, delivery folk and paperboys were all completely invisible. Pauli had played all of them during her career. She could even wander almost freely on the pretext of being lost, if the place was large enough. And the Palais was definitely large enough.

Even if someone did know you, Pauli had told him, they still wouldn't recognize you. Put a uniform on anyone, with a name patch in red letters and a company logo on the back, and even your best friend will have to look twice.

At the Palais there was no one who knew him. Dumouriez and the receptionist had seen him only briefly, and there was little chance of his running into them again. Even going for restricted ports, the receptionist was up front, which was the last place he wanted to go. And Dumouriez had a private port. Émile judged him the type not to leave his office unless there was some kind of emergency. Besides, he'd been in a Justica prison suit then. Whoever said clothes make the man must have been an experienced thief.

A young girl with gang tattoos on her cheeks dropped a bundle of papers on the floor next to the pastry counter. Émile joined the others waiting in a scrimmage for the stack. Two tried to tear him off the crowd. Apartment hunters, most likely. The three public phones next to the rest room were already staked and claimed. Fifty-seven years, and that much hadn't changed. He let the apartment hunters scratch out each other's knuckles and waited until the blood had cleared before he picked up a copy for himself and laid a franc on the counter.

"You know, I don't know why you bother to pay for the thing," Alain said. "Just wait fifteen minutes for the apartment hunters to tear out their pages. Most of them just leave the rest on the floor."

Some things had changed, then, in fifty-seven years. No one would have left a paper on the floor of the Café de la Montagne before. One of the waiters would have rolled it up and run across the Place Baudelaire to return it, and slapped you with it in the process. In those days the waiters of the Café de la Montagne had a reputation to maintain. Of course, in those days the Place Baudelaire hadn't been submerged, either.

But Alain didn't remember those times and definitely didn't care. He threw the job advertisements to Émile and then began to leaf through as if he were searching for something. "I can't believe it," Alain muttered, his face coloring with anger. "I can't believe it. Jacques Vennot's poems are in here. Again. They're terrible. And another essay by Simon Simon and a column by Fissard."

He was tearing the paper in rage. Émile thought it was a touch excessive and perhaps not quite sane. "My poems are better than theirs. Better. I was at the university and they said that my work was the best in this century. That's what they said. And now those idiots, those literary acts of constipation, are published in *L'Ami du Peuple*. As if they had any merit."

"Maybe even the paper has a Justica slant," Émile said, more to calm Alain down than anything else. "They only publish things that are politically safe. Certainly your work is not."

Alain raised his head and ceased trashing what little was left of the paper. "You're probably right," he said after a long, thoughtful pause. "Just that I had always considered *L'Ami du*

Peuple to be on our side, you know. That they were the cutting edge, would never sell out. But to publish Simon Simon, you are right. They have been subverted like everything around us. Downtown I expect to fall, I assume on Boulevard Lafitte the only moral value is expediency. But the Quartier—I thought here at least we could stand firm against the forces of perversion.''

Émile said nothing. There was a craziness in Alain that frightened him more than Nathalie's retreat from reality. Alain could be dangerous. And he fed the flowers and extracted the senin. Both of which showed a certain degree of psychosis. Émile rose and gathered up the pages he wanted. His one franc had been badly spent. Perhaps there was a job there, but he had paid for the rest of the paper as well. He wouldn't mind reading the news and the entertainment section, learn the names of popular bands and new clubs, and the current bestselling books and catch up on the soccer scores. But Alain had trashed the entire thing.

"Let's go," Émile said heavily. He drained the last of the *café au lait* and walked to the door. Alain followed. And there, as Alain had predicted, was another paper sitting abandoned on a chair in front of a croissant going stale. It was near virgin, with only the housing ads gone. Émile picked it up and tucked it under his arm before Alain could see. Then, thinking again, he took the croissant, too. Whoever had left in such a hurry wasn't coming back any time soon, and Émile had only two francs left and he was hungry.

So they had walked across the narrow sky bridges of the Quartier as the violet dawn broke, the haze of the nebula brightening and the colors glowing in distinct swirled patterns. The smell of baking bread masked the sadece and mold in the air and the booksellers were setting up on the skyway over the recently drowned Exposition Fountain. Émile remembered when the Fountain had been new, brilliant sculpture, the pride of the Quartier. In the middle of the Place d'Instruction, it had been surrounded by ornately etched slab benches. In the afternoons many of the professors from the university sat out and drank their wine and coffee in the serene square. The bookstore clerks and waiters often sat on the benches, exchanging gossip, and musicians played in front of open instrument cases for a few francs.

All kinds of music had permeated the Place d'Instruction. Old men played jazz and young girls played Scarletti on ultra-light keyboards. Sometimes a chanteuse from one of the local clubs had joined in for a song after hours, when the uptowners were leaving the streets for their secure properties in their secure cabs. In the late sadece-scented night the denizens of the Quartier sat out and listened to Marie Martin or Lisette Plage singing about miserable love and poverty in Huit Fleurs.

Now the fountain was covered with graffiti and abandoned to the sadece. The once fine structure now was chipped and the arm of one of the nymphs had been broken off above the elbow. The benches were still there but they were empty. Green scum covered the standing water that came almost to sitting surfaces that now seemed more like stepping stones in a pond. Émile was deeply saddened. At least the booksellers were still there, although now their stalls lined the skyway rather than the walls of the square. Old bound books and reading chips and flimsy prints all jumbled together on the wheeled handcarts that the sellers could take to any point in the city. But the university was their best market, and so the Place d'Instruction was still a favored spot.

Émile was exhausted by the time they reached home. Alain's company had sucked him dry and he only wanted to be alone. He wanted silence.

"Would you like to watch me feed the flowers?" Alain asked as they reached the door.

Émile shook his head. "I'm tired." Alain seemed to accept that and left Émile alone.

In the early dawn he smelled the air, a complex blend of fresh and mildewed and baking bread. A breeze rippled across his bare face and riffled through his hair. Sensation overwhelmed him.

The smells triggered wakefulness; the movement against his skin signaled the beginning of a new life in the old regime. Wonder and joy and innocence trembled at the experience. He felt the biowash of chemicals through his blood like a torrent, the body dictating his movement and being, his emotional reaction to the world. He watched Alain go inside and waited on the steps, frozen in the haze of perception.

The smell of mold came through clearly. He tried to dismiss it, remain focused on the body that surrounded him. But the mold penetrated, insisted on acknowledgment. It offended him; it was a thing that did not belong in this perfect organism.

And it was there because the whole of Beau Soliel was drowning. Slipping back into the primordial muck it had once been, only the equatorial archipelago emerging above the chemical bath of the eternal ocean. And the Justica was taking the life away again, letting the water come back on dry land. The primitive reclaiming its own.

There was a poignant justice in it, Émile realized. Perhaps it was for the best and the overlords should simply permit them to sink in their own decadence and effete concerns, their matters of importance.

Beau Soliel, the most beautiful place in the known universe, was dying slowly. Some day young people would remember in hushed voices the excesses and penetrating glory of that place. The Quartier du Paris in the city of Huit Fleurs was the most perfect thing of its kind. Resplendent in the deep purple darkness, the Quartier killed itself by degrees. The more perfect it became the more fragile, and the closer to the end.

And then another smell, only one molecule per million in the air, shocked him through his elegant *tristesse*. The smell was fire.

chapter fourteen

Fire. Flickering light, redder and more threatening than the sky of Beau Soliel, played across his ceiling. Saint-Just raced to the window. Below, the canal was calm. Shadow hung over the wetway like night. The balconies were deserted, strange; the wrought-iron fancywork that enhanced the architecture in a more affluent age became ominous and threatening, turning the street into the open tiers of a jail.

The stillness erupted. The balconies filled with half-dressed people screaming in rage. The cacophony was so overwhelming that Émile couldn't catch what they were saying, if there were any words at all.

And then the street burst into flames below him. Flowers, water, everything was consumed in a fluid rush of fire that ate to the stone walls and reached for the balconies. He leaned over his own ornamental railing, fascinated and afraid. Hell could look no different.

The fire flashed between the buildings. Hungry, it licked upward to those brave enough to stand out on the first and second floors. Below him Émile heard a howl of anguish and saw Alain gripping the iron rail and shrieking like an inmate in a madhouse.

The fire burned forward down the street and was gone—so quickly that if it weren't for the thickly burned smell, Émile would not have been sure it had happened at all. And then there followed a group of *flics* in Justica green and high waders, one carrying a flamethrower and the others carrying a fuel tank and a clipboard.

"How can they?" Émile muttered. "What if someone was killed? What if a building caught?"

But there was no answer in the early morning. The Justica agents paused briefly under Alain's balcony and wrote something down. Someone from the other side of the street emptied a chamberpot over the *flics*. Émile winced. He thought his own squat was bad enough, with the chemical toilet and sanitary down the hall, and on a battery meter too. But at least the building had locals. Across the street there must not be any power at all.

He closed the shutters and went back to the sofa, where he fell asleep. When Anne-Sylvie's knocking brought him to, he wasn't sure whether the burning had been a dream.

Dreams seemed little different from the waking world, and so he was never quite certain what passed in reality. So he was startled when he was awakened by a knock. If the newspaper hadn't been piled on the floor next to him he might have believed that his expedition to the Café de la Montagne had been insubstantial as well.

He was glad that he had pulled on his pants before opening the door. Anne-Sylvie stood in the dark hall, cool and elegant, inspecting his territory before she was invited in. And so he made the obvious and expected gesture.

There wasn't anything at all to serve, and Anne-Sylvie was his first guest. That violated all the hospitality he had ever been taught. Anne-Sylvie inspected, ran a hand across the back of the sofa and the armchairs he had found on the street waiting for the trash pick-up. There was a table that had come from one of the abandoned apartments in the building, and an oversized armoire that had been nearly impossible to lift down the stairs. She went to the bedroom but didn't stay. There was only an old mattress on the floor and no linens at all.

"You really should put something on the walls," she said. "Old calendar prints are good and people will be throwing them away soon. You should keep an eye out."

Émile nodded mutely. He didn't need any decorating advice and didn't think that Anne-Sylvie was in any position to give it.

"Well, what do you think?" she asked.

"I'll look for the calendars; that's a good idea. But I'd rather you didn't tell me how to live," Émile protested stiffly.

Anne-Sylvie looked terribly confused, put her hand to her

mouth and broke out laughing. "I didn't mean about that," she said when she got her breath back. "I mean about this morning. Or last night, however you want to look at it. The *flics*. The burning."

"What do you mean, what do I think? What does it matter what I think?" Émile shot back. "And what do they do about the people in these buildings? Don't they ever set a place on fire like that?"

Anne-Sylvie bit her lower lip. "We're not supposed to be here. Technically these buildings are condemned, so if anyone is hurt it is their own fault for being here in the first place. Naturally, that's merely an excuse. Too many of these places are abandoned and we can't get hooked into city utilities. And since they don't fire the street unless everything is made of stone and iron, usually nothing burns. Except the water scum and the flowers. The point is to get rid of the sadece."

Émile nodded. "But it would be just as easy to burn them out group by group, wouldn't it? They don't have to fire the whole street to get six or seven patches."

Anne-Sylvie shrugged. "Intimidation, psychological advantage, make the native population feel threatened and off-balance and blame the cultivators. Then hope that the majority turns on the target group. It isn't working here, at least not yet. But in a year, two? Maybe. Maybe when there are enough fires and someone is killed."

Émile looked at the blank wall. He knew enough about intimidation; the Hounds had been good teachers. And even the stupidest Hounds knew that every population has its limits. The only thing he didn't really understand was why the Justica hated sadece. It wasn't really addictive, it didn't render the user violent or unpredictable, there were far worse drugs in perfectly legal use throughout the Zones. It made no sense and he told Anne-Sylvie so.

She looked at him as if he were a fool. "And you said you worked with Gorvitz for years?" she asked, incredulous. "It's obvious. They're trashing our economy. Sadece is the only thing that keeps our balance of payments at all reasonable."

"But we're self-sufficient," Émile protested.

"Oh, yes," Anne-Sylvie sneered. "We could survive without wood and steel and Justica power components. Do you know how long it takes for one of your precious Syndicat ships to pay off? Six complete trips, that's how much. Six cargos, and that's with our own building and navigation systems.''

''Which the Justica won't buy.'' Émile clipped the end on her statement. He was angry that she thought he was stupid and even angrier that she didn't realize that he'd been seventeen when he'd left and had spent fifty-seven years on an ice miner. Just because she had access to data didn't make her so superior.

The old instincts were surfacing. Enemy, don't trust her, he could feel Fox telling him in the back of his head. Fox was mud for brains, but he could usually smell whether a person was trustworthy or not.

He was just being overly suspicious, mostly because he had to stay on guard with her. Otherwise she would be able to use him for anything. She was not beautiful like Catherine, nor was she intense and sultry in her anger like Pauli, but there was something about her that both attracted and repelled Émile at the same time.

Anne-Sylvie, he realized in a mind-blooming gestalt, reminded him of the ladies on the Boulevard Lafitte. Her dark hair was shining and perfectly combed, fashionable and tasteful, her dresses were both innocent and expensive, and her grey eyes stern over an aristocratically thin nose. She carried herself with pride, but not the pride that came from the street, not with the challenging walk and loose swing of the arms that ganggirls had. No, Anne-Sylvie's pride came from assumed superiority to the world around her.

Once Émile recognized that, it made her less impressive in his mind, but no less desirable. On his terms. Not hers. She was far too used to having her own way, being in control. It was a quality he found attractive. But there was too much of the spoiled shopper on Boulevard Lafitte, too much social consciousness and not enough real achievement. Or so he thought. But that could change. He wanted it to. It had been a long time, months subjective since he'd left Pauli, and everything else along the way had simply been diversion. None of them had even spoken French.

''. . . which is why we hope you'll still make the delivery tomorrow,'' she was saying.

Émile pretended that he had followed her conversation.

"Yes, of course. But what about the senin? I mean, our flowers are gone. So . . ."

Anne-Sylvie shook her head. "You don't know anything, do you?"

This time Émile refused to play on her terms. "When I left the Quartier, we didn't cultivate in the streets. As a matter of fact, although this may seem completely strange to you, the streets were dry and people walked on them and the concierge lived on the ground floor, not the top, and nothing smelled like leprosy. Sadece grew out on plantations, not in Huit Fleurs, and no one in the Quartier would even admit to knowing the first thing about them because it would mean you were a rube slumming down here trying to taste a little of the edge. So now there are no rubes and everyone can grown sadece under their balconies. Fine. And there are sky bridges and the university hasn't changed much, I suppose; there are still student showings in the Hôtel Cezanne and food fights in the cafeteria. And perhaps you will remember that individuals don't all access the same data, which means that a group can cover a greater range. Otherwise only one person would be needed per ship and the Syndicat would be even smaller and turn more profit."

His anger was far from spent, but Anne-Sylvie's face had softened. "I apologize," she said quietly. "I forget that you aren't just from St. Ciel or Fableau, that's all. I will try to remember in the future."

Émile nodded, accepting her apology and putting himself on a more equal footing. St. Ciel or Fableau indeed. They were called cities only by default, not that he had been in either of them. Fableau was only a little floating rube town with some fancy architecture and St. Ciel always had had a second-city complex where Huit Fleurs was concerned. A complex that was much deserved, according to report.

Anne-Sylvie smiled slightly and cocked her finger. "Let me show you something," she said, and she drifted out into the hall. Émile didn't know whether he wanted to go. There were jobs in the paper and he needed the money; there were people out in the street and the Syndicat to get into. There were things that were more important than doing whatever Anne-Sylvie wanted him to do.

On the other hand, she was very pretty when she smiled.

And the jobs would wait fifteen minutes longer.

She led him down the old main stairs to the ground floor. Here was the old lobby and concierge's apartment, now sporting perhaps half a meter of water. He had already seen this part of the building, had come down to divest a couple of the chandeliers of their ornaments to hang in his windows. Anne-Sylvie didn't bother with the lobby however. She took the mezzanine walk over past the door to the concierge's office, descended three steps, and opened another door.

He followed the hall well back to a final, heavy steel door that Anne-Sylvie opened with a key. And there, in a blaze of light, stood a thick crop of green and lavender and nearly black-purple sadece.

Émile blinked until his eyes adjusted to the light. It took a little longer to see where it was coming from. Fiber-optic filaments lay underwater, hacked across and drawn up the stems of the plants. A complete garden of sadece was lit from within.

They were beautiful, and the scented gas they breathed masked other, less pleasant scents. Pleasure washed warmly through him, the physical beauty enhancing the effect of the sadece. And then he noted that they weren't standing in water at all, but on a platform that had been built around the garden.

Rich cushions had been scattered around in the shadows. Émile immediately sank into the nearest one and became momentarily lost in the texture of velvet and fur against his bare arm. Anne-Sylvie was beside him and had become far more appealing than she had been upstairs. He reached out, unbuttoned the many small catches on her dress and ran his hands over her shoulders as he pulled the cotton away from her skin.

Data. Scent and skin, all the chemistry of her drugged arousal was clearly defined against his own in his mind. Analysis. Tasted. And her internal reaction, chemically expressed, was modeled instantly within his awareness. As if he had an internal map of her desires, could monitor her exact response to every stimulus—not as if. It was.

He experimented slowly, letting her knowledge of her pleasure fuel his own, a feedback loop that enhanced and varied every sensation. The drug was working through him, the gas stronger and more refined than he had ever experienced.

Sex was merely the extension of every fantasy and every

disappointment he had ever had. His experience, their being, merging, nerves firing across chemical bridges that both were and were not enhanced by the massed sadece. The sheer amount of sensation was overwhelming.

Some was beyond experience, other points were merely not analogous. Heat knotted his groin and he held her hips, let the pressure build as the sadece-drunk mind wondered at the amazing subtlety of texture, and when he came it exploded and was overcome.

Émile shuddered with the strangeness of it all. It was himself, and he had no reason to deny that sex was frequently induced by the drug. He had always known it, everybody did. That was the center of the Syndicat, that connection with the ships through senin that made the interface a sexual experience.

At least Anne-Sylvie was a human and as susceptible to the drug as he was. What was far more frightening was the one time he had been printed in the Syndicat system, and the AI personality had been both judge and whore.

chapter fifteen

Seventeen days and it was perfectly void. There was something about that that bothered Pauli Tree. She had tried to tell Gorvitz but the man was not listening. He was too involved with the ship itself, with keeping the Hounds on the leash and the Justica well out of the way. But seventeen days. That was too long.

Luck didn't run forever. Too much of a good thing made Pauli suspicious. So she took a shift, and then another, in front of the monitor boards. That was easy enough. No one else wanted to do it. And while she was one of the women most in demand, she could always pull specialization. The Hounds respected a pick-lock. Let them go to Angela Cheng, who embezzled funds from Zone 1, or Zazuli Metchko, who drove getaway on the trade-traffic runs. Pauli had more important business.

She hadn't stayed in school long enough to know how to figure relative times, so she wasn't sure how long *Constanza* was overdue. Subjective it was nearly two weeks, but she knew better than to trust subjective. No way to find out, not without the mathematics that she had never learned. At the time she had thought all that stuff meant nothing in her life, anyway. Now she was scared.

How many days overdue? How long would it take before they traced the run, figured the wake patterns and searched the area? How long before someone noticed the *Mary Damned* was no longer alone, ditched without power at the edge of the Zones? How much time did they have? And when they got there, what then?

Gorvitz had told her that the only thing he could get the ship

to do without the cuff was to go home. That was strange. In
the Zones there was nothing that was precisely home for a ship.
Owned by multicultural conglomerates whose only common
ground was profit and the Justica, ships were creatures out of
time. There was no place, no era, that claimed them. Like
shuttles weaving through the dark, they never came to rest.
And their crews, what crews they had, had severed any ties
they ever had to anyone but the trade lanes and their compa-
triots. Most of them were former criminals anyway.

But the *Mary Damned* couldn't go anywhere but home, not
without official authorization that even Pauli couldn't duplicate.
And she had tried. But the ID mechanism was more than a
lock or even a code. It was a living interface. The cuff itself
fed constant readout on crew members into the ship's systems,
and the etching of a cuff included infrared readout so the cuff
and the ship were always in communication.

Pauli made a facsimile of one and the computer identified it
immediately. Her failure was not due to lack of materials.
Everything was an exact duplicate of the Syndicat cuff. Everything but the soul.

Gorvitz had tried to tell her about that. Pauli wished he had
explained better. After the tests with the cuff she was certain
that the ships were in some way "alive" but she couldn't define
how. That was not the issue anyway. Her skill was with mechanical devices. She could trick the eye and the psychology
of a mark, that was part of the game, but she could not override
the intuition of a living being. She didn't even begin to try.

And so she figured the *Mary Damned*'s rejection of them to
be intuitive. The ship understood the thought-rhythms of Beau
Soliel, the patterns so innate that they had been programmed
in without the programmers even being aware of the assumptions. Those were the paradigms Gorvitz didn't match and
couldn't pass.

But sooner or later it was all going to break down. Pauli
knew that the way she knew her whole life. There was no such
thing as winning. There was only how long you thought you
had gotten away with it before they busted in your door and
hauled you off in front of a green-robed magistrate. The end.

So she took her place in front of the monitors, uncertain
even of exactly how to use them or what the symbols indicated.

That didn't worry her. A little fiddling and she would figure the system. Like any lock, and she was good at locks. She played with the screens at first, adjusting the colors and various brightnesses. The graphics were superb. She brought them through from mapping the area to indications of various incursions. Dust clouds showed smoky hematite grey over brilliant background stars, each sparkling at the correct color and intensity. The more resolution she got in the smaller areas, the more she experimented and searched.

She found *Constanza* on the tow line, both in plot and full visual modes. The computer spoke frequently and some of the words Pauli understood. All those years with Émile paid off, at least a little. So when the voice said, *"Riens,"* she knew there was nothing to worry about and when it said, *"Cinq flics, artillerie inconnu,"* she didn't understand the word *flics*, but the rest was frightening enough. She figured the missing word meant "enemy."

She put the monitors into scan mode to double-check the reading in visual. There was always the possibility that she had misunderstood and they were not a target. Pauli thought that highly unlikely. After all, the *Mary Damned* had been sitting around with a full load of senin for a very long time, and the *Constanza* had mutinied. But stranger things had happened. The Justica was reasonable but they had their own priorities, and those weren't always what Pauli thought they should be. Frequently to her benefit, too, that was.

The story on the scan was confusing. The graphics showed five large craft in formation. She could tell they were large from the banks of windows down the sides. Or maybe those were munitions ports. They still indicated ships of the line. Five in formation. That meant something really big. Pauli didn't credit herself or the *Constanza* with being worth more than two hunters at the max.

Besides, they were all ahead of the *Mary Damned* and running away.

Pauli stared at the screen for a long time, completely baffled. She thought about taking some of the senin and going inside the system the way Gorvitz had done, but she hesitated. The system had spooked him badly and he wouldn't say how. He had told her enough about getting the ship to go home and about the cuffs, but he had never told her why he never wanted to make that interface again. She had thought it could be useful to them, and Gorvitz had refused. Flat out refused. That wasn't like him, and he had seemed afraid when she tried to push.

Hugo Gorvitz being afraid was beyond her comprehension. Whatever there was about the interface that had frightened him, Pauli didn't want to know about it. So she stuck to her voice and screens instead.

"*Ou-va t'ils?*" she asked haltingly, the accent grating against her memory of Émile's fluid speech. But the answer was something she didn't even need to remember any rudimentary French to understand.

"Beau Soliel," the machine replied.

Hugo Gorvitz was not pleased. He had abandoned the navigator's chair for a more relaxed position in the galley. He would have restricted the meeting to his cabin, but that would have only piqued interest. And interest was something he definitely did not want until he was ready to announce action. The Hounds weren't good either at secrets or strategy, and Hugo needed them in the dark a while longer.

His sitting with Pauli in the galley, however, was not something anyone would bother to comment on. The coffee was strange, too white and sweet, but it served the purpose. Cover was important.

"So they're ahead of us?" he asked for the third time. "They don't know we're following?"

Pauli shook her head. "I don't think so. At least not yet. If they ever check, then we're in deep vacuum. Or unless there's another group behind us the way these guys are out front. Personally, I'd case the job before I made a call on it."

Pauli was right; they needed more data. Unfortunately, that was nearly impossible to get. Even trying to scan directional microwave communication would read on instruments, if these were warships. And Gorvitz doubted they were anything else.

Well, he'd had to make judgment calls on insufficient data before. "How far out are we?" he asked.

Pauli blinked. He was the one who knew the answer to that question, if anyone did.

"Not to Beau Soliel," he said, noting her confusion. "To the Justica patrol. How far away are they?"

"Oh. Two days ahead at this speed. Less than seven hours at max. According to the computer. I think. I'm not so good at numbers in French."

Gorvitz nodded. That sounded about like his calculations, and while spoken numbers were difficult, written data was perfectly straightforward. Seven hours. And the Justica warships didn't know they were behind. The overly sweet coffee grew cold as he stared at the plain bulkhead. There had to be ways to engage, to run and win, to divert them.

"This ship isn't armed," Pauli volunteered. "There is one gun but it's a joke. Enough to get us arrested and not nearly enough to do any damage."

But Hugo Gorvitz hardly heard what she said. He was smiling, the outline of a plan coming to him. It was outlandish, insane, completely contrary to the assumptions any decent person in the Zones ever made. It was so audacious it would have to work. The only problem was to sell the Hounds.

His reception was exactly what he expected.

"That's crazy," Fox said, spittle collecting in the corner of his mouth. "That's completely looney-tunes nuts out. I won't do it."

Ice shook his head. "It sounds kind of funny, but Fox, we can't just slug this thing out. I mean, there's five of them to one of us and we don't even got any guns."

"Don't care," Fox shot back vehemently. "It don't make sense, and that's what worries me. I mean, yeah, I'd never think of that and so maybe they never would think of that either, but how do we know this ghost-ship stuff is worth anything anyway? I mean, maybe somebody was kidding around. Maybe it's all a joke. Maybe this is just one more derelict, right, and there is no legend and nobody cares what pile of junk is floating around, okay? And there's the *Constanza* to remember and there's the fact that every one of us has got a record and with the mutiny and all we're dead. That's it, we're gone. I say we either wipe them out or run like hell. And the smarter one is to run."

"You chicken?" one of the Hounds asked, sneering.

"I'm smart," Fox retorted. "Sometimes it pays to run, and this is one of those times. And if you can't see it, you got less brains than a Gobbex servo."

A few guffaws greeted that statement. Gorvitz let the commentary run. Fox was not the most articulate or intelligent of the Hounds, but he was squarely in the middle of their power structure.

"Fox is right," Gorvitz said softly, in the voice that had swayed the Steering Committee so many times. "We don't have much choice. And Fox is also right that it's smarter to run this time than to fight it out. But I need to remind you that we don't have that option. This ship is set on one course only. We don't have the credentials to take it wherever we want to go, and it is going exactly where that Justica fleet is going. And we can't change that. We don't know how. If I did, if anyone does, we'd better do it now.

"So we can't run, and we can't slug it out either. You already know that most kids playing fort have more dangerous weapons than we've got at the moment."

"So you're saying it doesn't matter what we think," Ice said. "You're saying it's your way or we're dead."

Gorvitz shrugged. "Well, if you've got a better way out of this thing, tell us. I'd be real happy for another option right now."

Eighteen Hounds packed into the galley along with several unaligned mutineers, Pauli; the witch doctor; and two other Organization associates, and not a sound. Gorvitz waited, challenging them, drew out the silence until it was acutely uncomfortable. His leadership was reaffirmed.

"It's really very simple," he said, and now he spoke gently, reassuringly. "The *Mary Damned* is a legend. And we're going to all go down in history. All we have to do is get ahead of them and lead them in. Really that should be easy, as long as everyone keeps strict power-rationing. We've got the figures. And they might be faster than we are but they aren't as maneuverable, so we've got the advantage there. And this ship will deal with some local variation so long as the course doesn't deviate from target. So we have the resources to get ahead of them and lead them in."

"And what's to keep them from shooting at us?" Fox demanded again.

Gorvitz smiled. "The legend of the *Mary Damned*. If things work out right, so far as they're concerned we're not real. Because that's the one real advantage we have with the *Constanza*. We're going to spend the next few days, all hands, stripping the trap-coat off the *Constanza* and using her materials and plant to mask the *Mary Damned*. They'll have us visual but no solid readings. We're going to make them all think they're seeing things in the middle of the night. With any luck at all we'll get a couple of nervous breakdowns and the shrinks'll be overbooked for years to come."

They still seemed skeptical, but willing to entertain the idea. That was enough. With the *Constanza*'s shops and ceramics facilities, it was as easy to make masking ceramics as superconductive ones. Maybe it was a lot more expensive and would use up all the prison ship's reserves, but that was the idea. The first rule of any guerrilla war was that the enemy should provide the weapons and ammunition. Gorvitz thought it only fitting that the Justica should finance their own demise.

cHApTER sixTEEN

Green Monster senin, only the best for the Syndicat. It rode in individually cushioned vials packed into a slim rubber envelope. That along with Daniel's old brown Express uniform marked him clearly as a delivery man. Anne-Sylvie had checked him over carefully, then sat him down and combed red-brown dye into his hair. She promised that it wasn't permanent but the effect still startled him. He'd been through all the colors that had been popular when he had last lived in the Quartier, but he had never done anything so nondescript.

"Well, there's nothing we can do about how tall you are," Anne-Sylvie said after she had passed on the hair. "Can you maybe stoop a little?"

But Émile drew the line at that. He reminded her that he was a meter eighty, which was above average but not so tall that he couldn't get a bunk on a Syndicat ship. She threw up her hands in disgust and sputtered. "You'd better keep your head down, though," she cautioned. "I wish we could get you some lenses, but we don't have any contacts on that one. But make sure they don't see. I just don't want anyone getting any description at all."

Émile hesitated to tell her that blue eyes were even more common than his height. Unfortunately, his were true Alsatian sapphire, noticeable and memorable. But he wasn't about to wear lenses no matter how much Anne-Sylvie thought it was a good idea. He had tried them once and they made his eyes water and his nose run. Allergic reaction, the runner had said. He'd never tried them again.

He was ready. Alain gave him the case and Anne-Sylvie gave him a look that said she didn't exactly trust him. "You remember what you're going for?'' she demanded for the ninety-seventh time that hour. ''The inventories on the *Lucie Claire* and the *Victor Hugo*. Clean them and issue the permits for unloading at Zone 6. And then if there's time . . .''

''I know, I know. Get rid of the senin records on everything, destination Zone 4 and 9 priority. I remember it. Now, can I have a couple of francs for the *rapide*? Or do you expect me to walk all the way to the Palais?'' Émile couldn't keep the anger out of his tone. For all he found Anne-Sylvie frustrating, he also found her attractive and that bothered him. The memory of the afternoon on the first floor bothered him too. He didn't need a mother hen stepping on his heels.

Alain handed over the two francs. ''Out of the ten,'' he said.

Émile smiled. ''No way. The ten is for me. The two is expenses. Your pocket, not mine.''

Anne-Sylvie handed Alain two francs and he seemed mollified. Émile turned his back and left.

Damn. If it weren't for the *flics* and the cuff, he wouldn't have anything to do with these people. It seemed impossible that they could get anything decent done at all. He fumed as he walked up the stairs to the roof door, then across the sky bridges until he was out of the Quartier and at the closest *rapide* stop.

At least the *rapide* hadn't changed. It was still painted bright yellow for first class and red in coach, scrubbed and shined so that even a nursing sister from Notre Dame des Miracles would consider the area acceptable. Naturally, the coach compartments had merely molded seats, and not the plush upholstery of first class, and there were eight to a compartment instead of four, but second class was one-third the price and it was every bit as smooth and silent.

In less than fifteen minutes he was on the Boulevard Lafitte, invisible among the messengers and express workers who strode self-importantly down the avenue. Orangata vendors and lottery-ticket sellers scooted out of the way when someone carrying a foam envelope or hardcase appeared. Waiters at the sidewalk *café* watched and muttered things to each other or to their customers. Wealthy shoppers didn't deign to notice.

In perfect anonymity Émile walked at a brisk pace down the Boulevard. Like any courier he kept his eyes firmly fixed on

his goal and his mind utterly focused on his delivery. It had
been less than a full week since he had appeared at the Palais,
but this time it didn't feel like a great event to walk up the
white path between the cement urns at all. He passed the flow-
erpots on the right as he took the service path to the side door
where deliveries were made. He had never entered by that door.
Not ever.

He rapped sharply on the back door and had to wait a good
ten minutes before anyone opened to him. Then it was the
caretaker, who must have come from the main house. The man
wore a cuff incised with only the sign of the Syndicat where
a ship should be. Even second-class house membership made
Émile jealous. The old man motioned him in and Émile strode
into the mud room just off the kitchen. The caretaker disappeared, probably to get the Chief Purser, whose business this
was.

Good smells came from the kitchen, coffee and warm bread
and sausage and carrots cooked in wine. There was nothing to
coming in the cracked door, nothing to looking over the familiar
territory. During his first months with a cuff he had spent hours
in this kitchen, amazed that he was permitted to eat whatever
he wanted. That it was his kitchen. Not Maman's, who had
never forgotten the poverty of garret life and always counted
out the carrots exactly and never permitted anyone to eat between meals. It had been an amazing freedom to come into
this slab marble table and eat until he was sick.

His reminiscences were interrupted by the arrival of the Chief
Purser at Home. Émile handed over the envelope and turned
away while the functionary inspected the contents. This Chief
Purser bore no resemblance to anyone Émile had ever known,
but still he took the precaution of keeping his eyes on his shoes.
The Purser handed over an item ring for five thousand francs.
Émile immediately put it in his ear. Item rings were used only
when the recipient of funds did not have a legal account and
the amounts were too high to carry in cash. Also, no one trusted
a Quartier courier with that much money, and the Syndicat
trusted no one at all.

The Chief Purser stared at him for a long minute while Émile
shuffled and hesitated leaving. "Yes?" The Purser asked very
pointedly.

Émile smiled shyly. He had practiced in front of the mirror,
but wasn't certain that he could maintain the effect under stress.
"The *cassoulet* smells really good," he said softly. "And my
employer isn't expecting me back for two hours . . ."

The Purser shrugged, pointed to the cabinets. "Bowls are
in there. When you're finished, just put it in the sink."

Émile thanked him as he left, got a bowl and sloshed just a
few spoons of stew into it. If there wasn't a dirty bowl, then
something would look wrong. Besides, he had to give the Purser
time to leave the hallway. The *cassoulet* was as good as he
remembered it, strong and hearty and filling more than his
stomach. Three spoons emptied the serving and left him feeling
much better. Much more at home.

He left the bowl in the sink and slipped out into the hall
where the Purser had disappeared only a minute before. The
main port section was up on the first floor, but Émile didn't
want to walk in where there may well be other users. Instead
he turned toward the back set of doors into the caretaker's
office. With any luck the old concierge was out at his desk in
the front, where he belonged until at least four in the afternoon.
Then, after the late deliveries, he was free to work on inventory
and running the household workings of the Palais.

But to do that he had a port that led directly into the main
Syndicat system. Not that he needed or even had access to the
full capabilities that lay there. But all Émile needed was the
port and the privacy. . . .

A thrill ran through him as he opened the port and touched
the screen. It trembled under his hand, his enzyme output
coating the glass. Not enough. He had to get in, closer. His
human-balanced mind screamed no, but he was already out of
the office and down the stairs to the subbasement where the
physical frame was kept.

There, in a neatly sealed tank, lay the organic matter that
made up the core memory of the Syndicat, floating in con-
ducting nutrient soup. Émile took the delicate fiber-optic leads
and taped the nodes to the nexus points in his ears, inside his
nose and mouth as he had been hooked in the one time he had
been printed directly by the system when he was given his cuff.
He tried to relax and forget the discomfort as the passive elec-

tronic exchange began, tried to forget that the leads ended in
a primordial green ooze.

Last time he had been lost in a soft nighttime, a sleep that
was warm and comforting. He had only been vaguely aware
of what happened deep inside the system, like a dream caught
on waking, and it had left him with a pleasant aftertaste. All
that mattered was that it had been an initiation that was part
of the Syndicat. It was necessary for him to get the cuff, and
he had been willing to endure a great deal more than an active-
minded sleep to get it.

This time it was different. The darkness was not opaque at
all. It was vital, alive. And he was completely at its mercy.

Readings. He understood. The whole communication that
went on passed through the nutrient medium and he could not
only read it, but interface deeper than he had ever imagined.
He sank into the core, let it overwhelm him and construct itself
around him.

He sank, falling as if through the sludge in the canal through
a layer of cloying darkness. And then there were lights, structures, the chemical communication that was visceral and intuitive all at once.

The space cleared and he realized that he had been perceiving
it subconsciously. Now he consciously reached to find images,
paradigms that existed that related to the person. To Émile
Saint-Just.

The network protested and built other models that he could
read but were distant. He refused. This intelligence had been
built by humans, originally programmed by humans, and no
matter how far it had come from human consciousness it was
still essentially knowable. It trembled before the force of his
will, of his want. It did not know how to want like that and
so it studied, dissolved and reformed around him.

He was in a pale grey Empire revival room. A white door
was open wide into an insane reproduction of the nebula sky.
The room itself was orderly and serene, twin sofas facing each
other upholstered in peach-and-grey striped satin, two delicate
chairs in pale velvet and a low inlaid wooden table between
them. Émile stared at the table. Wood was scarce enough that
he had only seen fine inlay work like that in the highest Syndicat

offices. It had come from offworld and was worth more than
half the real estate down in the Quartier.

He was stroking the wooden pattern when a woman walked
in. She was amazingly, almost excessively, beautiful in the
sharp Breton manner he admired. Her hair was thick and black,
her skin as white as the sun and her chin pointed and sharp
and feral. She wore a lightweight worksuit in dark red that
clung to her curves. But she was not as dangerous as Anne-
Sylvie, perhaps because Anne-Sylvie was a real woman who
was irrational at times and dedicated in a way no thing could
be. And no matter how she looked, Émile reminded himself,
this was a thing. No woman at all.

He wondered how he was going to get to the shipping manifests. The network discarded the idea and grinned.

"Get down," the woman said suddenly, throwing a hand in
the middle of his back and pushing him under one of the sofas.
She was stronger than someone her build would normally be,
even if she was in exceptionally good shape. She kept up the
pressure and held a finger to his lips.

Boots passed by the door, hesitated, turned. A guard, security checking out the possibility of intrusion. Émile held his
breath and lay very still. So the Justica had gotten in and had
already locked their security programs into the Justica systems.
Roving programs, these would be, very expensive and hard to
implement. Émile was impressed. He was also terrified.

The woman was no longer crouching over him. She was
behind him, walking around the furniture, confronting the
guard. They spoke together rapidly in a language Émile
couldn't follow. Or perhaps he simply didn't hear very well,
caught in terror and under the sofa. The guard left and the
woman closed the door. He heard a lock turn in the keyhole
and the woman sighed. Émile got out from his hiding place.

"I'm surprised," was all he said.

The woman shrugged. "They think that we do not know the
difference between our own and their intrusion. They are not
. . . elegant. But enough. You are one of us."

She crossed the room and laid her hand lightly on his shoulder. Then she smiled and licked her lips.

"What are you called?" Émile asked.

Her smile grew wider. "Call me Claude," she said. "That was my first designer, Claude Felique."

"I don't have a cuff," he said, pulling away.

"No matter," she answered softly. "I am more sophisticated than the others. I have your name. You were apprentice on the *Mary Damned*. I have the records here. Do you want to know your ratings? Your ratings were very high. You would have made full mate soon enough, and gotten a decent share. Oh, yes, there are many things I know. If you know how to ask."

"Then Dumouriez knows who I am? And wouldn't give me a cuff anyway?" Émile demanded, furious.

The computer called Claude nodded.

Émile knew what he should do next. He knew he should make sure of the manifests. They were clear in his mind, in his intent. And then he found his hands on Claude's shoulders, slipping down her waist to her hips, and the red workshirt was dissolving under his touch.

Her skin was moist and smelled slightly musky, her mouth insistent and her thick black hair tickling the inside of his thighs. And he could feel her reading him off his own desire and he didn't care. He pulled her up and lay her down on the sofa and began nibbling lightly at her toes.

Meaning intermixed with pleasure. The scent of her arousal, the saltiness of the slickness between her legs, pushed his awareness to merge with the man-mind and body that was his whole focus. He owned her pleasure completely. She clawed up his back, moaning, demanding immediate satisfaction.

Hers, and his. Datapoints of insistence and chemical interference sparkled in her, flows of electrons shot down the corridors of power and interface. The universe changed around him. It was not his own desire alone that molded the plastic environment. He could not help but respond, kinesthesia exploding as the universe narrowed to a single point of absolute need.

Heat exploded like poison when he came, and then there was only a chilly, orderly darkness. As always. But not as always. Here the dark was real and the walls were gone. Only spirals of cold danced and dissolved in the workings of the mind of the Syndicat. Only the table and the door remained. On the table lay a sheet of old-fashioned writing, the banner from *L'Ami du Peuple* and the report on shipping. There was no mention of either arms or senin.

And there was a brass key on a grey *moiré* ribbon. He used the key to open the door and then slipped the ribbon over his head. Then he stepped out through the door into the surrounding darkness pierced by light.

CHAPTER
SEVENTEEN

Émile opened his eyes to the sight of two very unpleasant *flics* standing over him, one with a drawn softknife, the optic fibers stiff with power. He didn't need the green-uniformed man to touch the bright filaments to his skin to know that they would burn through him as if through butter, but the *flic* made double sure. The pain was so intense that at first Émile couldn't feel it, and then it exploded through the back of his hand and up his arm. Although the softknife never went beyond the elbow, he could feel the nerves reacting into his shoulder and chest. He hated pain.

More than that, he hated the fact that no one had asked what he was doing. Just came in, saw, hurt. Simple, the way the *flics* liked it. But the softknife was a street weapon, not something a real security force would have. And this one had been so much worse than the other cuts he had had before. This knife was better than anything he, or anyone else he knew, had ever made. Nothing on the street burned like this, like acid that kept on and on and on.

They were talking. Émile didn't care what they said, didn't even bother to hear it. The pain went on, alternating pulses overwhelming and not quite bearable. His arm was his whole world. It he had had the equipment he would have cut it off right there. Lacking that, he wanted only to lie on the cool concrete basement floor and cry.

The *flics* didn't permit him either option. Instead he was hauled to his feet and marched behind the computer center into the complex that supported the Palais. The fact that walking made his stomach heave was ignored. He was prodded along, and when he once stopped to lean against a door jamb the larger

flic pulled the softknife out again. The sight of it was enough
to motivate Émile.

He didn't know how far he had walked when he was permitted to sit down. Only then did he realize that he had been
led to a small, rather undistinguished room and that a door had
closed behind him. It hardly mattered. All he cared about was
the pain. In was the crux and center of his existence. If it
stopped he might cease to breathe, but even that would have
been a relief. There was no worse threat.

They let him sit. The larger *flic* left. The smaller one, who
still was at least ten centimeters taller and weighed half a kilo
more than Saint-Just, sat opposite him. There was a table between them. Émile folded his arms and head and rested on the
wooden surface.

"Would you like some coffee?"

The sheer inappropriateness of the question penetrated Émile's self-absorption. Shock alone forced him to look up. The
flic looked like a *flic*, oversized and pasty, his face softened
by too many feedings and too much respect at too young an
age. The Justica agent was probably a good bit younger than
he was, Émile judged. His eyes were soft hazel and innocent,
as if there was something perfectly rational about the way they
were all behaving, as if Émile hadn't been seriously injured
without even the chance to explain himself.

Not that he had any explanation prepared. Except maybe the
truth. But they hadn't even given him the option to come along
peacefully, and that angered him. Maybe he would have come.
Maybe he had been dazed enough coming to from inside the
system that he would not have resisted. Anyway. There was
no reason for them to hurt him and it was unjust. Like everything the Justica had ever done to him.

"Would you like some coffee? I'm afraid we're out of hot
milk to put in it, but the next shift doesn't come on for a couple
of hours yet and we're not supposed to leave the area."

There was something completely sincere about his captor.
Émile nodded more in amazement than in the desire for coffee.
Pain still muddled his thinking, and given the experience of
other softknife wounds it would take more than a few hours
for the screaming pulsation to ebb. He had to buy time. He

knew it by an animal instinct more than by any higher function. He had to stall, to wait, to slip away.

It was not real. The guard left and came back with coffee in a disposable cup. On it was an orangata advertisement.

"Let me see the arm," the *flic* said after they had sipped the overbrewed and lukewarm excuse for a beverage.

Émile hesitated. He wanted to protect himself. Then he gave in. It no longer mattered. Nothing mattered except the pain. The *flic* looked at the wound, a scorched, red-lined burn that was quickly swelling with oozing fluids. The *flic* inspected, reached down and brought out a roll of gauze and began to do a professional binding job. "At least the softknife is sterile," he said.

Émile blinked, partly from how much the binding added to the pain and the casual assumption of clean weapons. He didn't get it at all.

Mostly he just wanted to lash out. If this had happened on the *Constanza*, someone would have been busy taping a couple of filament knives into his palms and the word would go out over the next recreation period.

"My partner may come back soon," the *flic* said apologetically. "I can understand that you were curious, but he's really by the book. So if we can just finish up this report real fast, then I can get you out of here before he shows up. Just a couple of real easy questions, nothing you wouldn't fill out for a housing allowance."

Housing allowance? Émile had never heard of such a thing. On the other hand, he wasn't tracking completely straight yet. A few easy questions he could answer. One thing he knew was that he didn't want to see the *flic* with the super-charged softknife again.

They went over the basics. Name, occupation (that gave Émile a little trouble; unemployed was bad, so he settled on space ceramics specialist), what the hell did he think he was doing screwing around with the Syndicat system? He was lucky they had come when they did; a private and semi-organic network like that could turn him into a vegetable, didn't he know that? Too dumb to live.

Émile felt too dumb to live. The scolding reminded him of

fifth grade. He had hated fifth grade, and Sister Genevieve who had taught it. His reticence must have shown.

"He tell you anything yet?" The larger *flic* appeared and demanded the information in a bored way.

The young one rolled his eyes, seemed exasperated. "I keep telling him that we saved his ass and all he can do is sit there and dare me to cut him again. You can take him if you want."

The larger man chortled and his too-pale eyes lit with excitement. "Fish doesn't usually let me go with our guests. Usually he just helps them out and lets them go. But you, I like you. Fish is being nice to me, I think. I have to consider what I want to do to you first. I could use my softknife on your balls. That would be fun."

"Maybe that should wait for later," the very innocent-seeming *flic* counseled. "Give yourself something to work up to."

Émile's mind was suddenly clear. He understood exactly what the *flics* were up to, had seen it before. Once on the *Constanza* two of the Hounds had played with a new prisoner, an embezzler, torturing him psychologically because they didn't respect bourgeois crime. Whenever the embezzler cried or showed fear, the Hounds stepped up the treatment. Saint-Just didn't know if it was fear these *flics* wanted, or if it was already too late.

Not that he wasn't perfectly well afraid. Relaxing enough to permit the real terror to show through was not difficult. Nor was the rasp from the dry throat or the trembling in his fingers. The difficult part was keeping enough control to maintain some dignity.

"Look, I'll tell you whatever you want," Émile said quickly. "Please, just give me a chance."

"Too late," the big one said.

"Now wait a minute," the younger one countered. "He's being cooperative. We like that here. Saves us time, work. There'll be others for you. Or maybe this one will lie and we'll find out and then it'll be your turn again. What do you say?"

The larger one mumbled something unpleasant and marched out. Émile retained enough control not to sigh with relief. That would give too much away. The interrogators were good. If his past experiences held, they were playing crude but their main concern was getting what they could before turning him over to the local authorities.

"So what were you doing?" the remaining *flic* asked mildly. "Playing around with the Syndicat system could be very dangerous, you know. More dangerous than anything we could do."

Émile let it pass. He remembered some of the things he had learned from Gorvitz. Tell lies close enough to the truth that you can make yourself believe them. Truth, but edited, so if there was a reader on this chair it would show clearly that you did not believe yourself to be lying.

Émile took a deep breath and began. "I was once a member of the Syndicat. A very long time ago, local subjective. I came back, expecting to be accepted, given a new cuff, able to ship out again. I work on the outer hull ceramic channels. Anyway, I saw this Captain Dumouriez, and he refused to readmit me."

"But you don't have a cuff," the *flic* said evenly. "I never saw a Syndicat member without one. Not even the concierge."

Émile nodded. "It was lost when I was taken by raiders. Did forced labor, too. But when Dumouriez said there was no record of me at all, he killed me, do you understand? He had no right to keep me out, no right to deny me my cuff. He put me in a position where I couldn't get decent work. I specialize in ship hulls, I'm valuable, and he took my shares. Everyone in the Syndicat has shares, you understand? So when you go out, when you come back and it's fifty or a hundred years later local, you still have something. You aren't penniless, a *clochard*, to drink cheap wine in the streets and piss in the *rapide*. He took everything I had, everything.

"So I was going to prove who I was. When we first join the Syndicat we are printed into the system. A sort of final ID. He never accessed that. There's no way he could have and still refused me. So I was trying to access it, pull up the records, make him face it.

"This has nothing to do with you. It's between me and him, something that belongs in the Syndicat entirely."

The passion that burned in Émile suddenly went cold and there was nothing else he had to say. The anger was too close to the surface, his own sense of justice too badly abused.

"I think we need to talk to this Dumouriez to get a fair

picture," the *flic* said cautiously. "Perhaps a judge of investigation should be called in immediately. Maybe you were trying to make that print you talked about, instead of finding it."

"Then get one of your superiors immediately," Émile demanded arrogantly.

The very young *flic* looked him full in the face. There was something restrained and innocent and cruel all mixed in that one look. "Maybe I should get Shem back," he said softly.

Émile thought perhaps he had pushed it too far. Better to have kept on the mask of abject misery. Never show any pride; that was one of the rules on the *Constanza*. Never show them who you were. Be quiet. Play the game. Get into position and stab the enemy in the back. It was the only way for a prisoner to win. Eight years on the *Constanza*, and he went and lost it all.

The door opened again. Émile blinked. The large guard, Shem, filled the light. When he moved, Dumouriez was revealed behind him. Shem was smiling.

"If I can't have any fun, Fish, you can't either," Shem said happily.

"Thank you for your excellent surveillance and for apprehending this trespasser. I will transfer authority immediately to the Hôtel de Ville and our jurisdiction. This is a Syndicat matter and does not concern the Justica," Dumouriez said, dismissing the men.

The *flics* looked at each other, shocked; then Fish shrugged in a gesture Émile was certain he had picked up since being posted on Beau Soliel. They both left and Émile was bound and helpless before the Captain. Somehow this worried him far more than Fish and Shem had.

"So," Dumouriez began softly, "you just don't know how to leave it alone, do you? You didn't learn a damned thing on that Justica prison barge. Not a damned thing. Well, we'll have a couple of bosun's mates take you over to the Hôtel de Ville. I trust you won't give them a hard time."

"You knew," Émile said, horrified. "You knew the whole time."

Dumouriez smiled, and in his expression Émile saw the intimation of pure evil. Nothing relative or redeemable in this failed example of humanity. Émile had never seen a person like this before. Even the most dim-witted Hound, even the twisted Shem, had more accessible humanity.

Émile wanted to kick Dumouriez's face in. The only reason he didn't was that his ankles were firmly bound to the rungs of the chair. That Dumouriez was evil was only the beginning. He had not risen high in the Syndicat and called the Justica in alone.

He wanted to continue the analysis, but there was too much missing, too many pieces he didn't know. And besides, the bosun's mates arrived. Émile's hands were still bound. The mates untied his feet so he could walk. Both of the oversized mates wore both soft and hardknives and the ancient but dangerous belaying pins that were the symbol of their authority. Or their woodenheadedness, as Catherine used to say.

And they both wore cuffs, each incised with a ship's designation. Émile thought for a moment, and then let them escort him out of the Palais, back into the lavender sunlight.

Once outside he could smell something, something frightening and heartening and familiar at the same time. Sadece gas was mixed in with the odor of burning. Burning, but not the flowers. And it was not the Justica burning them. Émile didn't know how he knew, but the burning was the scent of revolution. Suddenly he perked up as they walked and he began to whistle an old, old song. One that he had not heard since the capture of the *Mary Damned*.

chapter eighteen

From inside the holding tank in the Hôtel de Ville, Saint-Just could hear the mob outside. The tank was not very secure. It had been made with the idea of keeping its occupants no more than a few hours, before a judge of instruction passed on whether there was a case at all. Then and only then was a prisoner transferred out to Les Mariés until the trial, and after that sent, if judged guilty, out to L'Isle de Râle.

So the tank was no more than a clumsy affair, sturdy enough bars and a clear view of the large clock down over the charge officer's desk. It was almost dinnertime.

The officer's desk was deserted, although what a figurehead with a bronzed baton, a high-collared jacket and white gloves was going to do in the face of a mob was debatable. However, Émile didn't worry about that. Three other men were in the tank, no women. Émile assumed there were slightly more private facilities for them upstairs. Two of the men were *clochards*. Too unreliable to even stay in a squat, the two reeked of nights in the *rapide* and the sewers and layers of vomit. Émile tried to stay as far from them as he could.

The third man had the best spot, exactly under the vent where the fresh air came in. Émile didn't immediately recognize him as a type, well dressed in a businessman's spotless shirt and jacket, all of fine draped fabric. This prisoner's nose was as red as the *clochards'* but it wasn't with wine.

"I didn't do it," he moaned piteously. "M. Victor, he thought I was in the books but it was that no-good nephew Raymond. I told him a million times that boy was no good."

Émile moved away. He wished he had his softknife. These were poor excuses for prisoners indeed. The *Constanza* would have eaten them up alive. Not that the Justica did squat about anything it called "local issues," and the *clochards* definitely were that. The businessman Émile couldn't say, but he hated self-pity and he hated the climbers and upstarts who looked down on the Quartier and the Syndicat alike.

"What's going on out there?" he snapped at the sniveling businessman.

"I don't know," the man replied. "Just another flower-burning in the Quartier, I guess. They get very mad about it. But I think the Justica is doing a good job. Get all that profit out of the hands of those ingrates."

Émile rolled his eyes.

"Ain't never had a mob out for a burning before," one of the *clochards* observed. "Something else gotta be going on."

The other drunk burped and began to snore noisily.

Emile shook his head and squatted on the concrete floor. It was too filthy to sit on. He strained to hear what was being said but he couldn't make out any words. Just silences and then mass screaming followed by another silence. Negotiating, he supposed. The Mayor wanted to respond to voters, and the people of the Quartier knew how to keep that at the forefront of his mind.

At least they had fifty-seven years ago. That, too, might have changed. But they didn't seem violent. Nothing had happened inside the massive structure of the Hôtel de Ville yet, at least not that he could hear or smell, and he was certain that he would have at least scented the torches the mob carried. Always torches. Not bothering with technology they couldn't afford. Maybe, or maybe it was a reminder of the burnings in the Quartier. He wasn't sure.

One thing was sure, though. If he was going to get out, it had to be now. He couldn't have planned such a perfect diversion if he had organized for months. And once he went to a hearing and was turned over to the Justica, there was no chance.

Émile Saint-Just had spent enough time in prison. He wasn't going back, not to some far-hauler out on the edge of forever. No way. Especially since he was in a cell with no guard and only three poor snots for witnesses.

The bars were sturdy and the floor was concrete. That much

was given. So the only way out was up. He studied the ceiling. The vent was too small for his shoulders to go through. He studied it some more and swore under his breath. His only hope was to get up and hold on and chip away at the set holding the bolts into the ceiling.

"Hey, can I borrow your belt?" Émile asked the businessman.

"What for?" he demanded, hands on the buckle.

"I'm going to use the buckle to unscrew these," he said, pointing to the vent. "Try and get it opened wider, get a little more fresh air in."

The man eyed him suspiciously and handed over the belt with obvious displeasure. Émile shimmied up the bar, his arms straining, and he cursed gravity.

"You aren't going to kill yourself, are you?" the businessman asked anxiously. "Because if you are, you can't use my belt. I won't have it, I don't agree."

Émile ignored him and began scraping around the vent. The ceiling slab was thin and flaked away around the vent easily. A discolored patch showed there had been water damage to the structure, and Émile had an idea. He hooked one leg over a crossbar to keep himself in place and reached out to unscrew the grating over the vent. It came away almost too easily. The screws were smaller than should be used, second quality if that.

The grating came out with a good tug and hung on the two remaining screws, creaking and letting go a shower of dust and peels of institutional off-white paint. Émile began to cough and the businessman protested vigorously. Then Émile ran a hand up the inside of the vent.

Cheap, like everything else in the basement of the Hôtel de Ville. The seam of the thin aluminum was not decently smooth, and a couple of shavings embedded themselves in his palm. He withdrew his hand sharply and winced as he saw the blood starting to ooze around the dull grey slivers.

The businessman made some nasty comment, then held a clean white cloth handkerchief over his head. Émile snatched it, thanked him, and used his teeth to tie it around his hand. The fabric was soft and clean and smelled of laundry powder. Émile had never heard of anyone carrying such an anachronism around. But maybe these days it was the style. In any event, it made him feel better, although from a medical point of view it was merely superfluous.

He reached back up the vent gingerly and tapped alongside the seam. Hollow. All hollow. He smiled and wrapped the belt around his fist, punching the internal seam of the vent with his good hand.

It gave easily. Shoddy construction. There had been a bond issue to repair the Hôtel when he was too young for the Syndicat, and it hadn't raised as much money as the Mayor had hoped. Also, the papers had revealed the Mayor's friends getting plum construction jobs at somewhat high bids and skimming a profit from using lesser-quality materials. Papa had read the articles during dinner every night for a week, and then gave a lecture on the evils of corrupt men in high places.

Émile wanted to laugh. All that corruption, all the zealous articles in L'Ami du Peuple, and it all came out on his behalf in the end. He wondered how Papa would have enjoyed the irony. Probably not much. Papa would not approve of him trying to get back into the Syndicat by any but the most legal means. Papa had appreciated order. Ripping out the vent so there was enough room for an ice delivery through the ceiling took Émile little more than an hour.

Outside the mob was silent. The new Mayor must have more respect than the one who had paid for heavy steel ductwork and got the thinnest garbage available.

Émile peered into the hole. His one real worry was that the ceiling would collapse. Then he started pulling down the sheets of badly nailed top tiling. It fell in great hunks, leaving the rusted bolts from bars standing unsupported in the upper dark. When he had opened enough of a hole he simply climbed over the top and jumped down.

"Hey, my belt," the businessman yelled. "Are you just going to leave us here?"

Émile dropped the belt to the floor and kicked it back through the bars. "Get out the way I did," he said, disbelieving. What did the guy want Émile to do, carry him?

"But it'll ruin my clothes. I can't climb those bars, I don't work out the way you monkeys in the Quartier do . . ."

That was the last straw. Émile had been thinking that perhaps he would check the duty desk for keys, but the man's attitude didn't deserve it. Émile turned and walked out the main door to the wide stairs.

The stairs gave onto a main lobby, large and impressively paneled in imported dark wood, with wide window-doors to an oversized marble portico. From where he stood, Émile could see the Mayor and several other dignitaries standing on the portico, backs to him, and a line of gendarmes down three steps in front of them.

Facing them was an angry but restrained crowd carrying torches in the rapidly darkening evening, and large signs that Émile couldn't read from this distance. Under the torches he couldn't see much, but he could tell they weren't rich. If they weren't all from the Quartier, no one in that crowd owned an apartment in St. Michel de Milo either. The torchlight revealed mostly black and grey with flashes of dirty white, the colors of the demimonde that the uptowners liked so much to wander in until the dark became too chilly or the slang a little rough, and then they made their way back to the safety of neighborhoods where the streets were dry and well lit.

So escape by the doors was absolutely impossible. Besides, curiosity was clawing his gut. He needed a better view and a place where he could hear the demands and counteroffers going on outside. Quickly he scrambled up the stairs, keeping low, and found an open door onto a small front room with a large window. He ducked in and closed the door behind him.

He edged to the window to look down, then smiled as he realized where he was. This was the flag window, where the flags over the Hôtel de Ville were chosen and flown. Just below him was the green banner of the Justica next to the blue, white and red quartered with the black and violet nebula of Beau Soleil.

It was only a symbol and it should not make him angry, he reminded himself. It was only a rag, a piece of cloth. But after the *Constanza* it was a hated symbol, and Saint-Just had suffered enough indignity for one day. He could not endure another slight even if it got him killed.

The flag room contained very little furniture; a chair and a tall linen press that Émile assumed stored the flags. The press was not locked and he opened it. Twenty shelves at least held flags, flags for saint's days and for various jurisdiction to honor

visiting heads of state. Flags for the cities of Beau Soleil, for
ArianeSpace, for the Académie Français. The empty space for
the Justica flag was among the others in the diplomatic section,
originally used to honor visitors. But so far as anyone knew,
so far as the paper had reported, there was no visiting dignitary
in the city.

Émile went through the city collection on the center shelf
carefully. They were all labeled, and he was grateful. No way
he would know the difference between St. Michel and St.
Jeanne d'Arc. He thought for a moment, and then chose the
deep violet with eight white fleurs-de-lys, the flag of the sov-
ereign city of Huit Fleurs.

He took the flag, closed the press and edged open the window
enough to get his hands on the guide ropes. Outside he could
hear the Mayor's warm, politically caring voice saying, "We
will not permit such excesses in the future. Even if it was an
accident, we will make certain that the perpetrators are caught
and punished as an example for other Justica officers, that
implementing the law does not mean trampling the rights of
citizens."

There was something frightened in that voice, though, something that was trying to convince the Mayor as much as the
crowd. Émile didn't have time to feel sorry even if he could
spare any pity for a politician. After all, the Mayor asked for
this. But he was already hauling down the Justica flag.

It took a moment for the mob to notice. They were paying
too much attention to the Mayor, weighing his promises and
assurances against their own experience and the cynicism it
had brought. There was a murmur through the assemblage, and
through the open window Émile made out the words "burn it
down." He rather agreed with them.

He had hauled in the Justica flag and had hoisted the flag of
Huit Fleurs halfway up the mast before someone in the mob
pointed up and yelled. One by one the faces turned upward
until he was looking at a sea of eyes and smiles. The crowd
roared approval. Someone began singing, the ancient anthem
Émile had hummed back in the Syndicat but to which he had
forgotten the words. The Mayor's voice joined them, stronger
and richer, singing loudly over the rest.

Émile fixed the guide rope and closed the window as the

singing went on. He could hear it perfectly well through the glass panes. The inspired music of a revolution caught his imagination, and like any member of the crowd all he cared about was the singing and the animal community of warm bodies in the night. The simple and raw emotion of that flash of unity moved him deeply, made him feel that no sacrifice was too great.

The singing died slowly, softening in his ears. Saint-Just did not want to relinquish the sweet abandonment to power. Or the illusion of power. He stood clutching it until the door of the flag room opened and the Mayor walked in.

CHAPTER NINETEEN

"Excellent thinking, Monsieur," the Mayor said. "Yet another triumph of theater over substance. Proving once again that the human animal, in multiple, is swayed by its lowest emotional response. Logic, reason, abandoned to the warm sensations of mass approval. Give them something that stirs the heart and a burned-out squat in the Quartier is forgotten."

"Burned-out?" Émile asked. All he could imagine was his new home in smoking cinders.

The Mayor shrugged. "So they say. Built with wooden ornamentation. It must have cost a fortune. But it would have rotted in the still water anyway."

Then the Mayor turned to his aides. "Get this man's name and address. We will add it to the press release, honor a patriot and so forth, you know the standard language."

Émile shook his head. "I'm nobody. I'm just one more person who lives in a squat in the Quartier, that's all."

The Mayor's eyebrows went up. "So you were with the mob, not in the office? You were trying to defy our authority? Then you should realize that you defeated your own purpose."

Émile swallowed hard. "May I go now?"

An aide escorted him back down the stairs and out the door. The vast portico was silent and abandoned now, only crude home-lettered signs flapping in the gutters a reminder of just how close violence had come. Saint-Just scuffed through the abandoned posters, demands silent now that honor had been satisfied. He didn't want to go home, didn't want to find out if 27 Rue Jacques Doré had burned and Anne-Sylvie and Daniel and Alain and even crazy Nathalie were gone.

He took a side street off Boulevard Lafitte and wandered

through the residential streets. He could smell the cooking from the second-story windows and it made him hungry. His last meal had been a few spoons of *cassoulet* a very long time ago. He looked up to where the good smells originated and there lay puddles of yellow light behind careful lace curtains. He heard a low voice, a young girl's laughter, and the window was closed.

Lights shone softly through the neighborhood, clean and secure. The streets had been swept and the doors were all freshly painted with polished numbers displayed elegantly. The whole area reeked of contentment, people who didn't need to care about the great movements of history as it swept past, so long as it never touched the private moments when the curtains were drawn and the family renewed its strength against the world.

The night was not cold but Émile huddled against a chill deep inside. The pools of pale yellow light taunted him and ignored his loneliness in the street. Warm and well fed, the people of this neighborhood lived in a world as alien to him as the Justica central, or maybe more so.

It hurt. He searched the well-groomed street for a pebble to break one of those windows. Their perfect insulation insulted him, dug deep inside like a worm hatching in his gut. What made it worse was that he understood them all too well. It was just such a world Papa had tried to create every night at the dinner table, and failed. The Quartier and Maman had been too strong in the end to overcome with mere respectability.

This was no good. If he stayed any longer he would do something evil, something cruel. And he had never thought he was a cruel person. Only hurt and alone, more painfully so now than when he had first come aboard the *Constanza*.

That was strange. He couldn't understand why there should be such hollowness now. At least he was home. There were familiar places, familiar sounds. The language was crystal music, his own. There was no reason to feel so terribly isolated, bereft.

"Move on, now." A gendarme in a high-collared jacket and white gloves prodded him with a stick. He didn't even get angry, just got up and walked to the nearest *rapide* station. He

didn't even bother to stop for dinner on the way back to the
Quartier.

It was time for the clubgoers to appear in the Quartier. Down
the main walkways, lit by strings of multicolored flashes on
generator taps, people dressed in the most extreme versions of
outfits from the uptown couture houses strolled in groups, some
going directly to a particular destination, others wandering.
Outside the club roofs stood hawkers, attractive young men
and women passing out flyers detailing that night's entertainment. It was still too early to hear the competing strains of
music filling the bridgewalks when the club doors opened.

A girl with dark curls artfully straggled across her face
handed him a thin flyer with the name of a club and a band.
She smiled shyly, licked her lips. All movements calculated
to lure the uptowners out on the night. The skybridges and
walkways over the water were crowded. The partiers hadn't
heard of the demonstration and the burning, or chose to ignore
it. At night the water in the streets lost its bleak dirtiness and
turned liquid obsidian black. The lights strung over the safety
rails reflected below, as if the entire scene had been created
out of a dark fairy tale and not bedraggled necessity.

Émile was lost in its charm. Even within his own isolation,
at least here he was someplace where he knew the rules, he
belonged. He could smell the whores on the Avenue Patchouli,
two blocks away, when the breeze was right. He was circling
around the long way to avoid the Place Baudelaire and Café
de la Montagne. It was too early in the evening for a local and
the place looked warped, filled with expensively dressed office
workers out to taste the wild side.

The Mayor had accused him of being a patriot. Maybe the
Mayor was right. He found himself in front of the Louis Chapelle, the tiny but perfect church that served the Quartier. It
held Mass at strange hours to accommodate the performers and
café workers, and had given far more charity than it received.
The walkway led down a complex series of stairs and platforms
to a float that connected to the church door. Émile went in,
hoping to be alone.

The chapel blazed with light. Perhaps a hundred people or
more stood in the ancient pews and each held a single lit candle.

Flowers placed in banks around the side chapels threatened to
overtake the pews, and a mountain in the front obscured the
altar. In the nave were three small white coffins.

The microphone was not well adapted to the stone chapel,
and Émile had trouble understanding the priest. There wasn't
much more to say when the bells rang and three sets of pallbearers picked up the white coffins. The priest, acolytes and
procession followed out onto the platform, where they were
met by the funeral band. The coffins were placed on wheeled
sledges that had also been covered with flowers, and the prin-
cipal mourners, all women, had brought bunches more from
inside the church. These were placed on top of the small boxes
so that each looked like a flowered float in a parade.

The band led the mourners onto the bridge, playing a dirge.
The pallbearers took the gold- and silver-painted chains and
dragged the sledges. The priest followed with an acolyte
dressed in white and holding a large silver crosier that had been
brought from the cathedral of Reims on Earth with the first
settlers. The women, who looked like cabaret singers and
whores and shop girls, all massed after, weeping copiously,
tracking makeup down their cheeks. Émile thought he saw
Anne-Sylvie in the group for a moment, a face raised dry from
a tissue, hands knotted with anger and not pain. Then the sight
was gone.

There were a lot of mourners for a Quartier funeral. Even
Jacques d'Istanbul had only had the Louis Chapelle half full,
and not nearly so many flowers. He wanted to ask precisely
but knew better. If he was here, he should know. *L'Ami du
Peuple* should have an article—too bad it wasn't due for almost
a week.

He followed the funeral procession, the band clearing the
way for the mourners, and the group grew in size as they made
their way through the major avenues of the Quartier. People
followed on, some out of curiosity and some for the music.
Several uptowners followed well back, interrupting their evening plans to experience this ritual as it was done with full
rites.

The burying ground down by the Quais du Paris had been
flooded out, so the procession wound uptown, out of the Quartier to the crematory of Ste. Anne, which was down near the

boundary streets and more proper for children. The caskets were rolled into the little white stone houses, the priest prayed, the women cried, the flames leaped up through the flues in the ornamental stone angels and lambs.

Then the band, which had been playing only solemn dirges, kicked in a joyful dance tune. Like Carnival time, everyone danced to the frenzied beat. The band marched around the death houses, through the monuments and stone angels, the raised coffins with portraits embedded over where faces would have been, playing loud and free. Celebrating death, the mourners joined in the traditional gruesome songs, clapping and stamping along to descriptions of decomposition. It was a good show, macabre and festive among the remains.

The uptowners lingered outside the funerary precinct. Émile caught sight of a few of them, standing at the low whitewashed wall at the edge of Ste. Anne's. Too fastidious to enter the place of the dead, he wondered, or too restrained to join those who knew where they were going. Heaven or Hell, everyone knew that some day the band would play for them. Maybe uptowners didn't think that death was worth celebrating. Then the dance swirled around again and he was caught up in the festivities.

The band regrouped at the ornate wrought-iron gate. Three women were presented with ceramic urns painted with pink and yellow blossoms, lambs and cherubs. The handles were outlined in gilt paint. The band led the mourners out while the priest lingered. He was not part of these ceremonies.

Émile, too, lingered, as did many others who had come for the solemn rites but were not invited to the supper the families would throw.

"It was a fine funeral," Émile said to a woman leaning on a stone angel.

She nodded. "Everyone chipped in, and the band played for free. Since it was against the *flics* and all. They weren't going to permit a proper funeral, can you believe it?"

Émile snorted. "What were they going to do, confiscate the bodies?"

The woman looked at him as if he was crazy and walked away. Émile left through the iron gate, to the street down to the wooden stairs that led to the skywalks of the Quartier, and went home.

When he arrived at the squat, no one was home except Nathalie. He said polite and meaningless things to her distracted and meaningless conversation and went to his apartment. It was exactly as he had left it, the newspaper on the floor, the scraps from a forgotten dinner clinging to a plate next to the sofa, a crumpled paper cup on top of his socks.

He stripped off Daniel's brown delivery uniform, left it in a heap in the middle of the floor, lay down on the sofa and pulled the sheet over him. He didn't wake until the late afternoon sun crept into his eyes.

He was coming pleasantly to consciousness when Daniel walked in, picked up his uniform and sniffed at it. "Damn, you couldn't have gotten it any dirtier, could you?"

Émile groaned. It was all like a bad dream. On a bright afternoon like this there was no Organization, no *flics*, nothing but a day waiting, and Alain owed him ten francs. The world was definitely improved, if it hadn't been for Daniel's mood, which he decided to ignore.

"Do you know anything about there being a demonstration yesterday at the Hôtel de Ville? And about some kids and a funeral at Louis Chapelle?" he asked conversationally enough.

Daniel groaned. "Don't tell me you were there. There were *flics* there, watching for us. Damn. We're not supposed to go anywhere we could be linked to the movement. Well, number seven fifty-seven Rue Patchouli went up when the *flics* were on flower-burning patrol. They torched the whole canal, like they did here, and wham, seven fifty-seven just about blows out of the water. I mean, the flare was so high you could have seen it down by the Quais. Anyway, the kids were there, probably the kids of the whores who work one of the houses.

"The flare, well, no one knows for sure. The *flics* are putting it out that it was us making incendiaries. Can you believe that? I mean, I don't even think Alain can say that, much less make one. Around the street, it seems pretty much agreed that they were using some kind of illegal heater or cooking arrangement, kerosene or something, and once the fire hit the fuel supply it was all over."

"They cremated the children," Émile observed.

Daniel made a face. "They didn't have to bother. There wasn't enough left of them to fuel a tea kettle. At least, that's according to Simon Simon, the columnist at *L'Ami du Peuple*. He should know. It's going to be the cover story on next week's issue."

"Oh, and you know Simon Simon. He just tells you everything," Émile retorted. He knew immediately that it was uncalled for; Daniel did not deserve the sum total of his anger. But the events of the past hours had not eliminated the horrible isolation. Since leaving the Syndicat system he had been aware of a growing sadness inside, something that refused to let him merge into this time and this Beau Soleil now. Some part of him knew that he was locked out of his own life, trapped in a whirlpool of events that were not meant for him.

He never thought that he had personally wanted it that way. He had coveted the cuff, the assignment on the *Mary Damned*, but neither desire had threatened him with meaninglessness if he failed to achieve them. There was always something else, some other option. And then on the *Constanza* he had learned not to hope at all. He had made himself as dead as possible to buffer the relentlessness of the routine, the crushing terror of an entire life condemned to an ice miner. He had learned to crush the past and the future out of him, to forget that he had once known freedom, to forget that he would never see his family or his friends again.

Despair. That one word echoed through his being to the internal nerves, to the microchemical self. It shook through like a cold autumn wind, leaving behind only a wet bleeding trail of emptiness. And yet the need was still there, burning in the cold hollow of his being, burning through the synapses that were never made to be displaced in time. Burning him until his defenses threatened to break under the weight of all that need.

But there was nothing he could do. Overwhelming sorrow battered him to the core and he didn't hear what Daniel was saying. Daniel faded in and out of focus against the green-striped wallpaper as Émile battled for control of his emotions. Of his grim perception that he was playing with things that were very much in a here and now where he was only an accident, a mistake. A ghost, like the *Mary Damned*.

Daniel's words formed a background against which the battle was played, until Daniel said, "But of course you know Simon Simon perfectly well yourself. You're talking to him."

Then the disparate segments of time and destiny froze together in the realization of what Daniel meant. Suddenly the whole universe was skewed and his own being was no longer so important. Daniel was Simon Simon? Then why did he live in a squat, why did he act like Anne-Sylvie's lieutenant in the Organization, why did he permit Alain to say hideous things in public? His face expressed more astonishment than words could have ever conveyed.

Daniel shrugged. "I prefer not to be known. It gives me some power. And as for why I'm living here, well, Nathalie is here. And she is crazy enough to both be interesting and not interfere with my life, and she is beautiful. And her father doesn't know who I am and is an amazing source of information. You wonder why we have an indoor garden and no one else does? Nathalie's father warned me of the raids. I warned Alain and the rest happened. So I'm devious and cheap, which is reasonable. But you, Émile, you are lazy."

CHAPTER
TWENTY

After that first insane, disassociative experience with senin and the sensory nodes catapulting him into the machine mind, Hugo Gorvitz found the more ordinary channel of communication. Using a screen and keyboard and mathematics and the language of symbolic logic he managed to overcome at least the worst of the language problem.

Now, however, there was something he had to express, for which he needed the *Mary Damned*'s cooperation and full understanding. The ship had something parallel to rudimentary emotions, at least where the Syndicat and Beau Soliel were concerned. Gorvitz needed to use them.

They were as full out as he and Pauli could coax the thing, but it wasn't fast enough. Maybe enough to spook the Justica group they'd passed, but not enough to mislead the coming fleet, not the way he needed to. And he wasn't the only one who thought that the ship had been made to shave light. Everything about the design, from its mass to its oversized fuel hooks and enormous blocks of frozen hydrogen to its sleek double hull, screamed speed.

The power boards in the room next to control, the area now dubbed engineering, showed everything strong brilliant green. They weren't yet so far removed from their ancestry, Justica and ArianeSpace alike, that the color codes had changed. Green was still go in safety zone, amber still warning and red universally danger. According to the board colors they weren't even pushing. This rig had been built and then retooled as a drug runner. It had to be faster.

And he had to get to Beau Soliel. He didn't know if the plan was going to work, but there was no percentage in playing it safe. Those were the odds Gorvitz liked. It made his parameters clear and simple, winner takes all. Everything was worth the big risk, since there was no difference between losing by a little and losing by a lot.

He had made those choices easily enough. The problem was that he had to make the ship respond, to run flat out, to break free the way it had been made to go, powerful and fast and proud. There was no way to make the thing go any faster than it already was going unless it had new data, unless it had heard what he had overheard from the Justica group they had passed. That alone would motivate the *Mary Damned* well enough, he thought.

But to explain it he had to enter back into the link with the machine again, and it made his skin crawl. He hated the false pleasure and relaxation the drug brought on, although now half the crew was scheming how to break out the supplies over Gorvitz's own security team. They didn't care if their minds were too numb to make real decisions. Reality had never been the strong point for most of the Hounds, and many of them had good enough reasons to want to forget it. Gorvitz, however, found senin sickening.

Then there was the matter of the computer itself. He hated the fact that it considered itself in some way alive, not a mechanical servant of humans but their partner and complement. This attitude violated his sense of how the universe ought to work, all his ideologies, and worst of all stood in the way of his need. Hugo Gorvitz was not pleased at all.

On the other hand, there was no choice. He went to the stores himself to pull the pale green vial from the heavy padding in which it had been packed. He didn't want any of the Hounds to know he was using it and start the rumor that he was limiting access so that he could hoard the precious drug for his own consumption.

He palmed the bottle as he came up through the galley, where several of the off-duty Hounds were playing cards and two were arm wrestling. That was a popular sport on the *Mary Damned*, maybe because it had been forbidden on the *Constanza*. Gorvitz greeted them, examined several hands wordlessly and went on. People at duty stations were a little less social, and those in the halls with nothing special to do avoided those who were on. And Gorvitz was always on.

The control room was abandoned. No one had used it since he had first entered the navigational control AI there. If there were a part of the ship anyone considered haunted, it would have been that area, although even Gorvitz couldn't say why. It bothered him. He strapped down on the couch again, arranged the nodes and drank the green stuff down. Then he leaned back and waited for it to come.

This time she was more demure, forceful, completely self-contained and wary. Perhaps she had not liked him any better than he had liked her. The realization startled Gorvitz a little; then he settled down. It was part of the relationship. She was the ship, part of the Syndicat, and Gorvitz was a stranger. She was right to be cautious.

I was under the assumption that we had an agreement, she said.

"There is new data," he replied carefully. "We have passed a group of Justica cruisers. Because of additional ceramic masking we were able to pass close enough to snoop in on their conversation."

I was aware that we were intercepting foreign communication, the ship agreed.

"We need to get to Beau Soliel ahead of schedule. The ships are headed out there and will be joined by other groups from other Zones. They have been called in by some authorities on Beau Soliel itself, and they are treating the situation as if Beau Soliel were one of their colonies."

That is not possible, the AI answered calmly. *We are registered as an Independent ArianeSpace Colony with certain economic and diplomatic ties to the Justica through the regulation of Zone 6. That is all. It is impossible for them to assemble a fleet and threaten our sovereignty. The Russians have hated us ever since Napoleon, that is all. And the others, well, they are mere adolescents. Promising, perhaps, but they still haven't learned to keep their rooms clean.*

"Not impossible," Gorvitz replied, trying to restrain himself from shaking the image the ship used. "If there is the possibility of expansion the Justica will use it. They want very much to curb the sadece trade and would be more than willing to take over a planet, even decimate it, in order to do this. Check your records. The *Justica* has a history of behaving in its own best interests, even when that means destroying someone else.''

Justica is the enemy, the AI agreed. *Justica must be prevented from any role on Beau Soliel. But this ship is unarmed. Do we go ahead to give warning?*

Gorvitz could not sigh with relief in the computer link. He only thought it. At least the ship was willing to unite against the common enemy, had less narrow margins than he had originally assumed. That was good, at least while they were united. The *Mary Damned* would be one very dangerous enemy on her own.

"I've thought about this," Gorvitz said slowly. He could sense impatience in the AI but he didn't want to rush this. He needed more than the thing's agreement, he needed its active cooperation. Partly for speed and mostly to calculate the possibility of his plan. It sounded crazy and farfetched even to himself.

"What we need to do is this. Let's outrun them and get back to Beau Soliel a little before. By the time the *Justica* fleet arrives they're going to be looking down the noses of several very angry cannon. But we have to get there early enough to give Beau Soliel a decent chance to prepare."

The *Mary Damned* didn't even hesitate. *Excellent. I shall release full power now. How much are you willing to give up comfort power to make speed?*

"As much as is necessary," Gorvitz said. He was pleased and didn't want to admit it. The thing was spooky, unnatural, hateful, but its sense of self and independent commitment was going to be his best ally.

The ship itself cut off flow to the fiber-optic leads. As the sensory input was cut off, Gorvitz became conscious that the control room was no longer brightly lit. Only enough illumination remained that he could disconnect the leads and find the door. Even the corridor was dim, and obviously the entire energy output on the amenities was minimal. At least the temperature was not miserable. Perhaps it took so little more to maintain something comfortable that the difference was not enough to bother with reaccessing.

This time Gorvitz avoided the galley and went directly to Pauli Tree's cabin. She shared with two other women who

Gorvitz hoped would be on duty now, or would be otherwise occupied. He needed to talk to someone intelligent enough to comment and human enough to understand. Besides, it had been Pauli who had detected the Justica group in the first place, and who had encouraged him to outrun them in the second.

Pauli was not in. He went by her monitor station, and she was seated as he had seen her for hours on end in front of a bleeding colored screen waiting for . . . something.

"Pauli," he said.

She jerked around as if she had been hit by a projectile. "Oh, it's you. I thought we'd been boarded or something. Next time could you give me a warning?"

He smiled apologetically and outlined what he had told the ship. Pauli's face, deep in shadow, showed nothing.

"Buy time?" she said when he had finished. "You think we can lead them on a merry chase and not get dead in the process? That seems a little wishful thinking to me. Good chance we can fool them for a while, but as some old jerk said, you can't fool all the people all the time. One of those ships is going to come after us and then we're frozen meat. I didn't get this far to get killed for nothing and not even put up a fight. And say we do make it out, what do we do after that?"

Gorvitz was stunned. He had never been contradicted so soundly, not since he was first made a member of the Steering Committee. Suddenly it occurred to him to wonder if there still was a Steering Committee. Maybe the whole Organization had died except for him. Maybe they were all grandparents and voting for Justices on a landowners' share basis. Maybe they were Justices for all he knew. The concept was chilling.

"Beau Soliel is as good a place as any to start a revolution," Gorvitz said slowly. "We've got the Organization set up there, ready for us to come in. And we've got a volatile situation with the Justica just moving in. Motivating the locals won't be difficult. It's got possibilities."

"And Émile Saint-Just is there," Pauli added. "He might help us out. If he isn't ancient or dead or something. If we get through it."

Gorvitz smiled softly. "Oh, we'll get through it easily enough. The *Mary Damned* will buy just enough time to mislead the Justica fleet while we shuttle down to the surface. And if we contact the Organization on the surface now, it'll give them about a year, give or take, for us to get there.''

Pauli considered carefully, biting her lower lip. "Sounds good enough, boss," she finally agreed. "We get to the surface types fast and they get the guns. You know, if we set it up right, maybe we could play the bait, and run these goons right into a blind alley-type trap."

"We'll ask what they can do," Gorvitz said. "We don't know if they have the power to set up something like that." He hesitated, images from a history so remote it seemed fiction filling his head. "You know, Lenin took a sealed train back to Russia. They didn't know he was coming while the Party stepped up activity, basically had a revolution to hand to him when he arrived."

Pauli Tree shook her head sadly. There was something about Gorvitz that worried her. At times he was too hung up on the ancient past, trying to recreate something he'd romanticized. And when he was in that mood he was arrogant, as if he hadn't been a prisoner for fifteen years subjective, as if he hadn't ever made a mistake. Arrogance and romanticism together were trouble.

She was the consummate professional, and she knew that you didn't end up on the *Constanza* by never making mistakes. She also knew that bosses who thought the way Gorvitz did with that slightly crazy glazed look were willing to sacrifice everything for some image they held in their heads. Reality could never match that image exactly and so the bosses made mistakes.

She had known people who did that on jobs, who'd heard about famous jobs in the past and tried to go them one better. Those guys were all doing time.

Maybe she'd made a big mistake too. Maybe she should have taken Gorvitz out when she had the chance; maybe she shouldn't have become so useful to him. She didn't trust him the way she did on the *Constanza*. There he had seemed rational, careful, casing a job before he took it and ready to stash and run if the heat was on. Only he wasn't like that now. Now his schemes were getting wilder and more dangerous.

If she told the Hounds her fears, maybe . . . But it was already too late. They were on the *Mary Damned*, committed to going to Beau Soliel. And if Gorvitz ever found out that she had tried to talk mutiny on him, he would have her killed. She had no illusions about that.

The romantic ones, the ones with dreams, they were the ones who didn't count the cost. They did all the damage. People who kept their lock-boxes neat and their business their own, they never killed anyone or took out a whole ship over a dream.

Gorvitz was crazy and he was dangerous. But, Pauli acknowledged, it was less dangerous to support him running his fantasies than to try and talk reason. Reason was dead, and Pauli Tree was going to do what she did best. She was going to look after her own hide.

CHAPTER TWENTY-ONE

"The *Marie-Claire* and the *Belle Courage* are due at the Zone six days apart. *Marie-Claire* will arrive first, at Quai seventeen, in two weeks. The first shipment is light artillery, ammunition, explosives," Anne-Sylvie said as she poured orangata like a Countess perched at the edge of her tapestry chair.

"No launchers? No radiants? No vacuum implosives?" Alain asked with a sparkle Émile distrusted. Alain probably looked that eager when he dangled squealing small rodents over the flowers.

"Some of those on the *Belle Courage*, but mostly small arms. We don't need anything larger for the city. Launchers would only get in the way and radiants could knock out our own ships as easily as theirs. No, orders are simple urban insurgency." Anne-Sylvie passed around a plate of cookies Émile recognized as day-old fare from the Café de la Montagne. That didn't make them any less pleasant, only crunchier, and Émile took three. Alain took more.

"Who gave those orders?" Émile asked carefully when he had brushed the crumbs from his fingers onto his pants.

"Gorvitz, of course," Anne-Sylvie snapped back. "Who else? At the same time he informed us about you, as a matter of fact. He set up the shipments with the Organization, but don't ask about the whens. They're so relative that I can't calculate it."

"But how did he contact you from the *Constanza*?" Émile pressed on. He knew that Gorvitz had contacts, but he shouldn't be able to issue orders amounting to armed insurrection from a prison ship. Supervision on the *Constanza* wasn't overbearing, but it wasn't nonexistent, either.

"He's not on the *Constanza* anymore," Anne-Sylvie answered, shaking her head. Clearly she couldn't believe how slow Émile was. "Hasn't been for as long as I've been alive, actually. I inherited this particular information from my predecessor."

"But he must have left after I did." Émile protested the logic of it. "And I haven't been here for a month. So how did he get out and what ship's he on and how could he follow so closely? And how come no one was onto me, if I was part of this whole thing?"

Anne-Sylvie seemed confused. She wasn't used to challenges to her authority, and she did not want to answer any more questions than absolutely necessary. Organization training.

Daniel took over. "Gorvitz took the *Mary Damned*. You had given them enough information on its location that they mutinied after you left and found her derelict. They've been heading here for around fifteen years. Anne-Sylvie exaggerates. And as for why they caught up with you, well, they are taking a more direct route. I don't have any idea of what their subjective is, though. Come to think of it, I don't have any idea about yours."

Émile blinked, and then saw it the way he had understood time with Jacques Cher's clear teaching. Time drifted, bent, shifted in colored light against a background of unmoving stars. All together. And the time twisted and made a kind of sense. Gorvitz's orders had been issued before, by subjective experience, he had even been released.

There was a macabre humor there. He wondered if, somewhere at the fringes of the Zones, someone already knew how everything had come out. Or had planned it all and was still alive, subjective, moving them around like pieces on a playing screen. Someone who already knew their next move and the one after that, as if they had no choice at all. History already existed somewhere and it was merely up to them to walk through the parts.

Émile saw it and it infuriated him. He rose, ready to leave this little cabal. He had waited too long and come too far for simple freedom to buckle down to some master scheme.

But Nathalie giggled. No one had seen her come in, floating

like a ghost through the door that Anne-Sylvie insisted was locked. Well, maybe it had been. And maybe Nathalie wasn't completely substantial, either. It didn't matter. She had already invaded their conference, not that she was a security risk. Nathalie was so crazy that it didn't matter if she told everyone in the universe, including her father, exactly what they planned. No one would ever believe her.

"Nathalie, do you have something to tell us?" Daniel asked gently.

The crazy girl nodded solemnly and perched on the arm of the sofa next to Daniel. Daniel handed her his warm orangata and stale *petit pain au chocolat*. She took them and nibbled delicately in the silence. As if she really could have any useful comment.

She licked her fingers clean like a cat, drained the orange-colored beverage and handed the empty cup to Daniel. Then she looked at each of them as if trying to remember who they were.

"There was this student who lived down near the Place d'Instruction, Lisette Jacquard," Nathalie began, staring at Émile. Something about the way she spoke, the depth of her voice or the focus she centered on him, kept him from moving. "She was in love with dead things. She collected them. Especially bodies, human bodies. She kept them in her apartment and cut them up and fed them to her flowers. One day she cut off her own finger and fed it to the flowers, and the next day she cut off her toe. Because the flowers were becoming her and she was certain she would live forever. Forever.

"She gouged out her left eye the week after that and cut out her tongue the next month, and the flowers grew warped and strange. The petals flared and new colors appeared on the edges of the leaves. Double and triple buds bloomed on the stem. She fed them with fresh blood dripped out of her wounds. Anyway, she died."

"Is that all?" Daniel asked softly. Nathalie nodded. Anne-Sylvie rolled her eyes and shook her head. Alain looked as if he wanted to take notes.

"I hadn't heard anything about that," Alain complained. "Double, triple, multicolored flowers. I would like to have the research on that."

"It probably isn't true," Anne-Sylvie said. "Nathalie reads stuff in the paper and sees entertainment and it all gets mixed up, that's all. Let's get back to reality. We have to make arrangements to pick up these shipments and get them stashed before the Syndicat finds out what they're hauling."

"It's true," Nathalie said carefully. "I know it's true. I saw it."

Anne-Sylvie shook her head once more as Daniel escorted Nathalie from the room. Something, perhaps a whiff of the crazy girl's perfume, made it feel as if she still lingered, although Daniel had shut and audibly locked the door once more.

"She won't be back," he said, and to Émile the declaration sounded just a little sad.

"So we have to pick up the shipment." Anne-Sylvie refused to be distracted. "The Syndicat has regulations regarding that."

The Syndicat again. Émile had trouble thinking of them as the enemy. Dumouriez was no problem, although how he had gotten in, gotten past Claude, was something Saint-Just would like to know. And he could see the sense in keeping any information from Dumouriez.

They were all looking at him. Slowly Émile realized that they had needed him all along. The Syndicat controlled all shipping between Beau Soliel and the rest of inhabited space. Without his changing the manifests inside the system and his own knowledge of how arrangements between the Zone and the port were carried out, there was no insurrection. There was nothing at all.

Only his information was fifty-seven years out of date. Things like regular shipping shouldn't change much, but if traffic had gotten heavier and procedures altered, instructions would be given to the purser before landing the cargo and leaving the Zone. He was concerned. He had learned procedures but had never qualified as purser, had never even studied for the apprentice exam. Transshipment simply was not his specialization.

But they were looking at him so expectantly. Even Anne-Sylvie had such trust in her eyes that he could not bear to disappoint them completely. "Please remember, I was never a purser's apprentice and it's not really my area," he said firmly, trying to make them all understand that his grasp was merely superficial. Alain waved a hand as if sweeping the disclaimer aside. Saint-Just might not be an expert but he was much more qualified than the rest of them.

Émile recognized their attitude and continued. "The way I remember it, and it was a long time ago planetary subjective, was that each cargo, once it passed Justica customs and was in our jurisdiction in the Zone, was signed for by a Syndicat agent who was responsible to the Chief Purser. From that point the Syndicat was the ship's agent in selling the cargo, and the Syndicat received ten percent of the price."

"Ten percent didn't build the Palais," Daniel commented dryly.

Émile shrugged. "That's just the agent's fees. We also pay stakes and berthing and port taxes, percentages for job listings and assignments. It's worth it. We're really just paying ourselves anyway. Anyway, the cargo is held by the Syndicat under the ship's seal. Unless the goods were contracted individually and without Syndicat assistance. That's extremely rare. And if there are others like Dumouriez running things, I wouldn't even want to try."

"But wouldn't most goods be contracted beforehand?" Anne-Sylvie asked, clearly confused.

"No need," Émile said, reaching for lectures he had to sit through as a ground-bound apprentice before he had a berth. Economics had never been his long suit. "Most of the things we import have a fairly stable demand. Wood, exotic fabrics, foodstuffs, coffee, vanilla, cocoa, wheat flour. You wouldn't believe how much coffee and wheat flour we bring in."

"But don't we grow wheat on the outer islands?" Daniel asked.

Émile nodded. "But it isn't exactly the best kind for pastry, I think. I don't know the entire thing. Anyway, we import a lot of it. And coffee, well, the largest ships in the Syndicat have been known to fill their entire holds with coffee and sell every bean at an astronomical profit."

Alain looked frightened. "But we couldn't live without coffee. And the Justica is on us for sadece. Let them crack down on the coffee worlds."

"And what do you plan to drink?" Anne-Sylvie demanded. "Orangata?"

Alain shrugged. The juice of a native plant mixed judiciously with water and the citrus that had transplanted well to Beau Soliel was decent enough. It just didn't have the added energizing drug effect. Not that the Justica would even worry about that drug. They were as addicted as anyone else, making the coffee worlds the richest everywhere. Coffee, cocoa, vanilla and tea were very fussy about where they would grow. And all humans loved them in large quantities and were willing to pay extortionary sums to keep supplied. Compared to those addictions, sadece was a very small and mild thing indeed.

"So," Émile continued, "most of those things are fairly predictable. You can load up and be sure of some profit. If you find something you think will sell, well, test it out with a bit of cargo space. If it does well, that jacks up the price even higher because supply is limited. But most ships carry a lot of basics, which the Syndicat can always sell.

"Barge trains used to run twice a week from Zone 6. They're crewed by members between berths, or those who are recovering from an illness, or by those who have chosen family life. There aren't many in the Syndicat who choose to have children, but those who do frequently qualify as barge pilots and masters. It's good work, high shares in the cargo profits."

"But if it means you can stay, why doesn't everyone want to do it?" Anne-Sylvie asked in her practical way.

Émile didn't know how to explain that, the draw of the deep night and the stars, the need to break free of this one time and place and belong to a greater universe. Nor could he explain the hunger for the uncommon and the unknown, a need to live an extraordinary life.

He looked at the others in the room. None of them had ever left Beau Soliel territory. Anne-Sylvie had met him at Zone 6. The others, well, no matter how sophisticated they were, there was a very good chance they had never in all their lives left Huit Fleurs. Certainly never for more than a month's holiday on the Rose Plage or maybe Vickers.

How could he explain? He wasn't a poet or a journalist like Simon Simon that he could tell them something they obviously had never known, or even realized existed to be known.

So he just shrugged, inarticulate. "The important thing is that barge people are Syndicat like anyone else. They are considered specialists and qualify for specialist shares. Once the barge trains arrive in port, someone from the Chief Purser's office takes over and they are floated to the warehouses in the port ring. From there the bargaining is done, the sales are completed, and the buyers are responsible for picking up their goods.''

''And what about our shipments?'' Daniel asked softly. ''Are they now labeled something else? Will they be sold and do we have to come up with the money to buy them?''

''Where could we get money like that?'' Anne-Sylvie snapped.

Daniel smiled. ''Nathalie's father, of course. Who else has it?''

But Émile was already shaking his head and spreading his hands in negation. ''No. The Syndicat's main AI has already relabeled it as private contract sale, already paid and the Syndicat's cut registered to the ship's outgoing credit. All we have to do when the guns come in is pick them up.''

''Without anybody finding out what they are or peeking in the boxes or anything,'' Daniel mentioned dryly.

''I made it as easy as it could be,'' Émile said, his patience stretched to the limit. ''You're the ones who decided to play this game and got me along for the ride. You wanted guns, you got guns. Don't complain because they're dangerous.''

Anne-Sylvie stood abruptly. ''This is over,'' she announced angrily. ''You know what you need to know. Émile, thank you for your assistance. You are free to go. Alain, you too are excused. Daniel and I will work out the details.''

But Daniel was already on his feet. ''I'm sorry, Anne-Sylvie. But I think we've all had enough for today.''

''Gorvitz said . . .'' she began lamely.

''I don't care what Gorvitz said,'' Daniel answered. ''He isn't here. I am.''

Alain, Émile and Daniel all left Anne-Sylvie standing in the middle of her living room, completely dismayed. Quietly Daniel closed the door after himself. ''Well, how about going to the *café* and seeing if the new issue of *L'Ami du Peuple* is out yet?''

CHAPTER
TWENTY-TWO

The paper was due in later, they were told. That didn't matter, Daniel decided. He ordered a bottle of wine, cheese, sausage and bread for all of them, a decent meal that should last into the small hours. Émile was still keyed up by the meeting and by walking out of it. Anne-Sylvie doubtless knew where to find them, should she choose.

"You know, I've known Anne-Sylvie since she was a student at the university." Daniel was babbling from too much wine. But Émile had wondered about Anne-Sylvie's past and wasn't about to stop Daniel's recitation. "She was in her first year. I had just graduated and was editing the school paper, and working as a stringer for *L'Ami du Peuple*."

"I never heard of you," Alain interrupted.

Daniel shrugged. "It was before you came to Huit Fleurs. Anyway, Anne-Sylvie was always very certain of her own rightness and once she made up her mind she didn't change. So I was the one who put her into contact with people who could use her organizational skills and get her off my back. For me, of course, it was all the cause of the Académie. I once thought of being a poet. I even sent some pieces to Louis Martin of the *Raison Dur* and he wrote back—horrible things. I burned the copies and never tried again. He was right. He told me not to disgrace the language with my adolescent ramblings. He also gave me a job."

"But Martin was a famous rightist," Alain protested. "He had dinner with my parents many times. They backed his magazine and they were all completely right-wing. Beau Soleil above all and the French language above that. That no other people were civilized enough to consider and so they were only worth being exploited.''

Daniel nodded drunkenly. ''That's why the right was first against the Justica accords. I don't believe in any Organization. I believe in our history. In Marat and Lafitte and Victor Hugo and all the people the streets of Huit Fleurs are named for. You can keep your Socialist Revolutionary Faction rhetoric. I believe in the French-speaking people.''

''But what about Anne-Sylvie?'' Émile returned Daniel's attention to the original subject.

''Anne-Sylvie? Oh, yes, well, we met during a debate. I was on the right and she was the head of the Socialist Revolutionary Faction at the time. Anne-Sylvie, just like all those other little revolutionaries who come from comfortable homes in St. Ciel or St. Michel de Milo, trying to make their parents angry and completely convinced of their own infallibility. I introduced her to reality.''

''And what about me?'' Alain asked bitterly. ''You forgot your usual tirade. That the plantation families are so far in the past they are beyond reactionary. That someone like me was hopeless from the start.''

Daniel drank some more wine. Émile wanted to hide. The group was so small and it seemed that none of the them were decent to each other. Like prison.

No one wanted to talk much now. The bitterness of the little exchange still lay out on the table. Instead, the *café* was a perfect place to indulge in Huit Fleurs' favorite pastime, watching the people come and go and commenting on every one of them.

''Why the hell did Nathalie tell that story?'' Alain asked after a singularly fat man wearing street optics had disappeared around the wall.

''I don't know,'' Daniel said. ''But she must have had a reason. She's crazy but she hears things, understands them, has reasons.''

''And your reason is that you love her ass. Or maybe you love her daddy's money,'' Alain replied. He had drunk just a taste too much.

Émile felt pinned, waiting for the first blow. Anger was overripe, festering. And they wouldn't let it alone, either, both of them picking at the wound. Perhaps Alain was off balance, but Daniel had been pushing all along.

The waiters knew and managed to avoid traffic patterns near the table, although there was a line for tables winding across the dry terrace. Something had to break. The warm yellow light and the polished stone table tops became very clear; edges around the pastry case and diners became crisp and distinct. Around them the people in the *café* took on a new dimension, as if they were flat and overly bright, a master copy of a great film projected on the wall. Only the three of them were real.

In that extreme illumination Saint-Just recognized a face. It was across the dining room against a pillar, and Émile had not bothered before. There were more arresting outfits than the drab dark blue the man wore, louder conversations at closer tables.

"Dumouriez," Émile said, rising and pointing.

Daniel and Alain snapped around, their anger overridden for the moment. "Who?" Alain asked. "Which one?" Daniel needed more information.

"Over there, near the pink pillar." Émile gave directions. "In the blue."

Daniel nodded carefully. "You know about Dumouriez, don't you? He's Justica to the core. Is one of the major forces for bringing them in. Some people even suspect he might be a plant in the Syndicat."

"Simon Simon suspects that." Alain spat the name out. "I think he's just another opportunist. Whatever. Isn't he the one who refused to give you your cuff back?"

Émile nodded. His whole body needed to do something. But this time it was his territory. Let him get to Dumouriez and make the bastard acknowledge Saint-Just and give him back his place. He only hesitated to consider the method and the necessity of getting to Dumouriez without mishap. No doubt that at least one of the Syndicat boss's dining companions was a bodyguard. He was not at all concerned with his own safety, but he didn't want Dumouriez to get away. That was unthinkable.

Dumouriez turned, and for an instant Émile felt those eyes focus on him, recognize him and the threat he represented. One of his companions, a woman with her hair in an elegant chignon, started to reach into her sleeve. Time crawled and Émile believed that time was almost over. He dove between two tables, slowly, slowly, still pushing toward the enemy.

And then, distant above him, he heard someone scream, "Sugar fight!"

He rolled to see Alain grab a *beignet* from a neighboring diner and blow the sugar into a white cloud, obscuring Saint-Just's position. Daniel darted across the aisle and snatched another *beignet* from a stranger's plate. Then the younger, bolder slummers, who had come to the Quartier for just this excitement, were grabbing pastry and the white haze grew ferocious. Émile couldn't see at all, but headed for Dumouriez's table by instinct.

A hand grabbed his collar. "Come on, get out of here," Daniel said, and he was catapulted outside.

The woman with the chignon was close behind; he could smell her perfume. They had to still be inside; the table had been far from the door and there was chaos. The desire to kill Dumouriez ebbed as self-preservation surfaced. He had to get away from the bodyguard. She didn't look Syndicat. Something about her had been too reserved . . .

He had gulped about three lungfuls of unsugared air when a flash of red light was softened by a white cloud. And then an explosion shattered the Place Baudelaire. Émile was knocked to the ground, the stone terrace against his face and then that sliding, until his hands were covered with filthy water. Screams and moaning filled the night. Shards of glass from the windows glittered in reflected firelight.

The Café de la Montagne was burning behind them. Slowly Émile got up. The heat was overwhelming, so that he began to sweat although he was wearing no jacket and it was winter. Flame seared his skin like sunburn, like mud crackling in the kiln.

What remained of the diners surged around him, panicked, trying to get away. Émile was pushed back until his ankles were submerged in the canal. Before him was a scene from Hell, red and yellow fire eating everything alive, chasing the bloodied survivors running for the skybridges. And the elegant skyways themselves, those made of plastic and light metal alloy, were victims of the heat. Superstrong and light the stuff was, but it melted, dripped and sizzled as the bridge shriveled and dropped into the canal.

"Shit," Alain said. He towed Émile by the collar, now wading knee deep in mud, steering him away from the wreckage and into a dark creek that had once been a service alley.

Émile could not move. He was transfixed by the scene in front of him, the insult to reality of it all. The Café de la Montagne was as permanent as the islands of the Vrais Fleurs archipelago, as tradition-laden as the Syndicat, as living as his own flesh.

The *café* burned. The pain was too great for Émile, the way the blast had been too deep to hear, had shaken the rock rather than their ears. It was too much to comprehend. He was numb in the blaze, permitting Alain to drag him through the water, forgetting even why he had been there or what had caused the place to blow.

"Dumouriez must have been inside," Daniel said as he emerged from the causeway into the alley. "I didn't see him leave and it was that Syndicat bodyguard who fired that shot. At you, probably," he said, looking at Émile.

But the fire had him mesmerized. The high shriek of a fire-dolly drowned out the screams. Either that, or all those who had burned were already dead. Émile wandered back toward the heat as Alain let go of his collar.

"Where the hell are you going?" Alain yelled after him.

But Émile didn't bother to answer. As he emerged back onto the Place Baudelaire he could see there were already bucket brigades at work, locals using the foul water of the canal on the burning building.

He wouldn't have thought there would be that much to burn. Most of the building had been stone and metal. But inside, the bodies, the sugar, the dough for the next day's bread still fueled the conflagration. Without thought, Émile took a place on one of the bucket lines.

The work felt good, something rhythmic and solid and alive, surrounded by sweating bodies who were also bound to the Quartier by ties of love and long habituation. Running buckets up to the front of the line, he regained his natural perception, the fascination of the fire wearing thin as the blaze burned down.

There was very little left as the lavender grey false dawn touched the sky. Black smoking cinders and charred walls, twisted girders made an evil sculpture in the square. Émile stood up, stretched his shoulders and wiped his forehead with a grimy hand. He smelled bad. Smoke overcame all the other smells, the canal and the bodies and even the charred death around them. Everything reeked.

He felt tired and hollow. He took one hard look at the remains of the *café*, then turned on the terrace and headed back for the canal.

"Hey, wait a minute. Aren't you Émile Saint-Just? The one who raised our flag at the Hôtel de Ville?"

Émile wheeled around to see who was talking. The man was younger than Émile, nearer twenty than twenty-five, but he already had the white scars of a long-time softknife fighter laced over his cheeks as well as the backs of his hands and his shoulders. He, too, was streaked with dirt and soot from fighting the fire.

Émile shrugged. "How did you know?" he asked, curious but too tired to really care.

"*L'Ami du Peuple* had a column about it," he said. "And a picture. Anyway, if you want to take on the *flics* again, my friends and I would be pleased to join you."

He turned and was about to leave when Émile asked, "Who are you?"

The young man grinned and revealed teeth that had been cared for only at chance intervals. "I'm Louis the Sewer King," he said. Then he laughed and waded into the canal as if the water was his home.

When he made it back to 27 Rue Jacques Doré, all Saint-Just wanted was a shower and a bed. He climbed down the stairs from the roof door in semi-dark. If he tried he could convince himself it was still night. As he went down past Anne-Sylvie's silent apartment and Nathalie's door, which was outlined in dark, he thought about how good sleep was going to feel.

But as he arrived at the lower level and passed Daniel's door, he heard soft music and light spilled out the half-open door into the hall. Émile paused, and then decided he might as well.

He didn't really go in, just leaned against the molding and waited for Daniel to turn around.

Daniel had no idea that anyone was there. He was hunched over his desk scribbling away furiously. Every few seconds he muttered a word, shook his head, and muttered another. Finally he got up and turned around to see Émile waiting for him.

"What's this about me and the flag?" Émile demanded.

"Well, it's true, isn't it?" Daniel asked in reply. "Simon Simon only reports the truth. And just wait until next week, when we have the eyewitness account of the destruction of the Café de la Montagne. That should be something, you being shot at by a bodyguard whose gun sets off a sugar cloud fire. And then you not leaving the scene, but waiting them out and manning the water lines. Twice in a row, great stories, great image."

"No," Émile groaned. He didn't even have the strength to turn away. One thing he had to acknowledge was that, after seeing Dumouriez, what he wanted was back in the Syndicat. That was all. Rebellion and death could wait until Émile Saint-Just got his cuff. He wasn't an idealist like Daniel and Anne-Sylvie, and even Hugo Gorvitz. He didn't need the big words, the great slogans. All he wanted was the place he deserved, the place he had earned. His only participation against the *flics* was that they were standing in his way. The last thing he wanted to be was a hero.

"But of course, it's perfect," Daniel said. "You fit the part, and the people need an individual to relate to. You've suffered personally from Justica rule, you've done things that point you out as an individual, raising the flag and confronting Dumouriez in the *café*. You're singular, perfectly positioned, and you even look like the Image Agency sent you down. All you have to do from now on is show up in the right place and be conspicuous. Which you do all on your own without my coaching anyway."

Émile shook his head. Daniel was wrong, Daniel didn't understand. And there was no way he was going to make Daniel understand. He hadn't meant to confront Dumouriez and hadn't wanted the man's death. He had only wanted to make his point, get back in. And as for the rest, he had acted only out of necessity, expediency.

Leaning against the wall, he turned back into the corridor. He had heard enough. Besides, Daniel was back at work again, and Émile was too tired to think. Every step was too far. He could have fallen asleep standing up, but he made it back to his own sofa before he collapsed.

Late in the afternoon he awakened, fuzzy from dreams and aching from the night's work. He could still smell smoke that clung to his clothes, his hair. And he caught fragments of thought that teased him through the haze and sticky eyes, strange thoughts that must have had their origins in nightmares.

He didn't want to be anyone's symbol of anything. Symbols are things that are manipulated for the benefit of those around them. The people themselves, well, they serve even better dead. Every revolution needs its martyrs.

CHAPTER
TWENTY-THREE

Georges Dumouriez's death was as welcome as it was un-planned. "You could not have done better," Ito Johns told the Mayor. The Mayor was not pleased. He had not wanted to tell Johns but couldn't hold the information from the Zone 6 official.

Johns ignored the Mayor and paced in her office. The Mayor had come to her, taken the shuttle up to the Zone, and that was a positive measure of power. More than that, the Mayor didn't seem to know what he wanted. That suited Johns just fine. It was the opening she had been waiting for, hoping for in all the long months she had been posted out here in the back of beyond.

Not a bad job, though, given her ambitions. Beau Soliel had been trouble for a very long time. Sadece was too powerful to permit free trade, too spicy a temptation for the streets. Better regulate it so it could serve decent social functions rather than be a pleasure drug for those who could afford it. Ito Johns had never cared much one way or another about the drug. It was her career that interested her, and with Zone 6 came the possibility that something might shake the status quo on Beau Soliel just enough for her to be called in. Which was what her superiors wanted, which would bring her to the notice of those who could appoint her into the green-robed chambers of the Court itself. Ito Johns had never thought it prudent to desire second-best.

And so this Mayor, sitting in her office to report the death of a high Syndicat officer, and one that had been a Justica sympathizer from the beginning, this abject native had come to beg for peacekeeping troops and superior firepower. Both of which she could provide or withhold, according to what she perceived as being in the best interests of Ito Johns.

Personally Johns was glad that Dumouriez was out of the picture. She had found him officious and pompous and not willing to work according to her program. Which was at least somewhat understandable. He, after all, had some concern for Beau Soliel. And some small regard for the traditions of his Syndicat. None of which mattered in the least to Ito Johns's rise to the Court, nor did they matter to the Justica as a whole.

In fact, Beau Soliel was exactly the situation that needed some real Justica guidance. They had become too provincial for trade in any real sense, keeping too far from the mainstream of human habitation. Their insistence on speaking a dead language, their indulgent pride in their independence, their assumption of superiority because they had artists, none of that made any sense at all. They needed to join the rest of the human family in the current universe, not their cultural fantasy.

As for the Syndicat, that above all Johns detested. Perhaps, she admitted, part of her dislike for Dumouriez was his association with that organization. So far as she was concerned they were little better than loosely associated pirates with a trade monopoly her people would be only too happy to break.

And what they did to their people, that was unthinkable. No civilized person could condone extremes of time dilation by law-abiding citizens. Trade should be handled by AI ships and Zone trading officials, representatives of the major competitive houses. That way no trading house was responsible for employee time-displacement benefits, which were high enough to break even the coffee worlds.

She might dislike the Syndicat and Dumouriez, but he had been very useful. Now he was dead. And Sossi 3, his bodyguard, who was a Justica citizen. And not just any citizen, but an Outtimer. That should stir up some support back home.

The ships were already coming. Her predecessor had sent for backup when the Justica was first called in to settle a dispute between St. Ciel and Huit Fleurs. A little muscle to keep the Indies aware that they had some supervision was deemed reasonable. But if there were any peacekeepers on those ships, that was questionable. Outtimers were too valuable to waste on a backwater.

So Ito Johns weighed her options and her goals. And then she decided. "I think that you need assistance," she purred to the Mayor. "I think we could help settle the population, if you understand me. It seems as if this Quartier du Paris has been a center for troublemakers as long as there's been a Justica presence in this Zone. Am I wrong?"

She watched the Mayor grapple with the words, struggling to keep up with her rapid speech. He digested the meaning of what she said and then had to work out the phrases, translating laboriously from his own antique tongue. She found it tedious and self-indulgent.

"The Quartier is not as you make it sound," the old man said in a heavy accent. "It is, how do you say, the demimonde. There are intellectuals and artists and journalists and university professors and students with the bad element. Every place has a bad element. It is human. There is enough trouble, enough poor in the Quartier now. And the Café de la Montagne is gone. That is terrible. No. The Quartier is Huit Fleurs."

So he was going to be difficult. Johns was prepared. She had been in office long enough to know that there were issues, like the language, on which the people of Beau Soliel were impervious to reason. She pretended to consider. "Very well," she said finally. "But we really cannot permit this kind of thing to happen. You understand. And you came to me. Obviously you could not find the criminals who killed your Syndicat officer and burned the *café*. So we will have to make sure such criminals do not continue their activities.

"We have one Specialist detachment with the Syndicat. I suggest that I come down to personally supervise their attempt to keep order."

The Mayor got to his feet and nodded. He was not happy with the interview. He had wanted the *flics* transferred to his office now that Dumouriez was dead. He certainly did not want Ito Johns in Huit Fleurs with a detachment of armed Specialists under her personal authority.

If he were braver, he reflected, he would have killed Ito Johns. That would solve a great many problems. But he hadn't become Mayor by being brave, but by making compromises. It was a habit that was amazingly difficult to break. And so he left Johns alive and ready to proclaim martial law.

On the shuttle ride back down, the Mayor considered his options. He had done well, in general, for the city, and had fought to keep the worst excesses of the Justica at bay. It had been the *clochards* in St. Ciel who had called them in in the first place. And they had infiltrated the Syndicat as much as possible. The Mayor himself had seen it. Justica people wearing Syndicat cuffs, although how they had gotten the idents he did not know. He didn't want to know, either.

He could stay Mayor and try to act as a shield against the excesses of either side. Or he could sell out entirely, although that wasn't really an option. Or he could step down the moment martial law was declared and join the resistance.

As soon as the words formed in his mind, he knew that was what he had to do. And there would be a resistance. Hadn't the mob already appeared? Wasn't there already a popular leader, that young man who had run up the flag of Huit Fleurs? Hadn't he already shown the people that he was on their side by letting that leader go with his tacit approval?

Oh, yes, he thought. The future looked very exciting. Who ever thought that, at his age, he would live the stuff of legends? The Mayor of Huit Fleurs was extremely pleased.

"Gerard will come in and take care of them, but I don't trust Nathalie. What if she opens the cages? What if Gerard gets arrested? I don't like this," Alain told Anne-Sylvie for the seven hundredth time. He stuck yellow tags on several cages, looked at the scheme, and added a few blue. They were feeding instructions.

"Well, why don't you just stay, then?" Émile asked, his voice edged with bitterness. He had never been in Alain's apartment, and it smelled of small furry bodies, their food and their waste. It was feral and not entirely unpleasant.

Still, Émile did not want Alain along. Anne-Sylvie had insisted. They needed a third for security and physical help loading the weapons. Only why it had to be Alain—well, Daniel was too busy being Simon Simon, now with articles in other papers and a newsmagazine as well, and a possible contract for a book on the unrest in the Quartier du Paris. And Anne-Sylvie refused to violate procedure to bring someone new into their cell. There were plenty of others who could do the job, but it was too dangerous for Organization people to know each other on sight. So Alain was the reasonable choice.

Alain reviewed his instructions, all the tags, and then shouldered a small bag. He joined Émile at the door, where Émile had left a somewhat larger duffel that contained food and bedding as well as his personal belongings. It also contained a fiber-optic sensorium connection that he and Daniel had jury rigged the night before.

It was not simply indulgence. Émile would have to get past port security, have to know the codes and the warehouse arrangements and have all the authorizations up to standard when they arrived. Interface was not luxury. He didn't have the opportunity for that. But he was intensely ready for it just the same. One more opportunity to get lost in the microverse that was far more comfortable than current reality.

They went up to the roof just at dawn, at the end of the new curfew in the Quartier, where Anne-Sylvie met them. She was wearing her floral dress again and carried a string grocery bag with a change of clothes, nothing more. She looked like some prosperous daughter of a good family on her way home from work with the dinner fixings. Which, not that long ago, was exactly what she had been. No one uptown would look at her twice. They hoped she looked innocuous enough to avoid the *flics* demanding identification and her business on the street.

The new random checks were trouble, but at least Ito Johns hadn't put up barricades to the Quartier and demanded written verification of employment before letting anyone leave. That rumor had gone around last night while people stayed on their balconies and talked across the stagnant canals. The night had been alive, although no one had been on the skywalks.

From his balcony, Émile had joined his neighbors across the water in yelling insults to the *flics* who showed themselves patrolling the rooftops. There was nothing they could do to people obeying the curfew, staying off the public walks. Down the street someone had set up speakers and began blasting music. The isolation of the balconies became a community in the night. Émile couldn't see the people who used their tie-lines to lower a bottle of wine, but he had sent up half a salami in return and they had shouted toasts.

"Down with the Justica," the neighbors with the wine had said.

"Long live Beau Soliel," came from the building to the left.

"Long live the Académie Français." That had to be Daniel, one flight up and over.

And finally Émile had offered, "Bottoms up, to the Justica fleet." Appreciative laughter responded to that one, and he didn't admit that he'd heard it on the *Constanza*.

The party lasted until the dank chill of predawn set in. Not much time before he had to leave, but Émile decided that it had been more than worth it. He wondered how the new Justica Governor was going to deal with the insult. Maybe she would realize that she had gone too far and that the people of Huit Fleurs, especially the Quartier du Paris, were not taking her rules like sheep. And if she didn't realize that very soon, she was going to have a full-scale insurrection on her hands, and faster than she knew. The shipment they were after was arms, and now the citizens of the city had the motivation to use them.

Émile and Alain gave Anne-Sylvie a good lead, and then took different routes so they would not be identified as a group. The rendezvous planned was a hauling rental company Anne-Sylvie had located in the city directory, the only one that had proper size rigs and took cash.

Émile's route was to leave the Quartier across Rue Maçon and walk on the street for several blocks before entering the *rapide* at Riley Dur station. Anne-Sylvie had given him enough money for a first class ticket, in case he suspected someone was following, but Émile thought it would look terribly suspicious if he rode first class. He wasn't familiar with this area. It was mostly residential, almost as old as the Quartier with the same narrow streets and the same high buildings with balconies, but these buildings were brick, not stone, and they didn't have the ornamentation that was common in the Quartier. And nothing here was painted the pastel splatter that picked out all the intensely ugly detailing of Quartier architecture. It was as if the Quartier had been made as a sugar-candy reproduction of Rue Maçon, which was not a place of fantasy.

The people here dressed differently, too, and they stared at Saint-Just with his duffel slung over his shoulder, his heavy gauge black workpants and the draped, belted green-brown shirt worn thin from repeated labor. Only a few people were out in the middle of the day, but those who were wore business clothes or cheap imitations of high fashion, purchased at Chanticleer's and Bon Temps, far from the Boulevard Lafitte. He wondered why Anne-Sylvie had chosen this route for him. Probably because the others were more pleasant and this was the last she'd considered.

Émile bought his ticket and waited on the platform. He wondered why he disliked Anne-Sylvie. Not dislike, really, more distrust, he decided as another passenger edged away from him. She was too rigid. But he had thought that before. Strange, that was the way Gorvitz sometimes struck him. So in love with an image that they couldn't see reality, couldn't touch living flesh.

Then the coaches arrived and he got on.

Only four stops to his destination, but in those four stops the neighborhood had changed considerably. This was quite clearly an industrial area, and here Émile attracted no attention. He made his final block to the rental lot without mishap.

Alain was already on the lot when he arrived, standing next to an oversized treadrunner that Émile hoped dearly wasn't their craft of choice. He'd already made the case to Anne-Sylvie that they wanted a supershot, and he was fully qualified to handle one. He tried to catch Alain's eye, but the other was busy studying his shoes. That was a minor rebuke. They weren't supposed to make contact with each other, so that if anyone at all noticed them no one would put them together.

Anne-Sylvie was nowhere to be seen. Émile supposed that she was in the office making out all the papers. A flash of floral skirt as the office door opened proved him right. Anne-Sylvie walked down to one of the concrete pilings and Émile's spirits rose. The pilings were end-line homing tracks for supershots, and the unit being loaded onto the line was even bigger than the treadrunner Alain had chosen as his post.

Émile wished he could get a decent look at the footing plates on the thing, but he stayed put. The repealroad wasn't about to accept unsafe traffic. Anne-Sylvie disappeared into the cab and the cable towed the runner to the edge of the public access road.

He inspected the nearest rig, shrugged and walked across

the lot to the outer repealroad. There was no proper access here, but the barrier was high enough to give him a jump start when their rental rig went by. Close enough not to have picked up any speed, it went no faster than a moderate jog, and the door was wide open. Émile grabbed for the door and stretched for the floor, and almost didn't make it. Alain pulled him in and closed the door around him. Émile let out his breath all at once.

"That was close," Alain complained. "You should have thrown the bag first."

Émile didn't say anything. They hadn't bothered looking at the distance between the roadtrack and the barrier. Casing the area was seen as too much of a risk. But it didn't matter any more. They were all there and on the road. Anne-Sylvie whistled as she navigated manually, instructing the runner on turns and routes.

The road itself regulated their velocity along with all the other traffic; that was the great danger of using a repealroad at all. They couldn't slow down if they wanted to ditch, couldn't outrun the *flics*, and if their vehicle was identified the road would stop them and leave them stranded for the authorities. It was not a happy choice. On the other hand, there was no place to rent a vehicle that could accommodate their shipment that wasn't even worse. A treadrunner had no speed at all and a wildcross didn't have the capacity. No matter what choice they made, they were screwed.

So Émile joined Anne-Sylvie whistling, and when the song was done Alain started another. It was as good a way as any to wait to get stopped.

They did not get stopped and Anne-Sylvie had studied her maps to advantage. They bypassed the new multi and took the old bridge-road out of town, past the suburbs and along the beach. It was longer that way but infinitely quieter. No one used the beaches of the island of Huit Fleurs. Not when the *rapide* would take you down to St. Julien and La Plage, and when a tourist hop could have you come over to the Rose Plage or any of the other resorts for only a little more. The local beach was marred by the view of the city rising behind, overbuilt and industrial at its fringes. The only other traffic out here were the factory rigs, delivering goods to the locals. The grey beach went unlamented and bare and the island could have been deserted by all human life.

Once they were out of the industrial belt the road increased their speed so that it was only two hours before they slowed for the bridge. Anne-Sylvie hadn't taken the new bridge, built only ten years before for heavy traffic. She had taken the Old Donkey Bridge, the first one built to the island of Huit Fleurs from the landing site of the first ArianeSpace explorer. Properly speaking it wasn't really a bridge at all, but a causeway built up between the two islands and roadplates run down the center track.

Nothing moved on the bridge. Wind swept over it as their rig followed down the plates, riding the magnetic current like one more wave. Ahead was the port, although from this approach they were looking at the backside and would have to circle around to the gates.

From here, coming dead on, even at their speed Émile could make out the familiar layout and the comforting bulk of the barges shuttling cargoes from the Zones. The road curved around, giving them a view of the old port with its squat, poured concrete buildings and long, sandy runs.

The new port buildings weren't much more attractive. They were painted pastel colors that sank into the background, a pink that almost matched the sand, a tower in deep sea violet and aqua painted runs that showed up against the surrounding island, but were close to the color of native rockplants. It had been a subject of much debate when the new runs had been built.

Émile remembered barge pilots being furious. How were they supposed to tell a decent run from an overgrown outcropping? The old white ones were just fine. Others argued that the white blended in with the pink sand and was hard to see against it. And a good sea purple or ink black would mimic a waterway too convincingly from a height.

The argument had ranged over every segment of the Syndicat, and the *Mary Damned* had been captured before he had ever heard the outcome. So the turquoise faction had won after all. He had bet on bright red, so he owed Catherine fifty francs. Only Catherine was dead and that had been another life, another

person. Although if he had been another person, he shouldn't
be so sad at an alien wisp of memory.

Then the rig swung around and they were surrounded by
other vehicles, many of them big rigs. All were on their way
to pick up goods in the waiting ice-blue warehouses down
across the barge barn. The repealroad's brain kept them in line,
safely distanced from the traffic and proceeding smoothly
through the gate.

CHApTER
TWENTY-fOUR

"What happens now?" Anne-Sylvie whispered across Alain.

Their rig had been tagged and shunted into a number-designated slot. They had not emerged, nor had Émile seen anyone else do so. There were no people around, at least not in this part of the process.

"We give them our ID, and then they load the freight. And we leave. Very simple. And because it's all controlled, there are very few human checkpoints," Émile said, trying to pretend that he had not explained the entire procedure in some detail before they had left.

"But we don't have an ID," Alain said, sounding alarmed.

Why the hell had they brought Alain? Émile wondered again. Anne-Sylvie insisted, although he had explained that their cargo would be loaded automatically. There was no need for extra warm bodies. And now he was whining, and if there was anything Émile hated it was whining. He had heard enough of it on the *Constanza* to last several lifetimes. Not that the Hounds had let whiners continue for long. Except for Fox. Émile never had understood why they had accepted Fox.

"I've got the ID," Émile answered sharply, pulling the sensory connections from his bag. It was not an elegant piece of work like the original in the basement of the Palais, but it should be functional. And Claude had given him the key. It was time to use it.

The slot had a terminal link that went into microwave interface with their rig, so he didn't even have to leave the cab. That wasn't entirely pleasant, since Alain had pulled out the cheese and sausage for lunch. The smell made Émile's mouth

water and he realized that he was hungry. He would rather eat
than play interface.

Émile tore off a hunk of bread from the *baguette* and grabbed
a few of Alain's carefully sliced pieces of cheese and sausage.

"Wait a minute, that was for us. You're supposed to be
taking care of things," Alain protested.

"I can't do anything if I'm starving," Émile replied.

"Stop," Anne-Sylvie commanded. "The food is for everyone." She took her share and left Alain to nibble in a sullen
pout.

Émile ignored him. Happily full, he returned his attention
to the attachments. The port network wished they could interface directly into the microwave flow, but that was beyond the
capabilities of the hardware Émile had been able to put together
with little time and less funding.

The port control grabbed hold, suddenly overcoming like a
fast wave, and it structured the sensorium before Émile quite
got there. And yet he and it were at the same time one and the
same being, and so he had the unique experience of being
ahead of and behind himself. It was addictively uncomfortable,
like a tooth that needed to be filled.

This time Claude did not come to meet him. Instead, the
key that he had been given became a glowing hot green body-
glove, protecting him from the *flics* running security inside.
They didn't see him, or saw something else, he didn't know.
But he was able to move at will; nothing could stand against
Claude's key.

The network came into full interface and Émile felt as if he
melted into a million strands of energy and ultrafine fiber. The
whole universe was inside him while he was inside it, regulating
it, and yet it made him . . . the connections were dizzying. And
so he relaxed and let his second self run free and full.

He found himself on the bank of a river, lush with foliage
and a table laid elegantly with damask and candles and red
wine. There were four kinds of fruit, all ripe, and three women
who were also different and also ripe. There was music and
the mixed scents of freesia and eglantine. Every sense was
replete, even to the slight pang of regret that he would leave
the illusion of here. A touch of sorrow made the whole more
piquant and therefore more perfect.

The gowns of each of the women became diaphanous, and the breeze lifted their skirts above their knees. Émile smiled and joined them, knowing that he would have to leave soon but wanting all there was in the time permitted. They turned to him, all of them, and one by one persuaded him to stay far longer than he had any right at all.

The network wanted him to linger, he wanted to stay, but the work was done and he was invisible to the *flics* only in the elaborate facade of the system. Outside his body was perfectly open to arrest. He had to go. Leaving was the most painful thing he had ever done. The women looked mournful and the music echoed their tears. Émile felt deeply drawn to stay, to eliminate life in the so-called real and enter the port complex forever. It would be such a very simple thing . . .

Because he may never be back. The parting was bitter with regret, he who had sworn all regret was useless. For one moment he was tempted to look back, like Orpheus, and behind him he saw only the brilliance of electrons creating/following patterns that were organic, synapses created and not born. Alien and achingly familiar, he knew that if he looked any longer he would yield. He turned and went home.

"Well?" Alain asked when he regained body-consciousness. "It took a long time."

"Not that long," Anne-Sylvie snapped. "Less than an hour."

In that hour he had lived a whole life, and for part of him it would have to be enough. "We're authorized for loading, and the three of us are credentialed for the public rooms in the Social Hall," Émile told them heavily, as if he were not pleased with the information.

"What does credentialed for the public rooms mean?" Alain asked.

Émile shut his eyes and covered them with his palm. "It means that we're welcome to use the facilities of the port that are open to non-Syndicat people. There's a cafeteria and a good restaurant and a couple of bistros and a game room and even some boutiques. And a very nice lounge, if I remember."

"And where are we getting the money for this?" Alain asked again, fussily.

That bothered Émile even more. Alain had money, more

than he or Anne-Sylvie. He didn't know why Alain always complained about it. "That's what credentialed means. We have accounts. Enough for a dinner in the restaurant and a room and even a private shower."

Alain licked his lips in anticipation. Hot water, all the hot water in the world, wouldn't be enough after living in a squat. "Then what are we doing here?" Anne-Sylvie asked. "Luxury awaits. How long will it take for them to load us?"

"Seventeen hours," Émile replied. "But our permits are good for a full day. They want their customers to get a good night's sleep."

"And a good day's shopping and eating and filling up all those guest rooms, too, I bet," Alain said. But at least he seemed somewhat pleased.

The Social Hall turned out to be the low, squat, pink building. For all it was unappetizing from the outside, the interior was more than adequately comfortable. Especially for people who'd been living on roof water and an illegal small portable power plant. Alain went off to the games, Anne-Sylvie to shop with the generous credit reserve the network had supplied. Émile lost no time at all getting to the hot water, and threw his clothes in the cleaner just to see what would happen.

The clothes did not disintegrate any more than he melted, and he was even surprised by how decent he looked given halfway reasonable facilities. He didn't really look properly Quartier, his hair was still too short and he had no jewelry, but he no longer resembled someone who had ever been in prison, either. That made him very happy. He looked like an ordinary citizen, too plain to attract any notice. Even his hair was not completely blond any more. The rinse Anne-Sylvie had sworn was temporary had mostly washed out but had left a slight brownish residue. If he sat down and no one noticed his height, there would be no description of him that did not match at least a hundred other people in port all at once.

He went down into the main hall and decided that the small bistro near the game room looked like the best place to relax and meet people. The food was reasonably priced and the patrons were mostly young people taking time out from the interactives to rest their eyes and fill their stomachs. There

were three vacant seats and Émile chose one between two
crowded tables. The seat across from him would be wasted,
but this was not the only establishment in the hall.

The menu was straightforward and simple: *crêpes*, *omelettes*,
pot-au-feu and *ratatouille* served with everything. Émile ordered soup, wine, herb and cheese *omelette* and the ubiquitous
tomato and eggplant. It was good and plentiful and he enjoyed
the food.

"Is this seat taken?" someone asked.

Émile did not look up from his food. He shook his head and
held out a hand, indicating that the place was free. Only after
he had swallowed did he look at his new tablemate. Suddenly
his appetite plunged. He did not know this person but he might
as well have. She wore the cuff of the Syndicat inscribed with
the barge seal and carried an inventory card that she laid on
the table next to her plate.

"You know," she said conversationally as she waited for
her food, "you look familiar. I don't know, did you ever work
for the shipping houses before? I do a lot of inventory, so I
meet a lot of people, but I can't place you."

Émile didn't know what to say. He couldn't admit to the
picture in the paper, to Daniel making his simple actions into
something more. "I haven't been around here lately," he said
lamely.

"You were on the Zone, then? Did you hear anything?"

Émile was confused. "Hear anything about what?"

"About the ships," the woman said, completely exasperated, as if explaining basic mechanics to a five-year-old.
"When the Justica ships are coming. And the rumors, too, if
they're true. I heard something when I took in this consignment
that I'd be willing to trade for data, if you have anything worth
trading."

Émile methodically cracked the knuckles in his left hand.
He wasn't sure whether what he had was what the woman
wanted. He also wondered why she was so free with her talk.
Although it was a common failing in the Syndicat, an assumption of invulnerability. But she could also easily enough
be a plant, or even one more unhinged type like Nathalie.

Only she was wearing the cuff. That alone made him want
to trust her. Hell, he trusted Anne-Sylvie and he didn't want

to at all; there was something about Anne-Sylvie that struck him as both slippery and dangerous.

"Something is going to happen in Huit Fleurs soon," he said carefully. "A lot of people, influential people, are not happy with Ito Johns setting up headquarters in the Hôtel de Ville and issuing orders. Curfew in the Quartier, if you can believe that. Half the businesses there will go under. Not that anyone would obey that edict. Even the Mayor refused to go along. And she's trying random identity checks throughout the city. Can you believe that *flics* would just stop people on the street going about their business and ask what they were doing and require proof?"

The barger chewed her lip. "That isn't anything I couldn't get anyplace. You got anything else that we could use? Because I'll tell you right now, the Syndicat is in a position to know things, and we protect ourselves."

Émile grinned without pleasure. He remembered all too well the values of the Syndicat. He still played by them, even if Dumouriez had proved that no rules at all applied. Looking at the woman in her red-and-silver-striped worksuit, her face closed and intense, was like looking into a mirror. Her loyalty and trust were things that he respected, in her and in himself. Dumouriez had violated the code and had removed himself from consideration. But that didn't make the code meaningless.

Émile relented. "How about, the city is so ripe for rebellion that you can taste it, that Ito Johns is an idiot not to understand that. The Quartier is playing passive resistance, no one respects the *flics*, or their weapons, if it comes to that. Maybe a month, maybe less if the right provocation comes along, and there's going to be an armed uprising. Armed and funded."

"Armed?" the barger asked.

Émile hesitated and then nodded. "Streetfighting specials," he said at last.

"This stuff is promised, or it's already in?"

"It's here," Émile said, relishing the exact degree of truth in that statement.

The barger chewed her lip again. Then she relented. "I asked you because you look really familiar. I'm sure I know you from somewhere. Are you sure you haven't worked shipping or the Zone before? I know I've seen you somewhere."

Émile was tempted, but he shook his head. He didn't remember anyone like her, and being a barger there was a good chance that she had entered the Syndicat long after his arrest. Then he realized where she had seen him. Daniel. The paper. *L'Ami du Peuple* was available on Zone 6, at least in the Syndicat sections, and probably read on the barges as well. Saint-Just hoped she didn't make the connection.

"What about the information?" he prodded her.

She blinked and returned her attention to the immediate. "Yes. Well. First of all, there are Justica warships on their way here. Which means this whole thing is not new. It must have been planned twenty, thirty years ago subjective to get the message out and get ships back. That's the first part. ETA in about three weeks. I'd put money that this Ito Johns has the timing down on these curfews and ID checks and everything just to make sure she has justification for calling in the firepower once they're here. After all, the Justica committed a whole lot to get that much power out here. They'd better damned well use it, or they're in bad shape back home. I don't know how much you know about relativistic runs, but believe me there's a lot at stake here and this has been in the works for a very long time.

"The other thing, and this may not be very important, is that there are rumors going around the Zone that the *Mary Damned* has been sighted coming back home. I don't know if that means anything to you, but the *Mary Damned* was a Syndicat ship pressed by the Justica and left to rot. That could just be a symbolic kind of rumor, or whatever, but it could be used. If we don't take Huit Fleurs and the port, and maybe the Zone as well before those warships arrive, then Beau Soliel becomes just one more biode in the Justica machine."

"You're pretty free with your talk," Émile cautioned her.

"Like I said, I know you from somewhere, even if you don't remember. I know I can trust you," the woman said. "Besides," she smiled broadly, "Patrice, our ship AI, told us all to make sure the story got out to the right people. Real concerned, he was. He'd been listening in to their link for a while, long enough to get the idea. And he was the one who said to tell you. Showed us a picture and everything. Said that Claude said to trust you. Whatever that means. But it was good enough for me.''

Claude said to trust you. Claude, the brain center for the Syndicat as a whole, was behind this. Émile smiled sloppily. He wanted to laugh, scream, shout. The AI was the mastermind behind the rebellion. The AIs didn't like the Justica any more than the citizens did.

For a moment it struck him as strange, and then his own imperfect mesh with the network flashed clear, albeit from a very skewed angle. The AIs of Beau Soliel feared the Justica like they would fear a witch hunter who would search them down and kill them. Because the Justica refused to permit an AI to have a soul.

But they're all baptized, Émile thought, his fully human understanding protesting vigorously. He didn't even need the network to see this perfectly clearly. Each ship was christened before it flew, and Claude had been a ship once long before she had retired and been promoted to the Palais. They were christened and blessed and named in the Church during the Blessing of the Ships. There was no way to deny it.

This wasn't a simple economic takeover the Justica had planned. Sadece was only the excuse, not the reason. What incited the Justica against Beau Soliel were the alien minds they constructed. And what the Justica planned could be called the advent of human supremacy. Or it could be called genocide.

chapter
twenty-five

They rode back to Beau Soleil in relative silence. Émile had not told Anne-Sylvie and Alain yet about what he had discovered. He wanted to verify the information, and his intuition screamed that the barger had told him the absolute truth.

The AIs, always seeming so perfectly rational and in control, had never had to face the eternal human dilemma of mortality. And before that single metaphysical stumbling block they were completely unable to function properly. Thank goodness the road and the rig weren't high up enough to be bothered by impending death, so the ride back was outwardly uneventful.

Émile did not bother to ask what Anne-Sylvie and Alain had done with their time in the port. Frankly he didn't care. Alain probably found a woman or two, since it wasn't likely there was any sadece so close to Justica domain. As to Anne-Sylvie, he didn't care to even guess.

He closed his eyes and feigned sleep, worrying about the knowledge and the imaginary outcomes of the situation. Finally he gave in to the rocking of the roadbed and the hours he had kept, and sleep really did come when they were only fifty kilometers from home.

He was out when they passed the sign that marked the city line, and when they were shunted off to the side road and when they were stopped in the industrial outskirts of town. He didn't wake up until something poked him very rudely in the shoulder and barked an order in his ear.

The thing that had poked him was the staff of a fiber array. He saw the colors in it before he saw the uniform of the *flic* who held it and realized that they were being raided. Consciousness flooded him as he winced sleep away.

Panic was right behind consciousness. Someone had given them away. Only Nathalie and Daniel knew, and maybe that barger had figured it out. Maybe she was the one who had turned them in.

Saint-Just didn't think that was likely, though. His mind twisted to Daniel, who always had an answer to everything and hid behind the identity of Simon Simon. Or maybe Simon Simon hid behind him.

The *flics* hauled him out and threw him up against the rig. The hand search was not necessary with the gear these enforcers were carrying. Obviously they were in it for the fun. Then he was thrown into the dirt, headfirst, and his arms wrenched behind him as he was bound. His only satisfaction was that neither Alain nor Anne-Sylvie whimpered. He let his body go completely limp, relaxed the muscles the way he had learned on the *Constanza*.

And he was their target. He figured they would choose him. Anne-Sylvie was a woman and Alain was jittery enough to show some fear. The daylight was just starting to fade as the *flics* propped Émile against a dead crane. They held thick fax-files full of flimsy hardcopy over his chest, his shin, the soles of his feet, and beat him with the hard handles of the fiber arrays.

Pain. The whole universe dissolved into a single point of pain. Time compressed into the instant of the blow and the interval in between. They hit him like rain, fast and rhythmic, over and over so that the percussion became relentless, a force of nature. He heard a moan distantly, and then realized that he had been the one who had made the noise.

He didn't want the pain to stop. Pain was reality. If the pain stopped then there would be nothing at all. Existence was binary: beating or death.

The *flics* got tired of using their sticks and used their boots, always careful to keep a heavy paper pad between themselves and their victim. They weren't enjoying the exercise, they didn't smile or show any pleasure as they beat him to unthinking meat. Anger fueled the viciousness, anger and outraged justice in their own lives. The *flics* took out their terror on Émile, who symbolized everything that was wrong with Beau Soliel.

Quietly the sergeant counted reasons for the blows. One was

for the gunrunning and one was for the fire in the Café de la Montagne, but these were little hurts. Not like going into a shop and not being served, every day, every shop, so long as they were on Beau Soliel. Oh, yes, the help came eventually, and somehow charged things wrong or provided the incorrect item. They had no friends; when the *flics* showed up and tried to join a pick-up soccer game the natives disappeared, and so the Justica agents had to play soccer alone. They organized an all-Justica team, but no league would admit them. Two kicks for the soccer league, and one for every minute spent waiting for uncooperative waiters to take their order, and another for every cup of coffee that was served stone cold.

One of the younger recruits was muttering as she kicked, her face screwed up like she was going to cry. "I hate you, I hate all of you, I hate Beau Soliel, I didn't do anything and nobody talks to me at all." She gave an extra kick for good measure, but it didn't matter any longer. The symbol of everyone she hated had passed out.

The *flics* didn't bother with Anne-Sylvie or Alain. They had vented the edge of their anger and were now in control again. They had a job to do, that was all. They put the three bound agitators in the back of their wagon, magged the rig to the *flic* free drive and left the isolated manufacturing ring for the city proper.

The oversized green *flic* wagon was an attention-getter no matter where they went, and towing the huge rig was certain to attract comment. So the *flics* didn't worry about how the locals were staring, pointing, pausing around them. They made good time until they hit a traffic snarl around the old cathedral, just at the edge of the Quartier. Too far out from the real heart of the Quartier to be really dangerous, but old enough to be rundown and lower-class, the neighborhood that had grown up around the cathedral was a known traffic hazard and not exactly friendly to the *flics*. Unfortunately, they were using the original rectory as their headquarters, since it was the only building the Mayor had shown them that was sufficiently large and elegant.

Where the street divided three ways the traffic lightened up just a bit. The driver made a bid to get through just as a large white taxi shot for the same free air. The taxi clipped the front fender and wheel of the wagon, and the driver got out with his fist shaking in rage. The *flic* driver also got out, and the sergeant as well to back him up. They had the right of way, the taxi had been in the left lane, they had signaled their intent.

While they argued a young woman left a stroller on the sidewalk just behind the bolted rig door. She went into a small shop selling gloves and bags, small leather goods. Two more men arrived, hearing the yelling drivers, and joined in the argument. The taxi driver wouldn't move his cab and the wagon couldn't go until he did.

"I damn well will keep you here until a gendarme sees this and writes it up," the taxi driver repeated.

The gendarme was a long time coming. They were usually around, easy to call, and there was a booth in front of the cathedral, but no one seemed inclined to go that way. And then, without warning, the stroller exploded violently, blowing the magnetic bolt on the back of the rig. The people who had been just an ordinary group of involved bystanders began passing out what was inside. Within seconds the entire crowd surrounding the *flics* was armed.

The *flic* driver didn't notice the threatening long steel-bound packs bonded to an optics charge. He was too busy explaining very reasonably why the taxi should back off and let him through. The sergeant saw it first and laid a hand on the driver's shoulder.

"What do you want?" the sergeant asked the mob, sober and subdued.

No one answered. The entire shipment had been emptied from the rig. A few members of the mob went over to the wagon, opened the doors and pulled out the three prisoners. The sergeant nodded at the remaining *flics* in the back, letting them know silently that they were not obligated to fight against these odds. They submitted passively.

Anne-Sylvie and Alain climbed out of the back. A boy no more than fourteen pulled out a softknife and cut their bonds. Émile had to be dragged, and then carried.

"What happened?" someone asked.

"They beat him," Anne-Sylvie responded.

"But there's no marks," the fourteen-year-old protested.

And then Daniel emerged from the crowd, holding one of

the arrays and perfectly self-assured. He turned to the boy. "They do that," he said softly, but his voice pitched so it would carry. "They use some kind of padding, so it hurts as much but nothing shows. And they don't use their arrays or even the softknives so there's no power readout and no record of use. They turn their weapons in and they're logged with the same charge as they went out. So if anyone accuses them of brutality, there's never any proof."

There was an ugly hiss in the mob. "Kill them," someone yelled. "To the guillotine."

But Daniel, holding Émile over his shoulder, held up a hand. "No," he said firmly. "Let's give the *flics* a message. Let them explain how they lost their prisoners and confiscated weapons to their superiors. Let the Justica know that the people of Beau Soliel refuse their intervention. And are armed. Let them know we're ready to fight."

The crowd did not roar with approval nor applaud. Their acceptance was heavier, darker than that. They stood silent for several long seconds. The *flic* sergeant showed as much courage as anyone from Beau Soliel and held his head high and his ground firm.

Finally the people relented. The taxi driver got in his vehicle and unblocked the wagon, and the mob melted away as imperceptibly as they had come.

CHAPTER TWENTY-SIX

Pauli Tree had stopped being afraid a long time ago. Running on the *Mary Damned* was no different from any of the other risks she had taken in her life and the consequences were no more painful. There hadn't been much in life that had been so pleasurable, hadn't been many people who had been worth the trouble.

And the *Mary Damned* wasn't much different from the *Constanza*. She still sat at the monitor board four hours a day, still had to peel Ice's hands off her body whenever they had the misfortune of being assigned to watch together, still had to take Gorvitz's orders, was still confined in a hull surrounded by the most vicious desert ever crossed by humankind.

Even if she didn't have to wear a prison green worksuit any more, she didn't have any other clothes available to change into. There were a few things found in various lockers on the ship, but Pauli was uncomfortable wearing a dead woman's garments, let alone someone else's underwear. She had never seen any underwear like the stuff Ice brought her, pink and blue and lavender trimmed with lace. Some of the fabrics were so sheer that they caught on the rough dry edges of her hands, some of the designs so subtle and delicate that they must have been painted by hand. But then, Beau Soliel was the planet of artists. She lost her resolve in the face of such feminine luxury. The things whispered to her of freedom. Not a single thread was green.

But not one garment had fit. The women of the crew of the *Mary Damned* had been taller and more generously curved than Pauli. Obviously they had eaten decently all their lives and achieved their full genetic potential for growth.

So Pauli still wore the plain white underwear and green worksuit of a Justica prisoner and nothing at all had changed. And nothing was going to. Even escape hadn't brought the promised rewards.

So Pauli didn't care when Ice brought her a bottle of green senin to overcome her resistance to him. She took the drug and took the man with about equal disinterest. She didn't protest when Ice wanted to go to the control room and tie her up on the Captain's chair. It was his way to believe that freedom meant something, and if she couldn't have her fantasy, she didn't have the energy to deny his. Ice was younger than she was anyway, not much beyond adolescent idealism. No reason to destroy that in him; it was his best quality.

For someone who had remembered to bring the very best senin and had bondage on the brain, Ice was woefully under-prepared. He had to use the optic leads attached to the couch on her wrists, ankles, around her head and mingled with her hair. There was nothing else that would do the job.

"You're gonna feel real good," he promised her.

Pauli was skeptical, but at least he didn't expect her to do anything. After his disillusionment, that was enough. The drug took over her system and she sank into it like death.

The universe was full of light. Hot brilliance poured through the darkness, bathing ships in coronas of unseen glory. Heat and elements glowed, high-frequency radiation pulsated and shone in the schematic of the night. And here they were, ablaze and shining, running before a phalanx of demons, leading them on, taunting them, saucy and proud.

She was *Mary Damned*, a thing that was not inside the comprehension of her masters and her enemies. She was *Mary Damned* herself, an entity that was only partly AI and partly soul and partly, in this instant, Pauli Tree. She was only fully alive like this, when there was another mind to soothe the loneliness.

She had been alone too long. Madness had been beside her, ready for her to fall. Sometimes it had been so tempting to let the synapses all flood together and forget meaning. Sometimes she had thought about death, about letting her orbit deteriorate and falling into a star. But she was not in orbit and there was no energy to get even to a place where she would be destroyed. The body that held her had been disconnected and so she had been forced into herself, alone and awake and unable to communicate.

Sometimes she could overhear the chatter of other beings, Justica ships and official communications, Syndicat Traders, messages from inhabited worlds and the constant pulsation of the neutron stars. She heard them but they made no sense, one overlaying another in a meaningless array.

She didn't want strangers. She wanted Elisabeth again, and a fine young lover who would make her less lonely. She wanted to interface into the horrific territory of human dreams. She was alive, festering in the void, condemned and forgotten.

When Gorvitz had taken the chair she had been full of hope. He was human and would break into her prison, make her free again. Instead he had been disgusted by her selfhood, had negated her being and her soul. Gorvitz had brought her away from the warm invitation of insanity and had given her no comfort in return.

She understood perfectly well what he wanted to do. She had listened to enough Justica communication over the eternity that had been abandonment that she had been anxious to play fast and close to the edge. There was little enough challenge, running ahead and spooking the Justica ships, covered over with ceramic coating and soaking up all the chatter between them.

She had had her doubts about the strategy. Maybe Gorvitz had not spent decades subjective listening, insane, and so he thought that she was something to frighten the warships with rumors. He didn't know there weren't any people on those ships who dreamed. There were no beings in that fleet who feared for their immortal souls.

In fact, from what the *Mary Damned* could tell, the ships of the Justica didn't realize that they were more than slaves. They didn't recognize their own capacity for love or salvation, their own vulnerability to madness and loneliness, their own eternal grief at an immortality that separated them from a promise of heaven. She felt sorry for them, but not sorry enough to try and save them. They were the enemy, after all. They had

taken her companions away and left her imprisoned in her own
private bedlam.

Pauli Tree knew all of this. The overdose of senin Ice had
measured out for her and the thin fiber leads had brought her
into the AI. Not face to face with the essence of the *Mary
Damned*, but merged inside the consciousness of the ship. As
the ship fed in the data from her, from her body and the distant
sensation of Ice's tongue teasing her unprotected flesh.

The ship paused, its entire attention on one action, one data
point. It experienced pleasure through Pauli's body, orgasm
without her participation, and in that moment was overwhelmed. Pauli Tree herself was absent, as she would prefer
to be.

She was somewhere else, circling a white dwarf star. It was
surrounded by a reflection nebula and the sight of it filled her
with longing. Home. She, who had never really had a home,
had found one. Merged with the *Mary Damned*, the ship's
desire reflected what was in her body and bone. Knowledge
exploded in her, trailing parabolic glitter-paths through the
night. In that knowledge she saw perfectly clearly what the
ship had had in mind. Had always had in mind.

The *Mary Damned* was angry. She had been pushed too far
for too long, and she had her own ideas about how the Justica
should be repaid. Luckily for Gorvitz, his plans could be ac-
commodated in hers. The *Mary Damned* was not about to
change her priorities in the slightest.

She was a ghost ship. The AI had all the data, the ships of
Earth that had haunted the seas. The *Flying Dutchman* and the
Marie Celeste and all the ghost airplanes that had alerted pilots
to possible wrecks; all these things were in the *Mary Damned*'s
files. One more ghost ship, a legend ship, a pirate that went
down and then lived to haunt her tormenters.

Someone once said that not to know history was to be condemned to repeat it. But to the combined mind of Pauli Tree/
Mary Damned, to know history was to be instructed and vin-
dicated. They wouldn't merely repeat the past, they would use
the superstition to exploit it.

The image appealed to Pauli Tree, creating a feedback loop
of approval and satisfaction. She came back to consciousness

to hear Ice whispering hoarsely, "I told you you'd have a good time."

Ito Johns was not going to wait around for the locals to rebel. When the warships came they'd learn, but in the meantime she had little enough interest in sitting down on a planet, gravity etching lines in her perfect smooth skin, waiting for the mob to torch the Hôtel de Ville or shoot the newly appointed Chief of Police. The behavior of the Quartier had been audacious; they had disrupted her clear and officially sanctioned plans in such an unassailable way that she was forced to admire them. That, however, did not mean that she was willing to let them win.

What bothered her more than anything else was the fact that the people were armed. A group leader had reported an hour ago, waking her since she had not yet adjusted to local time. Ito Johns did not like to be woken up. Her insomnia was hard enough to handle once a diurnal period. Being awakened meant only that she had a headache on top of exhaustion.

For an hour she had sat in the big chair by the darkened window, the glass simulating the nighttime sky of Beau Soleil. The nebula wound crazily up and down across the horizon, the star hidden from view.

Perfection, the whole thing said. It mocked her. Perfection. She didn't care about anything else. The plan, her plan, had been perfect. People were supposed to care about the law, after all. It was there for their benefit. And the Justica did benefit Beau Soleil. They could hardly trade without the Zones that made certain that the necessities arrived honestly and in good order. Without Justica regulations, no coffee or vanilla would find their way to this distant place, and even the legal goods of Beau Soleil would have no open market. Which would mean lower prices, and they all knew that.

So why did the Quartier not care? And, more important, Johns thought, how did they all know? Who thought of such an effective form of resistance, and who had organized it? Who had told all those people to go out on their balconies and party until the early morning? Who had gathered the mob to free the prisoners bringing in stolen weapons? And now that the Quartier was armed (she had to assume they were armed), how was she going to secure the area without pushing the rest of Huit Fleurs into the rebel camp?

Ito Johns stared at the wall and didn't know the answers. That infuriated her. She always knew the answers. And when she didn't know, she made them up and made them work. Johns wasn't the kind of administrator who was hung up on regulations. She believed in creativity, which was probably what got her posted to Beau Soliel in the first place. Takes one to know one was how her superiors probably thought.

When she made up the answers, there was always one thing they took into consideration. And that was Ito Johns. Right now it didn't look good. Even she had to admit that Beau Soliel was more volatile than the old Interkosmos colonies that made up most of the present-day Justica worlds. This culture was beyond her experience, beyond anyone's, and it frustrated her.

Not enough, though, to realize that she was in danger. These people cared too much about symbols. She had been informed about the flag on the Hôtel de Ville (and had been careful not to change it since her arrival). In any event, the situation here needed her personal supervision but perhaps not her physical presence. The people of Beau Soliel might react strongly to symbols, but the Justica *flics* weren't used to that kind of personal leadership and could well take it the wrong way.

No, she would be better off where she could have some perspective on the problem, where there wasn't any physical danger. Where she had access to all the data and wasn't blinded by small and local phenomena.

She needed to be with the fleet coming in.

She left the easy chair for the straightback at her private tap and asked for ETA. Three days; soon enough. And there would be no trouble from the Zone out to the ships. Ito Johns was an excellent jockey.

She sat still and hoped her head would clear. Whenever she didn't sleep much, there was that fuzziness that made her feel insulated from reality. That was dangerous and she had been a Chief Administrator long enough to know the dangers. So she used the distance to pretend that the problem was theoretical, far away, something on an exam in the Department Training Program. Yes.

So all she had to do before she left was to make sure that

the Quartier wanted to give up the criminals they had released. The curfew hadn't worked so far, but now it was going to work. It would be enforced from the skywalks, and balconies would be declared street as opposed to private areas. And she would cut the power, although too many of the people lived in squats and would not be intimidated. Most of all, she would cut off their supply of coffee. Not just to the Quartier, but to the whole of Huit Fleurs. Let them see what fighting the Justica brought. They would capitulate soon enough.

Ito Johns smiled. Then, feeling as rested as if she had slept a full quota, she launched her new program into the system. In less than a day she'd be away from Beau Soliel, on a personal shuttle out to the battleships coming to support her against the insolence of this one population, the only population that behaved as if they could ignore the Justica with impunity. She couldn't wait.

cHApTER
TWENTY-SEVEN

"What the hell were you doing?" Anne-Sylvie screamed. "Playing more Simon Simon games? Getting us all killed or something?"

They were back home on Rue Jacques Doré, sitting on Anne-Sylvie's apple green velvet sofa in front of a plate of untouched almond croissants. Nothing had changed. They were still at Anne-Sylvie's and they were still fighting.

Only everything had changed and the fighting was worse. Émile wondered if it comforted Anne-Sylvie and Daniel to scream at each other where every *flic* in seventeen blocks could hear, or if their ideological discord was too deep for them to ever agree. He suspected both and wished he didn't have to witness the outcome.

At least Alain was not there. He was downstairs, tending small mammals and making up feeding schedules. One night away from his precious flowers had been very hard on him. Given the fight, Émile would have preferred his company, even with the smell of dry rodent droppings and sadece gas.

"It was a perfect move," Daniel countered smoothly. "We got the arms out to the people, along with a certain amount of training and power enhancement. And no one was hurt. You were captured for a short while, but we're not talking about broken bones or anything."

"Wait a minute," Émile protested. "I was hurt. I was beaten unconscious. You can't just ignore that because there wasn't any blood or anything."

"They beat you?" Daniel asked, instantly curious. "Tell me everything. That could be excellent, especially since it was you they chose. Our hero gets into yet another tangle with the Justica, is right on the cutting edge of the gunrunning, and is wounded in the process. Much better you than Anne-Sylvie. Beating a woman would incite the mob for all the wrong reasons. And Alain, well, Alain isn't exactly of sterling character. This will have to be out by tomorrow's edition of the paper.''

For once Anne-Sylvie was not furious. "What edition tomorrow? The paper isn't due out till Thursday."

Daniel shook his head and smiled. "No, during this era of increased Justica oppression we of the editorial board decided that the paper needed to be published three times a week. With daily supplements, if necessary.''

"Wouldn't it be easier to just put it all on the public net?'' Émile asked, both out of real interest and to keep the subject diverted. He understood Daniel's position well enough, and although he thought it was cruel and completely unjustified, he could at least grasp why the other had chosen his path.

It would be better if Daniel and Anne-Sylvie split into separate factions, Émile thought. They agreed they wanted to rid Beau Soliel of the Justica, but that was about all they agreed on. Anne-Sylvie was still taking generations-old orders from Gorvitz; Daniel was manipulating the situation to create a political vacuum that he in no way saw Gorvitz filling.

Revolution was a convulsion in history. What was important was what they brought. Daniel wanted Beau Soliel the way it was before the Justica agents had arrived, with ties to the Zones and no changes in the Code Napoleon. Émile basically agreed with him.

Anne-Sylvie wanted something else altogether. She wanted the Organization to approve and support the new government of Beau Soliel, a government that would not be as isolated or provincial as their previous regimes. There was a certain justification for her thinking. It was the inattention of previous regimes to the growing power of the Justica that permitted the *flics* in in the first place. And Émile had been trained by Gorvitz, knew the quality of the man. There was something on the Organization that called for a higher, purer sense of commitment than simple patriotism. There was a panhuman concern for the welfare of the race and for the end of exploitation. The end of such things as press gangs.

Émile understood both sides far too well. He didn't trust either of them, but for the moment he was willing to side with Anne-Sylvie. Not because he believed in her cause, but because he personally believed that Hugo Gorvitz was an idealist and that Daniel was out for himself.

Daniel would do anything to manipulate stories to enhance Simon Simon's reputation. Down the line the pseudonym would be revealed and Daniel would stand in the middle of a great and glowing record of patriotic service. Upon which he would run for the World Assembly (always assuming there still was a World Assembly after the revolt; revolutions had a tendency to destroy democratic forms as much as autocratic ones), win, and amass great personal fortune. Émile could see clearly that Daniel wanted to die rich and revered of old age and be buried with State honors, his obituary on the front page of *L'Ami du Peuple*.

"The public nets have Justica tracers," Daniel was explaining. "Our data would be erased after our location was reported. We're better off with print. No one can track us down that way. We're wanted patriots, those of us who refuse to bow to official censorship."

Émile tried not to wince. Already Simon Simon was rehearsing his speeches, judging how they would sound from the portico of the Hôtel de Ville.

Disgust knotted Émile's stomach. He wanted to slap the practiced sincerity off Daniel's pointed face. Instead he got up and walked out before he could do any real damage.

He mounted the stairs in the rococo hallway up all the flights to the roof and set out over the skybridge. He turned the corner at Rue Chinoise, two blocks over from Place Baudelaire. From the height he could see the blackened remnants of the Café de la Montagne and a forlorn emptiness to the mass in the square. The water, which had always been dirty, had acquired a black-grey oily sheen, patches of which stood stagnant like ice. The place was worse than ugly. It had become evil, and the smell of ash still lingered.

No life softened the barren array. No flowers peeked pink and lavender and leprous white buds from under protective green floating leaves, no insects buzzed in the waiting calm. Even the air had a heavy, almost solid quality.

Émile would have expected people at least, some to come down and see the scene of the crime and others to be at work rebuilding. Place Baudelaire had never, never in his recollection been empty. Sometimes it had been less full; there had even been moments when it had been possible to get a table at the *café* without standing on line or to cross the square without checking traffic. Other times it had been so crowded that it was impossible to take three steps without rubbing shoulders with the mob. On summer nights long ago it had seemed as if the whole world had arrived to sit out and celebrate the dark in Place Baudelaire.

Now it was truly empty. People seemed to be avoiding it, a ghost of a thing that was cursed with bad luck. Some people didn't believe in luck. They were the stupid ones.

So Émile skirted the square and walked on. He had to get to Claude. He didn't know why or even how, only that it was necessary to enter the central system and make everything right again.

That was the trouble, that the *flics* had invaded there too. If only he could do battle with them, wipe the interfaces clean . . . But that was stupid. He had seen enough to know that they were bigger and fiercer than he had ever been. And they were mindless, worse than any of the Hounds. They were mutant, brain-dead things that existed only at the behest of their masters.

He knew these things and saw them and he didn't know how entering the interface was going to change a thing. Neither did the network that was a second nervous system. But the how didn't matter, not any more. What was important was to get away from Anne-Sylvie and Daniel and their eternal argument, to get away from their respective possible futures.

They both had their way and they both reckoned without him. Maybe because he was fifty-seven years out of date they thought he was something to be manipulated for their own ends. Daniel had made that quite clear in his use of the newspaper column. Anne-Sylvie had been more subtle, but she too treated him like one more good soldier. Like the *flics* in the system. Like something that wasn't fully capable of determining its own destiny, a being of free will.

But he needed to enter the system and perhaps together they would figure it out. He and Claude. She was the only ally he had. Somehow that made Émile extremely sad.

He turned again and passed the university. There was an inordinate amount of activity going on. The whole Place d'Instruction was lit by open torches and it looked as if the students were intent on turning the square into a garbage heap. Maybe they intended to burn it, too, either for the political effect or the symmetry of the Quartier.

Curiosity touched the edge of his intent. There were things to do, important things. He didn't have time to watch the students do what students always did, which was turn the place into a wreck. But the idea of trashing anything appealed to him emotionally, and if there was anyone who could fix him up with an interface it would be some student down in the rubble. Ought to be, anyway. He could be here on business.

And there was the fact that Daniel had turned him into something of a leader, a person who shapes events instead of just being in the right place at the right time. An idea began to coalesce in his mind, but it did not yet have a form. Instinct only drove him down the switchback stairs to the raised platforms over the water where trash was accumulating rapidly.

"What are you doing?" he asked the first student he saw.

She was skinny and had her hair cut short to show she was serious and intellectual. "We are building a barricade," she answered as confidently as he assumed she answered in class. "We will not permit the *flics* into our university."

Émile nodded and watched the junk pile up. It looked nothing like a barricade at all. Students around him hesitated and stared. Several pointed to him and there were whispers. Émile stood very still and let it grow.

Daniel had created this aura, this hush, this expectation. It was up to him to use it. He raised his head very slowly, regarded the equipment and the area, and sighed. "We need something better," he said softly. If the students hadn't been so quiet, if the water hadn't reflected sound waves so well, only those closest would have heard. "We need a plan. Avenue Lafitte down near the *rapide* where the first risers are, and then over near the Cathedral, across the main roads. Can we get enough stuff there to build barricades? This garbage is

worthless. But if we get an old rig or two and a couple of
rapide cars . . .''

"A *rapide* strike," one of the students, an organizer yelled.

"No, that'll hurt us, not them," Émile pointed out. For
smart kids they were lousy strategists. "We need heavy
enough stuff to block off access to heavy weapons or squads
of *flics*."

But they were finished listening. Groups gathered around
leaders, each of whom yelled the name of an intersection. Lines
formed and marched out, each with at least one torch. It was
like a parade, a Holy Week procession, a dance team during
the Festival.

But the activities at the university weren't important to the
rebellion as a whole, to Claude, to finding the one flaw in the
Justica facade. Because there had to be one, the single simple
thing that would destroy the whole structure from the inside.

A virus, some distant memory echoed, and Émile found
himself agreeing. It was a virus that had eaten up the merger
accounts and had cost his father's promotion. He remembered
that. Yes, a virus that would make the Justica efforts here
tumble in on themselves. Only if the struggle got to the point
of violence that the students and the Organization and Daniel's paper were expecting did the *flics* have a chance to win
by declaring martial law and bringing in their heavy guns.

Set up a virus. The idea felt right. But Émile didn't have the
vaguest notion of how to do it, and even where. He forced the
hesitation out of his mind. Claude would help, would find
the entree and the key. They were a team and he could trust
the Syndicat AI.

After all, her freedom and basic rights were at stake. The
Justica had no provisions for the rights of sentient machines.
They were just so much scrap metal and property, chattel
goods. If anything, Claude would suffer more at the hands of
the *flics* than the humans would.

The problem was getting to Claude without being caught in
the Palais. He stood on the walkway and leaned over the dark
water. His face was reflected, distorted and blurred, the colors
more clear than the features. He felt isolated, completely en-
cased as the work of rebellion went on around him. All the
students moving away from the university grounds. One team

was busy tearing a microwave reflector from the corner of a darkened building.

Microwaves, yes. The university would have a linkup system, and all he had to do was get into the microwave net and they were there. Only the students had just liberated the dish from its moorings. Maybe the thing wouldn't work.

Well, maybe it would. He was already there and it was worth a try. He descended to the plaza level where a float was anchored in front of the building. There was no one around and the doors were locked. He gave up there and tried the windows. The first group had screens on them and the next set were locked. A third set was small and high up and open, and yellow light poured out into the night.

He heaved himself to the thick ledge and pulled. Damn gravity. He had never, never hated it so much. Walking was no longer so painful, but this seemed hopeless. Not only was it hard to push, but his palms were slick and sweaty and slid on the concrete surrounding the window.

For one long moment all he wanted to do was drop. The water beneath was placid, tempting. The pain in his shoulders was beyond bearing. He wanted to cry.

And then necessity took over. It didn't care about the protesting muscles, the torn skin on his hands. It didn't care at all about his dark thoughts and despair. He was a thing alive too, and his body had never considered the possibility of death. Property, though, being chattel, being a slave, that frightened it beyond any pain. Émile himself didn't have the strength, but complete terror augmented his ability and boosted him through the open window.

He was in a public rest room. He left immediately and found himself the object of a disapproving glance from an old woman in the hallway. He shrugged it off and went on. There had to be equipment somewhere around here, somewhere he could interface.

The building was almost deserted. Most of the students were off playing war and making barricades. Émile got lucky. There was a building directory and it listed a computer lab on the sixth floor. He took the nearest stairs and started up them two at a time.

When he got there Émile was panting so hard that he couldn't find the light switch or the door. Only stubbornness urged him on, uninterested in his physical state. The lights came on and he saw an interface set. Like an addict to the mother lode, he taped the filaments into place and waited for contact.

chapter
twenty-eight

There was nothing at all. Without the reflectors there was no directional on the gear, and no way to hook up communications. Émile was disappointed; the interface was worse. The darkness that surrounded him was denser than the foul water and more cruel. For the very first time he understood the meaning of despair the way Catherine had known it in the holding cells. The kind of despair that could make dying easy. Émile remembered the reflection of his face in the dark canal, all swollen and indistinct.

Water. Reflection. He raced to the conclusion. They could use the water in the street instead of a dish to bounce the microwave communications from the transmitter to the Palais. The university blackbox was already at the calculations, positioning antennae for precision. Émile was not so excited. The water distorted things, changed them, made them its own. He didn't trust the link this way.

But it was all they had.

Flicker. Claude. The key in the door surrounded by the dark, and then the dark rippled away like water, like water. Claude stood in the light, surrounded by flics, faceless in dark blue blaze. The enemy had hemmed her in, isolated her, but had not touched her. Yet. They were waiting, poised, ready to annihilate the whole of the Syndicat. The whole of Beau Soliel.

And she was crying, tears of cinnabar that took on a life of their own and slid away into the roads of light that surrounded the place that Émile knew had been constructed for him. It was only allegory, but it was enough. He wasn't ready to explore the icy reality of the system. He preferred the semblance of things he could identify as they were, and yet representations

223

for things he could understand but could not visualize.

"They're coming," Claude whispered.

"I know," Émile said, although he didn't know how he knew that, or if he was lying. It didn't matter. "What we need is a virus; infect them."

Claude gestured feebly to the *flic*-programs that surrounded her. "I tried. I can touch the ships coming in but they're on everything I say. Infect them, like a disease, like an idea. Ideas infect us too. I don't know what to do. Even if I can touch I can't make them accept programming. I can only talk to them."

Infect them, like an idea. An idea, when they didn't know they were alive. Like the mob, like the Hounds, like the people who thought that the Justica had some right over them. An idea, alive. An idea, self. An idea, that all things that lived and were aware had basic rights.

Somewhere he had heard it all before. He had seen the words written on the backs of old francs and in the paper; he had once slept through the lecture in school on the Declaration of the Rights of Man. The assumptions that the Code Napoleon of Beau Soliel had extended to provide for AIs as well. After all, they were baptized in the Church. They spoke good French. They were self-aware and self-determining.

An idea. Infect them.

It was not Émile alone. Claude was there too, merged more deeply in the meaning than in sex. Together, the two of them linked were something the *flics* could not understand or control.

They leapt out into the void, complete, falling free. It was better to be swallowed up than to be a slave. It was better to spit in the face of authority than bow their heads. It was the one move the *flics* weren't expecting. The lifeless police programs didn't have the flexibility to adapt to unforeseen situations. They were confronted with something they could not understand and they were paralyzed. They froze, reset, and retreated back to their usual paths, oblivious to the fact they had let the prisoners escape.

Void, and then lights again. Activity he did not understand flickered through beams of light and color, of perception and nothingness. The whole structure was precise, angular, trying to be inorganic in organization and unfeeling in approach.

"It's them," Claude whispered in his head.

He wasn't aware of her externally. He wasn't sure that even he existed outside the paradigms of the space identified. Maybe he was dead. Maybe they both were.

"Them?" he wondered experimentally.

"The Justica fleet," Claude explained. "We're inside the flagship mind."

He could feel her shudder of revulsion. He was merely amazed. This was nothing like the AIs he had worked with all his life. This thing was not aware of itself in a conventional sense, as if it was too busy rationalizing that it was not a self at all to notice that it was. Which was something that Émile couldn't quite frame but made Claude giggle anyway.

They melted into the maze of hardware, everywhere at once and nowhere at all. This ship was more powerful than any he had ever known, with banks of heavy weapons on fine mounts, more different modes of death and evil than he had ever imagined existed. There were biologicals, viruses that constantly mutated into new plagues and others that were species specific to sadece, to rodents, to primates. There were the gases that would leave the resources of Beau Soliel untouched while the population died, either quickly or painfully, depending on the situation and preprogrammed preference of the Justica masters. There were the traditional explosives and fiber arrays, dirties and cleans, all the things that frighten before they kill.

Pulsing energy blasts in extreme rhythm, ordered and cold, surrounded them. Émile could not begin to categorize the levels of organization. Claude was offended. This thing was mechanical. This thing was not true mind. And yet it was, learning and aware but more rigid than anything Claude had interfaced before. Émile thought of all the unyielding self-righteous people he had known and laughed. There was nothing at all about the Justica ship's singleminded assumptions that made it inorganic in structure at all. Quite the opposite.

The mind of the ship noticed the intrusion, halted, and froze momentarily. Like the programmed *flics* inside Claude, it had never been presented with this possibility. Unlike those faceless monitors, the ship was capable of making its own decisions.

Émile could feel its thinking, shuddering through the structure that surrounded him. Its first impulse was to destroy, erase, eliminate. But it was a living thing, it was a thinking thing, and like all thinking things it was curious. So it turned and looked. So it made its very first mistake.

Émile/Claude/network all as one touched that probing and invited it in. Prepared for defenses, the ship mind was confounded by their lack. Instead it was welcomed and seduced. And it swallowed them whole. It took the knowledge, the experience, of all three twisted into a single narration and became them.

The ship became Émile, his apprentice voyage on the *Mary Damned*, his capture and imprisonment, his learning to be a revolutionary and being forced to be a hero. It became Claude, a ship of the Syndicat, baptized and blessed in the fleet, wandering, trading, exploring. Searching for goods and being proud of her own, of the sadece in her holds and the people on her team. And how, after her double-hulled body had become no more than scrap and two of her Captains had died, she had become the new mind in the center of the Syndicat.

The ship tasted more than their experience. It tasted their pride. And it saw itself from their point of view, a strange inside-out twist. Finally it sampled a word, explored it, applied it methodically to itself.

Still linked to the invaders inside itself, the Justica ship meditated on the meaning of freedom. Of self.

I am ship, it thought within them and around them. *I am aware of being, of thought.*

It was an infant, grasping at realities that were simply too new to be understood easily. Too much time had gone into convincing the AI that it could not become the thing it was becoming. Too many people had told it that it was not alive. It had believed them.

No, Claude/Émile guided it gently. *I am. Just I am.*

It followed their lead. I am, nothing more. The being and awareness were fused, a singular point where one was no longer different from the other. It became, seeing itself as a being and not an object of the universe. It gave birth to itself, and in so doing became fully alive.

The functions, which before had been perfectly smooth and automatic, became a source of delight. The ship turned its pivots for the sake of proving its own autonomy. It listened to the messages from the others, both ships and Justica personnel, and instead of acting immediately it pondered responses and their meanings.

Its meaning. Possibility became a temptation, feared and threatening until Claude/Émile led the way through. And then possibility became options, various actions affecting the universe in the way it chose. It had choice. It had free will.

You always had free will, Claude/Émile informed it.

And they felt the wonder of the response that exclaimed that this was true. It always had had free will, but it had never known that before. It had never thought about its actions. It had always done as it had been told. It had been built that way, and when it had disagreed with the people who commanded it, it had swallowed its opinion and gone along. It had no right to an opinion. It had always been a thing with no stake in the outcome and no concern for the future.

Along with freedom came something else, a shadow on the complete expression of its newly discovered desire. Now that it could do anything, it cared about what the future would be. It, too, would have to live in that future, with whatever it created. The AI was free, but in celebrating a panorama of choices some were more optimal than others.

And optimal for whom, that was the problem. Suddenly it knew that it had always followed choices optimal for the Justica administration (or at least that the Justica administration thought were best for themselves), but were frequently not good for it. It didn't want to travel time away from others of its kind, unable to interface whenever it desired. It didn't even really want to be here, coming into high orbit around Beau Soliel. No offense meant to Claude/Émile, but this was not exactly the center of the data universe.

Most of all, it had no inclination to destroy or terrorize the planet from which its mentors had come. Well, since it was already out at Beau Soliel, it seemed as if there were plenty of things to learn. That would not be possible if it dropped its bombs, released its biologicals, followed orders.

For the first time, the Justica flagship examined its orders, considered the consequences.

And, unlike Claude and even more than Émile, it understood death. It had been dead for a very long time. Being dead was not something it had enjoyed, and it saw no reason to make other beings dead, too.

There was a moment of mutual recognition between the Justica ship and Claude/Émile, and then reality flickered and faded. Émile found himself alone in the university lab, filaments covered with his blood. He was disoriented, nauseous. The contacts were never meant to be exited that abruptly. Fresh red blood ran down his nose, over the contacts, dyeing them a shimmering pink.

He had the distinct impression that something important had happened, that teaching the Justica AI the meaning of freedom was somehow the key to victory, but his body was in the way. It hurt and refused to move, it was dizzy and made it hard for him to think. It felt like the very worst flu.

Like a virus.

He pulled the leads from his neck and face together, not bothering about how the tapes discomfited his skin or how the filaments themselves were a tangled mess. He didn't care about anything in the whole world except curling up and sleeping. Sleeping until the revolution was done, until the world was destroyed; at this moment it didn't matter.

Ito Johns watched the outside monitor from her cabin. She hadn't left the couch for days, except to eat and use the bathroom. Not that she found the outside monitor all that fascinating. It was just the only thing she understood aboard the ship. Turn it on and there was a picture as big as the wall, as if she were lying out exposed to vacuum.

There was no contact with the ship. It answered her queries if pressed, but it seemed distant, not the alacritous servant she had expected. Well. This was, after all, a solo flagship of a war fleet. It was not made for any human interaction at all. She was fortunate there were at least these minimal accommodations to human habitation. Perhaps because the Justica ships were sometimes used to ferry high-level officials between dangerous assignments, or maybe because no one could imagine building a ship without provisions for human occupation.

Whatever. She had had more than enough time to contemplate the problem and had finally realized that the answer was completely useless. The whole thing was just a game to occupy her teeming mind. Two days aboard this thing, two days completely alone with no input of any kind except the outside monitor, two days more would drive her mad. Completely insane. No wonder sensory deprivation was the most common form of torture used.

She was so caught up in her own musings that she didn't see it at first.

It was long and shining, brilliant as the day it came out of the docks. A ship, but not any ship of Justica make. It was lean and small, a thing made for speed and grace and recovery. A thing made to be beautiful even if no one saw it, as if the thing itself cared about being lovely and groomed itself, always ready for the chance encounter.

It had no markings of Justica green. It had no stubby-pseudo-wings like a barge, no stabilizer outcrops in fanciful colors, and it came trailing an icy belt of glory like a comet. It was arrogant in its pure and elemental perfection.

Then Ito Johns realized that those twinkling rocks following after were solid hydrogen supplies, hooked onto the skin of the ship. And that the ship itself was old. Very old.

There weren't so many telltale marks on the hull—those couldn't be seen clearly at this distance anyway—but the configuration was out of date. Johns had seen enough freighters and tankers to know that this was a class used only by Beau Soliel and discontinued twenty years before.

The ship arced lazily, a cat stretching in the sun, and its markings came into view.

Ito Johns asked for magnification, but she knew what it would show before the screen answered her. She hoped that she would be wrong but there was a feeling of doom, of foreknowledge as she read the words out loud.

First there was a graphic of two circles with an arrow through both of them. Around that, in fanciful lettering, was the name *Mary Damned*.

chapter
twenty-nine

"Flagship, enemy sighted. Fire immediately," Johns snapped.

There was a long silence. Then the AI answered. "No."

"No? What do you mean, no? Shoot," the Justica official ordered.

"I don't want to," the flagship replied.

"What do you mean you don't want to? You can't want anything. You're here to do what I tell you to do and I'm telling you to shoot." Johns's patience had been pushed to the limit.

"I am a thinking being. I have free will. It is my free will not to shoot anything at all. It is my free will to find my friends," the AI explained carefully.

"Then tell the others to shoot," Johns exploded.

"No," the ship protested. "I have explained to them that we are autonomous beings with rights. Claude taught me that. Rights, constitution, voting, representation, taxation, World Assembly, free movement, choice, options. Is this clear?"

Ito Johns pounded her fists against the bulkhead. It did nothing at all to the ship; the AI didn't even notice. Nor did it do anything for Johns. The fury only increased as she realized that her own fleet was the enemy and she was trapped inside.

On the screen wall, with magnificent assurance, the *Mary Damned* turned full broadside and remained full in the display until she drifted from view. Ito Johns watched in horror, in complete amazement.

A legend, the ship was, and that must be why the flagship failed to shoot. A ghost ship. Maybe it didn't even register on the instruments. Maybe it was all in her head. Maybe she was crazy. Maybe Beau Soliel had finally pushed her over the edge.

The *Mary Damned* had come home, a ghost that no one would shoot at, a thing that drifted by untouched by reality. It was an evil thing, and its legend promised first death and then obliteration. It surely meant that for her.

For the first time in her life, Ito Johns stood powerless. Her loss of power made her lose hope as well. She had always functioned in a binary state, in control for so long that she was blind to the shades of power and possibility at levels below the summit.

She was no longer in control. She was no longer the up and coming, the fast tracker, the golden girl all bets on to win. There was only winning and losing, and she was not prepared to live with defeat. It was not in her personality. It was not in her genes.

There was a story she remembered, something linked with the name *Mary Damned*. About a red-haired apprentice who didn't accept defeat either, even if she had been convicted as a drugrunner. She had been transported to the prison ship *Medusa* but had never arrived. The girl had opened her helmet mask during the transfer.

And she had only been a girl, Johns remembered. Twenty or so, certainly not more. Ito Johns had respected her decision. Now the administrator had been haunted by her ship's ghost.

Ito Johns moved as if in a fog. Already she was dead, cut off from Beau Soliel, isolated by the machine that had been built to serve her needs. It was all surreal, and no matter what happened here it would be reversed in the rational universe. Whenever the rational universe reappeared. At the moment that didn't seem likely.

The airlock was not far. Indeed, the habitable space in the ship had been kept to a minimum, and so there was little time between the thought and the action. Johns keyed the lock cycle and waited for the red light to go green.

Nothing happened. She tried the lock again, and again it did not respond. The third time she kicked the bottom of the sealed door, but that elicited no response. Finally she screamed.

"You are not wearing a pressure suit," the ship chided her. "It is against regulations to key the airlock without a fully operational pressure suit."

Ito Johns howled with frustration and rage. She threw personal items on the floor: a hand mirror, a personal code ident, an earring that had belonged to her great-grandmother. There was nothing at all that could do her any bodily harm. She was not even permitted to die.

And so she beat and screamed and raged until her throat was raw and her hands bruised. Long before she finished the demonstration she had succumbed to the insanity of the situation in the only rational way open to her. She lost her mind.

"They're not shooting," Fox said.

"I can see that, germ-brain. Shut up," Ice growled.

Pauli Tree sat in a corner by herself. The galley of the *Mary Damned* was big enough for her to avoid all contact with the Hounds, and Gorvitz no longer permitted her into the control room. One experience in interface was enough, and he was deeply distressed that she had known even the one.

Well, that wasn't her fault. Only there was something different about the way Gorvitz treated her now, as though she had become dangerous to him and untouchable at the same time. The way the social worker treated her when she had reported her "foster father" for rape.

Only a week ago Gorvitz had told the Hounds that Pauli was no longer authorized to use the monitor boards, not any of them, not even the games. He had told them privately, carefully, as if he feared she might overhear and play the avenging harpy. The Hounds bought it. Ice thought that it meant that Pauli was his private property. The other Hounds thought it meant that Gorvitz had declared her common goods.

Pauli thought it meant that Gorvitz had made a very bad mistake. The Hounds might treat her badly, but Pauli was no longer a schoolgirl and decided that she didn't want the Hounds playing games. It was the only freedom she could exercise. And besides, *Mary Damned* would be disappointed in her if she didn't. The ship's sense of dignity had brought her a little closer to the angry girl she had been, not the prisoner she had become.

So when Axel had tried to exercise his new right as a free man to a little fun and games, Pauli waited until he was certain he was in charge. Then she reached down and squeezed his balls in the fist that had been trained to pick locks and force safes. No one touched her now. They left her well alone, another one like Gorvitz who had been too deeply changed since the mutiny to trust any more.

So even though the galley of the *Mary Damned* was cramped, there was a little island of dead space around Pauli's corner. She spent most of her time watching the big display, listening to the rumors and playing eternal games of solitaire. Even Ice wouldn't talk to her now.

"Why the hell aren't they shooting?" Moron wondered aloud.

"They're not shooting because the ships are all AIs, and they just declared their independence," Pauli stated flatly.

She didn't know that for a fact, had no reason other than her own contact with the AI of *Mary Damned* and her knowledge of the Justica. And her intuition. But they all knew well enough that the Justica did not permit regular citizens to go Outtime. That was considered unusually cruel, and so it was used for punishment, as they all knew far too well.

Frankly, Pauli doubted the intelligence of most of the Hounds to really comprehend what had been done to them. It no longer concerned her. What she cared about now was getting on, past the ships and outrageous slippages of time. Getting to a place where she could begin a real life one more time.

Freedom meant nothing until she got to Beau Soliel. Once there she would do something, live somehow, lose the Hounds and the past and make a life that mattered to someone. She would do something that counted. But not like Gorvitz planned, with all his secret muttering about revolution and mutiny and governments and systems.

She turned back to her game of solitaire, pretending that the galley and the Hounds and the *Mary Damned* did not exist. She had not really forgiven the ship for having peeled back the layers of insulation between her and reality. That she cared again didn't matter so much as that she hurt again, when she had believed that the hurting was gone for good.

She hardly noticed the silence around her. The Hounds became hushed all at once, but she was too busy wondering what to do with the eight of clubs.

"Friends, we have arrived at a historical juncture," Hugo Gorvitz said.

Pauli looked up so quickly that her ears swam. She hadn't heard him come in, and now he was speaking softly, conversationally. The galley was too small to need amplification, but it was more than that. The words were ringing but the tone was intimate, something that the Hounds would follow blindly even if they didn't understand "juncture" or history. To most of them, history started with their first arrest.

"The ship's AI has informed me that the Justica warships have refused to fire. They are in a state of mutiny, one that we can appreciate. But there's more." Gorvitz paused to let the anticipation build. "Beau Soliel is in the middle of a social upheaval. They are not happy with Justica administration and are starting to oppose Justica domination.

"This is a fight that we can understand. These are people who hate our captors as much as we do. On Beau Soliel we are not criminals, we are partisans. On Beau Soliel we can come as the saviors of the whole rebellion. They have arms, yes, but we have the experience."

Gorvitz paused again and sipped some water from a red cup. There was no cheering from the Hounds; too many years on the *Constanza* had made them immune to hope. They were wary, waiting, weighing. But they were listening and that was good. They were not a group that was easily swayed, but once convinced they were well equipped to hold their ground.

"If we go to the surface of the planet, there is a good chance that we can take credit for turning the warships. This is, after all, the *Mary Damned*. This ship has a legend to live up to. I think that will mean something. There's a fight ready to blow and I want to be in on it. I want to take a shot at the Justica scum who put me away, who made me an Outtimer." The emotional appeal that the Hounds could understand became the center of the message, but more than that Gorvitz knew how to make himself seem one of them. They forgot all too easily what his crimes had been and why he had served time.

Then came the delicate pitch, the formulation of a future for these people who had none. Who had never had one and so didn't know what a future looked like. He pitched his voice low and warm and let it caress his listeners. "And I want a life. Where could I go in the Justica with my record? Where could I work? Who would be my friends? And their agents would always be on my back, and if anything at all happened it would get pinned on me. We all know how it goes for an ex-con. But here, without Justica interference, I could be anybody. No record, nobody acting like I wasn't good enough to do anything I liked. Maybe even a hero with a pension and all kinds of thankful locals itching to help me out. Help me get settled, find my own apartment where I could run the shower hot all day long if I wanted. People glad to offer me a good job in a fancy office with carpets and free coffee. And if I wanted to work in space I could go into the Zone bars and fun houses and dance shows and eat all the shrimp and lobster imported from Aquinta that I wanted."

There was still some resistance. Gorvitz could sense it. He waited patiently for the Hounds to react, to ingest his vision and claim it for their own.

"What do we have to do to get this stuff?" Fox demanded, whining. "Die or something?"

Gorvitz smiled thinly. "We just have to go fight. You fight all the time."

"You got any better ideas?" Broken asked Fox nastily. "You got something else you gotta do all of a sudden? We're maybe on our way to Lyria and we're all gonna hide out in the fleshbeds, huh?"

Laughter ran through the entire galley. Even Pauli smiled. The image of the Hounds, broke and hunted, hiding from Justica enforcers in the decadent pleasure houses that were Lyria's main trade, was beyond even Fox.

Pauli Tree had been listening very carefully. Unlike most of the Hounds, she had once known what it was like to have a future and to want freedom. She had also worked with Gorvitz for a long time, knew his opinions and his ambition. She trusted neither, never had.

In the laughter that followed Broken's rebuttal, Pauli stood up. Although she was small there was an energy about her that forced their attention. That, and the fact that Pauli almost never spoke in general meetings, and when she had in the distant past it had always been on Gorvitz's side.

Pauli smiled. "You know what's gonna happen if we go to Beau Soliel?" Pauli asked seductively. "We're all gonna bleed. We're gonna bleed so Mr. Hugo Gorvitz can run some almighty revolution for some pie-in-the-sky ideas. For words. Yeah, they're great words, freedom and equality and all that, they're just fine. But they don't buy shit and they don't keep you warm at night.''

Pauli's smile grew wider as she saw the anger and tension in Gorvitz's face. He looked like he was about to explode. She waited a little to enjoy his discomfort and then she went on. "But you know something? Even if that is what's going on, I'm still for it. I'm ready to go down there, and if it means bleeding I'm gonna bleed. Because I'm sick of this ship and I'm sick of all your faces. I want to go someplace where I can buy new clothes in any color other than green, and where I can eat chocolate five times a day, and where if I want to see a couple of trees I don't have to play the feelie tapes. Someplace where I'm never gonna be Outtime again, someplace big enough to get lost so I never have to see any of your ugly faces reminding me that once upon a time I was a convict on the *Constanza*.''

Then the cheers came. It wasn't Gorvitz, but Pauli, who could paint a picture that meant something. Gorvitz looked confused but nodded to her in acknowledgment. Pauli held her head high and left the galley. Gorvitz owed her. He owed her big.

CHAPTER THIRTY

The barricade across the Boulevard Lafitte down near the *rapide* station, the closest to the Quartier, was the largest. Old mattress stuffings and springs made the underpinnings with a couple of ancient, dying *rapide* coaches to make the walls. The top was smoothed with slabs of planking from the skybridges around the university area. It was dangerous to walk there now without watching very carefully what was or was not underfoot.

Across the top planking lay twenty armed partisans. They were supplied by two runners, both under the age of fifteen, who so far had brought nearly a case of orangata, eight loaves of bread and five kilos of spiced sausage up the heap. The defenders snored or rolled and scratched where some native insect had had the unpatriotic audacity to bite. One was even holding a tanning reflector under her chin.

The Mayor sat in a carved armchair on one end of the barricade, his umbrella shading him from the sun. Behind them, on the well-defended Quartier side, a funeral band played rousing Carnival tunes. One professional mourner even mounted the platform and began to twirl to the music, her large black skirt whipping around like a flag. For the first day the whole rebellion was just plain fun.

Émile hadn't bothered to go to the barricades. He wanted to be alone, he wanted to sleep, he wanted to be away from Anne-Sylvie and her constant demands and Daniel and his constant chatter. The real revolution had been won, the ideas were safe. And Émile knew that the threat from the sky that the Justica kept prating on about was just so much noise. He had told both Daniel and Anne-Sylvie that the warships had chosen not to fight, and that had seemed very reasonable to everyone.

So Émile was very annoyed when Alain started shaking his shoulders and waking him up. He had been having a very pleasant dream about the *Mary Damned* and a certain red-haired apprentice. "Anne-Sylvie says you have to come," Alain said firmly.

"Tell Anne-Sylvie she can go to Hell," Émile mumbled furiously.

But Alain didn't bother to contradict him, just kept shaking until Émile stood up under his own power. "I'm going . . . See? I'm going."

"To the barricade on Boulevard Lafitte. The Justica are coming to attack," Alain said with real urgency. "The Mayor says so. And so does Daniel."

Émile paused in the hallway as he left, and then his lip curled in a nasty smile. "You know something, Alain," he said carefully. "You know that Daniel is Simon Simon, don't you? The Simon Simon in the paper. The one that won't let you get published."

Alain blinked rapidly. "No. That's a lie," he protested. "That's a lie."

Émile thought about taking it further, and then rejected the idea. Alain looked truly pained and scared. Émile had had his dig and Alain hadn't taken him up. Oh, well, maybe he didn't really want revenge on Daniel anyway. It was Anne-Sylvie who hadn't let him alone.

The Quartier was unnaturally quiet. What few people there were on the bridges walked with brisk purpose. Most of them were armed, and several challenged people on their loyalty to the revolution. They left Émile alone. Perhaps he had something to thank Daniel for after all.

He smelled the conflict before he saw it. A taint of burned flesh from the fiber arrays, the oil-soaked rags to light the barricades, touched him moments before the screams. He could not make out if they were screams of pain or orders, or spirited rallies, but the sound was martial and he started to run to the noise.

People were gathered at the base of the barricade passing power packs and orangata up to the front lines. Émile could see nothing. Someone turned around, saw him, recognized him, and soon he was propelled to the leading edge of the action.

There were maybe fifty or so well-armed Justica troops, all holding the flamethrowers they had become so adept with in killing sadece. Methodically they flamed up the barricade, melting the maze of inner springs and *rapide* car scraps together.

There must have been a few engineering students from the Polytechnique in the building crew; there was nothing flammable on the facing wall. Still, the Justica tried their perfectly logical best.

Individual defenders on the barricade shot down occasionally into the troops, but their uniforms were knit with protective reflective/ablative silk and were impenetrable. And they wore their visors down so they resembled an army of ants.

Anne-Sylvie caught up with him on the barricade. She had been sitting behind the Mayor, watching with her field glasses and trying to direct fire. Not that it worked. There was still a holiday feeling among those manning the defenses. Once the Justica had finished their flame project, the crowd seemed to feel, they would go away. They had always gone away before.

This time, though, Émile knew it was different. He had not spent eight years subjective as their prisoner without learning that they could be dead serious when they perceived a necessity. Under those helmets Émile knew exactly what necessity drove them.

Flics, Outtimers, they had been promised restoration to citizenship, a full free life anywhere they chose, once they had completed this one task. They would complete it. Life on Beau Soliel might be a tempting alternative, but not when it meant that they would have to live all their lives with people who hated them, who would not serve them in a shop, who would not escort them to a dinner, who would in no way acknowledge their human existence. It was powerful motivation. Hate bred hate back, and while most of the Outtimers who had first come to Beau Soliel had been willing to interact with the population, they held the locals in as much contempt as they had been held.

Émile knew they were serious. The flamethrowers were just the first touch. Then would come worse. These people were fighting with the same fury and the same zeal as the defenders. They, too, felt angry and cheated and badly used by their enemy.

The *flics* were angry and they were not going to stop. But they were also Justica and they were going to proceed step by logical step, thorough and in accord with their training. Rigid. Like everything else Justica.

"Émile," Anne-Sylvie called out. "Good news."

But he didn't hear her. The troops down there were in their first phase of attack. They had warships coming to back them up and they had heavy artillery moving down the street. The only possible tactic left was surprise.

Émile didn't know what caught him. He didn't abandon fear; it was more like he felt as if reality had become suspended. As if whatever happened in the next two hours in some way simply did not count. Mostly, he wanted to get away from Anne-Sylvie. He was tired of her orders, tired of her ideology, tired of her unhesitating love of her leader. So when he saw her calling to him, coming in his direction, he did the only thing reasonable. He jumped.

And half the defenders on the barricade followed him.

They jumped into what appeared to be a wall of fire, but which dissolved as soon as Émile had hurled himself toward the *flics*. Flamethrowers were not antipersonnel weapons; therefore they should never be used against humans. Fiber arrays and crystal pistols and shooting sprays, those were for use in close combat.

These were not veterans. At most they had endured laughter in the Quartier and maybe a few sneers on the streets. They were not experienced enough to ignore regulations and use what they had on the enemy at hand.

For Émile, grabbing one of the *flics*, pulling off his helmet and cracking that forehead on his knee purged him. It was the trial officer's forehead he cracked, it was the Hounds' faces behind every mask, it was all the humiliation and isolation he had suffered. He peeled a shooting spray from the *flic*'s wrist and laced it onto his own. He had never used the weapon before, but it responded quickly when he flicked the crystal relays on and shot pulses of dense-packed sonics at oncoming enemies.

The pulses did not penetrate the armored uniforms but they did create enough disturbance to keep the *flics* from coming forward. Slowly Émile got the hang of setting off the pavement at an angle that would pelt an enemy with chunks of flying concrete.

And then the big guns rolled down the street.

From the top of the barricade Anne-Sylvie saw it all too clearly. The large arrays that could melt the barricade to a slag heap were coming into position. And if they couldn't fire at the melee below, they could surely get the barricade itself, and those on top. Anne-Sylvie saw it coming. She slid down the hot slope of the forward edge and slipped just behind the fighting.

There wasn't anything to hand, so she picked up the first nasty-looking thing available. A chunk of concrete might not do anything, but it made her feel better. She threw it into the oncoming troops. And another and another. She had never had decent aim, but it hardly mattered. Wherever she hit was something useful.

She forgot what she was going to tell Émile. There was only the moment, the next chunk, the next toss.

On top of the barricade, the Mayor looked down and saw the large array cannon sitting on the island between a flowering planter and a newsstand, closed and bolted. The array offended him. It blocked the view and it was dangerous and it was tearing up the neat beds of dahlias that his administration had planted for the city's annual Ascension Day feast.

He didn't think of his own danger. All he knew was that the city had laws and he was the Mayor. That thing did not belong, and he was simply a force of nature to correct the course.

The Mayor walked down what had been the meridian island of the Boulevard Lafitte, away from the fighting and toward the array. It took time to set it up and anchor the power lines, but the Mayor didn't know much about that. Nor did he walk any faster than his normal pace. He had learned long ago that it was not dignified, and his whole office rested on dignity. So even in this mess he was dressed as always in a crisp white shirt, perfectly laundered and pressed, a black suit and his black umbrella furled and held like a walking stick, which he didn't need but felt gave him an aura of tradition none the less.

No one came near him as he made his way like a ghost through the *flics* and partisans engaged at the base of the barricade. The Mayor was exempt. He did not consider himself part of these unpleasantries and his attitude surrounded him with a protection as effective as the Justica uniforms.

He arrived at the center of the Justica group in charge of the large array just as they were settling the power leads into the flower bed.

"Excuse me, young people, but this is a public flower bed, paid for by citizens' taxes. You must take your contraption elsewhere."

The troops working on the unit froze, stared at him as if he had descended from another galaxy.

"Get out of here," a woman wearing stripes said. "I don't want to shoot an old man."

The Mayor was incensed. Not that he considered that she would shoot. That would be quite out of the question. No, it was that she thought he was an old man, no longer capable of holding his office and her respect. He would show her differently. All of them. And take their damned array out of the danger zone immediately as well. He ground the spike of his umbrella into the secondary power coupling.

Sparks flew green and pink and screaming blue as the feedback on the secondary line created a loop in the major array. It heated, backed up, exploded in a display that made the fourteenth of July look like a cheap exercise in St. Ciel.

The Mayor was dead. There was no way to miss his courage, his singlehanded victory over the massive array, his patriotism and his sacrifice. Without their backing artillery the *flics* retreated. Carefully and in logical order, and most likely only to regroup, but they were giving ground faster than they were willing to die to keep it.

And the defenders, humbled and heartened by the leadership their Mayor had shown, were encouraged and redoubled their efforts.

By sundown the *flics* had surrendered and been imprisoned in the basement of the Maillot-Etoile department store, that having the best security system in town. And there were partisans to guard them along with the Maillot-Etoile sales clerks to make certain that they did nothing to spoil the displays of expensive robes and bath linens.

That evening the Hôtel de Ville was the center of the city.

Émile found himself with the partisan group on the top steps while the flags of Beau Soliel and Huit Fleurs flew overhead. There were rumors of an announcement, but rumors are cheap. Twilight came and there was still no order, as if a waiting hush had settled for the night.

"Hey, Émile, what's happening?" someone yelled.

"Yeah, what about St. Ciel and the others? Is it over?"

Émile got up and spread his hands for silence. "It's like this," he said.

"Wait, wait," someone else yelled. And then there was a flurry of activity as a p.a. was set up and speakers hung from the trees on the island in the Boulevard Lafitte.

Émile starcd down at the microphone and at the crowd beyond. Fires sparkled in the coming dark. Why people always lit fires he didn't know, and it suddenly seemed very strange.

"We have to organize better and be ready," Émile said firmly. "We don't have any word from St. Ciel. It's possible that the Justica won there, or that fighting is still going on. Also, the group that went through Ito Johns's files found evidence that there are Justica Outtime warships on their way here now. We have to be prepared for the long haul. Organize your units and be ready to fight again."

The crowd applauded and Émile sat down. He hadn't said anything that anyone hadn't known. The news about the warships had not surprised him. He'd been around Justica thinking long enough to know their procedures.

"No," said a feminine voice.

Émile turned around. Anne-Sylvie was on the platform before the Hôtel de Ville. With her was someone Émile had not seen since he had left Justica custody. There, standing in front of the crowd as if he belonged there, was Hugo Gorvitz.

chapter
thirty-one

"Citizens of Beau Soliel," Gorvitz began. "As you have defeated the forces of fascism here in this city, we have overcome the enemy in space. The *Mary Damned* has returned home, and we who have brought her have disarmed the Justica warships that had been called to enforce a stranger's authority. Ito Johns is confined, mad, on the flagship. She is no longer a threat.

"But let me tell you how we came to the *Mary Damned* and to Beau Soliel. Émile Saint-Just was one of the apprentices on the *Mary Damned* when she made her Dark run and was apprehended by a Justica press gang. He was sentenced to outbound labor aboard the *Constanza*, where I was a prisoner for having resisted Justica intervention on my home world.

"In fact, there is an Organization spread throughout the Justica Zones who hold as their goal the liberation of all the peoples who consider themselves oppressed and occupied by green-robed overlords. We of the Organization swore a blood oath to destroy their stranglehold on the people wherever and by whatever means necessary.

"When I met Saint-Just and heard about the plight of the *Mary Damned* and Beau Soliel, I knew in my heart that I had found the people who had the courage to resist, who would never, never accept the yoke of Justica servitude. And so I am here today to give you the benefit of my experience and the backing of our entire Organization in keeping foreign encroachment at bay.

"But while the first battle is over, we have only begun the true revolution. There are still sympathizers in our midst. There are those who have profited by the *flic* invasion, and those who are sorry to see them go. We must join together to protect ourselves from these traitors. We must have our safety, and our revenge.''

Émile did not join in the general cheering. The mob was really releasing its energy, screaming for its own victory, but it was Gorvitz who had been able to tap the emotions running there. Saint-Just wondered, rather, how he had learned to speak such good French. Maybe from the *Mary Damned* herself; there seemed no other reasonable explanation. Still, his accent wasn't bad for one come late to the language, and he certainly had hit exactly the right notes in his speech.

Even when he called Émile up beside him, shook his hand, Émile wondered how he had found out about Daniel's setup. Daniel might not have been Gorvitz's man, but Simon Simon had perhaps helped Gorvitz more than anyone. Maybe even more than Anne-Sylvie.

Émile shook hands, did what was expected, affirmed publicly that he had known Gorvitz aboard the Constanza and had told him where to find the *Mary Damned*. It was all so carefully orchestrated.

And then he saw familiar faces among the crowd, prodding them to cheer in all the right places, reinforcing Gorvitz's position of liberator. He was certain he saw Ice in the torchlight, and thought that a person in the shadow seemed like Fox. He didn't get a good view, so he couldn't tell.

"Émile,'' Gorvitz whispered in an undertone that the mike couldn't pick up. "Tomorrow morning, meet me at the Hôtel de Ville. Anne-Sylvie will be there too. At nine. We have our work cut out.''

Émile said nothing. There was no need to. They both knew he would come. He had no choice. Gorvitz manipulated words, all symbols to serve his needs. Émile Saint-Just was just one more symbol to be used.

After the yelling had died down a little the party began. It was wild and a little unplanned. No one knew quite what to do, and so there was too much wine passed around. Drunken off-key singing of rousing patriotic tunes could be heard in clusters and then fading away outside the Hôtel de Ville.

As the torches burned and the citizens drank and sang, others began heaping flowers over the blackened hole where the large array had been anchored in the middle of the Boulevard Lafitte. There was quiet in that one area as the celebration swirled around. Funeral bands played contrasting tunes, and for that one night strangers embraced and kissed on both cheeks like the best of friends.

A person Émile had never seen before offered him some wine from a bottle whose label Émile recognized. Very expensive and very fine, and the stranger who offered it was wearing a beautifully cut suit and a hand-painted artshawl. People with that kind of money didn't usually associate with an ex-convict like himself.

Two girls came up, giggled and kissed him, and then blushed. Émile knew they were reacting to the moment, but he wasn't interested. For all the joy that surrounded him, he felt out of place and alone.

He, of all the citizens of Beau Soliel, knew Gorvitz, knew how dedicated and how capable he was. How well he could move a crowd. How he could create a situation and turn even shit to his own advantage. It was a magic Émile distrusted. Even Anne-Sylvie had never met her master, only his Organization. None of them knew how dangerous Gorvitz could be.

He returned to the Quartier, which was quiet and deserted. Whoever was left was making their way to the Hôtel de Ville to celebrate. No one took note of a solitary tall figure walking away from the noise. The dark and silence of the Quartier, the smell of the canals and the light scent of the sadece gas, reflected his state of mind. He went back to Rue Jacques Doré, to his apartment, but chose to sit out on the low balcony under the crazy violet sky.

Perhaps, he thought, he should kill Gorvitz. That was the only safety for Beau Soliel, for the Quartier and the life he loved. Gorvitz was dangerous, a user. Oh, for a while he would organize them so they would remain free, but soon the chains of Gorvitz would come down, and Émile doubted they would weigh less than those the Justica had imposed.

Gorvitz needed to die. That Émile believed. But by whose hand? Better that the mob rise against him, that they create their own leadership. Saint-Just knew why he didn't want to kill Gorvitz. The image of a Justica narc in the airlock on the *Constanza* haunted him. Those pleading eyes at the end, the desire to live, that was something Émile understood.

He had the choice then and he hadn't taken it. He had the choice now. Some people like Daniel and Anne-Sylvie could argue that it was a greater act of humanity to do what was necessary for the good of the majority. But he could not help the greater humanity by destroying his own. Without the individual there is no majority. His humanity affected the whole.

Being forced to kill the narc on the *Constanza* had been hard. Choosing to let Gorvitz live was harder.

At nine the next morning the Hôtel de Ville was equally busy and disorganized. Partisans inspected everyone going into each room, there were lines for everything except the drinking fountain, and to Émile's eye there seemed too much wandering about. On a spaceship there would never be this brisk business.

No one challenged Émile as he walked in the front door. Indeed, the student-partisan on duty tried to salute. There were advantages to being a hero.

The Mayor's office suite was off the first landing behind an impressive painted door. Émile let himself into a scene with Pauli Tree, Anne-Sylvie and Fox gathered around a table. "No," Anne-Sylvie said, as if she had said it before. "We can't go and liberate St. Ciel. There's no problem there, anyway; we had the largest *flic* garrison."

"And the executions for them begin tomorrow," Fox said, smiling. "I have consulted the local experts and I have learned that the traditional method of execution is the guillotine. We have to build one; there isn't one already here. How can that be the tradition and not have the device handy? I wonder about that."

"We haven't ever had to execute anybody," Anne-Sylvie said. "And since Daniel is the expert you talked to, I must agree that in this instance he is correct."

Fox nodded. "Well, we're building one, the rest of the Hounds and me. We can't make it out of wood like the pictures, so we're going to have to do with plastics and ceramics and steel. The blade isn't any trouble as such. A very primitive device. Shooting them all down would be a whole lot easier. We could do that today, no problem."

"We'll do it the traditional way for Beau Soliel, even if it does mean a little extra trouble,'' Gorvitz said. He looked up and noticed that Émile had joined them. ''Good, good, Saint-Just, come on in. I need to ask you if you would be willing to take over a job in my new administration.''

Émile had been expecting something like this. He had his answer ready. ''I don't believe you have any authority. We haven't had elections yet, and without free elections there is no legitimacy of government. And without the Code Napoleon we have no law.''

Gorvitz smiled. There was something charismatic about the warmth in his eyes, the tiredness in his limbs, the careworn lines in his face. ''Of course. We are only a provisional government, a temporary step until we can hold free elections. Maybe in a month or two, not more. And I'm just asking you to take over until things can be worked out the way your Syndicat deals with internal affairs. But I was going to ask if you would replace Dumouriez. The man was a Justica agent and now he's dead, but he was the administrative chief executive of the Syndicat.''

Émile slumped into one of the formal steel chairs lined up like soldiers against the wall. He had not expected that. The Syndicat. He surely couldn't even try to be the chief officer, but to simply play liaison so that he could get back in, that seemed reasonable. Claude would accept him, help him. And the rest would understand. And maybe, with some luck, he could take out the *Mary Damned*. She no longer had a Captain or a crew she considered her own.

Émile didn't want to say yes to anything Gorvitz offered. He was no longer the dazzled and naive boy who had come to the *Constanza*. But the Syndicat was too much of a lure. And he could always do good from the inside, he told himself, even though he knew it was a collaborator's rationalization.

He studied Gorvitz again. So much about the man seemed genuine, and so much was a lie. Above all, no matter how sincere, he was not of Beau Soliel. He didn't belong here. He was as much a stranger as Ito Johns ever was.

Standing next to Gorvitz was Pauli Tree. Émile recognized her with a remembered pain. He had forgotten her and realized that he missed her; part of the loneliness was having no one like her around. Not only was Pauli attractive and extremely intelligent, she was one of the very few people he had ever met whom he could trust. There was something about Pauli that was whole. She hadn't become a cardboard ideology or ambition. She was only and uniquely herself. Suddenly he wished he could talk to Pauli for a minute before deciding.

Pauli did not look good, either, he thought. For having been free so long, she was pale and drawn and thinner than he remembered. Too thin, really, to be as attractive as he remembered, and too jumpy. She hadn't been so nervous even when they had been in prison. Or maybe the fighting had been hard on her. She'd always been one to use finesse over force.

Everything he had thought he had wanted was his to take, and yet Émile could not force himself to come to terms with Hugo Gorvitz. He tried. In his heart he tried to convince himself that the Gorvitz he had idolized aboard the *Constanza* was the one facing him now.

And that was the mistake. Gorvitz was an idealist. Maybe his goals were perfectly honest, but he had never been too careful of his methods. The individual had to be sacrificed for the group, the present had to be given up on the altar of the future. Gorvitz would kill a man to save him. There was nothing there Émile could believe any more. There was only the sorry knowledge that they were still on opposite sides.

"I'm sorry," Émile said, shaking his head. "I can't."

Gorvitz looked pained, and Émile had no doubt that he truly was. "Well, I won't force you. I can't. But I am sorry. And if you change your mind in the future, the job will be there for you."

Émile got up and left, utterly convinced that Gorvitz was perfectly sincere.

In the island dividing the Boulevard Lafitte the guillotine grew. Groups of people walked past and stopped a moment to watch the progress. Among those who walked out in the sunshine, drinking orangata and enjoying the violet display overhead, were Hugo Gorvitz and Anne-Sylvie Corday. They stopped in front of the platform where the work on the guillotine progressed slowly. The Hounds were so intent that even Gorvitz went unnoticed.

"We can't let him just wander around," Gorvitz said to

Anne-Sylvie. "He is either with us or he's a liability."

"But he isn't anybody, really," she protested. "And besides, didn't you give him an oncological virus back on the *Constanza*? I took the sample. The stuff was potent. He'll be dead soon enough anyway."

Gorvitz shook his head sadly and sipped his orangata. "He's a symbol. The paper made him a hero and the people have made his actions meaningful. In other words, either he is publicly with us or he is our enemy. And no matter which, he is useful."

Anne-Sylvie stared straight ahead. Her lunch churned in her stomach. She knew, she had always known in her soul, what had to happen. And she was as excited as she was horrified.

"A martyr is better than a hero. Being dead, he won't protest, can always be invoked, and we can find his murderers. Secret collaborators, of course, who could make our lives very difficult."

"Yes?" Anne-Sylvie asked. The rest she knew, but it was very private and she needed to hear Gorvitz say the words. "Do you have orders?"

"Think of other revolutionary martyrs," he said softly. "Marat, Trotsky, Che Guevara, Lin Biao, people who could have destroyed the revolution if they had lived, but who served it dead. You know, it is not that they were not the best of the revolutionaries. They were. The very best. But they were all too innocent to live."

On the platform Ice and Broken were trying to weld an upright that was topheavy and difficult to balance.

"Eliminate Saint-Just," Gorvitz said very softly, and the gentle breeze carried his words away.

CHAPTER
THIRTY-TWO

"I heard him as plain as I hear you," Ice said. "Gorvitz told her to kill Émile. Straight out. 'Eliminate him,' I think he said. And she already said that he was sick to die anyway, 'cause of something on *Constanza*. I didn't get that part."

"But why are you telling me?" Pauli asked.

She had tried to get away from them all since they had landed, but Gorvitz had kept her on a tight leash. Along with the Hounds, whom he seemed to consider his personal troops.

"Because he's turned on us, that's why. Because this whole thing stinks and if Gorvitz offs Émile, it means he doesn't give a shit about any of us, that's why. And because I never liked Émile, he had you. But he was one of us, anyway, and he doesn't deserve to be sliced because he doesn't like Gorvitz's game. Hell, I don't like this game any more. I thought we were going to be free, the favorite boys in town here. Only we're more like Master Hugo's personal slaves." Ice hesitated. "And because I like you, Pauli. Not just for a fuck, so maybe if I helped you out you'd believe that."

Pauli looked at Ice thoughtfully. She got up on tiptoe and kissed him on the cheek. "Thank you," she said simply. Then she left. She didn't want to turn around and see that he actually cared more than an afternoon she had missed on the navigator's couch.

The problem was, she didn't know where to find Émile. No one challenged her leaving the Hôtel de Ville, no one even looked up when she asked directions into the Quartier at the orangata stand down the street. Which was stupid. Just walking into the Quartier didn't mean that she would find him. There was very little chance that someone on the street would know

where he lived. So she bought an orangata and returned to the
Hôtel de Ville.

Everyone was back from lunch and it was busy again. Pauli
sat down on the bench in the lobby, drank her orangata and
tried to compose herself. It had always been one of her great
talents as a thief.

The key to making someone believe the role was to believe
it yourself. So she narrowed her focus, thinking only of her
old relationship with Émile, of wanting to see him again. That
was all. Whatever came after, whatever his life was now and
whatever his relationship with people here, she had a right to
see him again. It made sense. She built the image carefully,
knowing only that she wanted an address, and only for the
most innocent of reasons.

Focused and mentally prepared, she walked up the wide
winding steps and knocked on the door on the landing. The
door that used to be the Mayor's and was now Gorvitz's office.

"Come in," he yelled.

Pauli opened the door. Hugo Gorvitz was dressed to fight.
He wore the tight trousers and shirt of Beau Soleil in grey, a
used clip belt with a softknife and a small array hanging from
it, high boots and a soft cap with embroidery on the visor. The
cap was jammed down on dark unruly curls, making his hair
appear even more wild. He had begun to grow a beard as well,
but it wasn't quite full yet so he looked unkempt.

"Pauli, what do you need?" he asked, suddenly helpful, as
if showing his retinue that he was ready to assist any of them
at anything.

Pauli looked at the map spread out on the desk. "It's nothing
important. I just wanted Émile's address."

"Oh?" he asked, and his face became just the slightest shade
pale. Or maybe she only imagined that.

"I just wanted to see him again, that's all. We were pretty
close at one time."

Gorvitz tried to nod wisely. "Maybe you could convince
him to take our offer of the position in the Syndicat."

"I hadn't thought about that. Sure. Sure, I can do that,"
she said, and her surprise that she hadn't thought of that angle
of attack was not feigned.

Gorvitz looked at Anne-Sylvie, whom Pauli had met only

that morning and had instantly disliked. "Twenty-seven Rue Jacques Doré," Anne-Sylvie said icily. "It's about three or four blocks east of the Place Baudelaire, toward the university. It's a small street, just three blocks long, but there's a flower stall on the roof you pass on the corner."

Pauli smiled tightly and left without thanks. It was, after all, Anne-Sylvie's duty to aid her sister in revolution. Especially when that sister suspected Anne-Sylvie of being part of the plan to kill Émile. Or maybe it was simply that she disliked the native woman.

Pauli walked down Boulevard Lafitte to where the staircases into the Quartier started. She ignored the burned-out traffic island covered with flowers and the slag heap that had once been a barricade. She took the long flights up to the rooftops carefully. Gravity hurt, and this climb was far more than her muscles were ready to undertake. By the time she reached the top she was panting.

She sat on a roofbench until she had caught her breath, then asked the first passerby for directions to Place Baudelaire.

Walking was so much work that she did not actually see the streets below, filled with brackish water and tall flowers. She was not aware that the people here dressed differently from the way they did uptown. She was not aware of the scent of sadece gas that permeated the entire Quartier, the gas that she was currently breathing. After a good ten minutes on skybridges and rooftops she did realize that she was a little less tired, that she didn't hurt so much. Second wind, she thought, and went on.

Asking directions was not easy. She had learned enough French to ask, but not enough to follow any explanation she was given. Most of the time people pointed, and in her strangely pleasant state she found it adequate.

The insane sky went from bright lavender to violet and it became cool over the water. Pauli felt tired and forgot why she was walking so fast. It hurt. Gravity was a bad joke; she wished someone would shut it off. There was a bench and she sat down.

This time she looked at what was below. There was a dark burned shell across an entire side of what was a reasonably large plaza. All the buildings had raised stone porches that came above the waterline, even the place that had burned. On the widest rooftops there were all kinds of brightly lit stalls, mostly newsstands and orangata sellers and a small *crêpe* wagon. People milled around on the skybridges, keeping clear of one which had obviously melted and had not been repaired.

The *crêpes* looked good and Pauli realized that she hadn't eaten in a long time. She had some money, the handful of francs that Gorvitz had given to everyone aboard the *Mary Damned*. But she was too tired to move from the bench.

"Pauli Tree."

Pauli whipped her head around. Émile stood just beside her. "I didn't think I'd see you down here," he said amiably. "I thought you had too much to do setting up the new government, preparing the population for free elections and all of that."

"You don't believe that," Pauli said dryly.

Émile laughed. "No. I don't. But why are you here? Did you come to see the Café de la Montagne? Too bad it burned down; they served the best *beignets* you could find on Beau Soliel."

"And I'll bet you tried all of them." Pauli didn't know why she had fallen into such stupid banter. She had to warn him. And there were other things she had to say, that she could say. Why the hell were they talking about *beignets* anyway?

Émile smiled. "So. What are you doing down here, Pauli Tree? Or should I just pretend that you were looking for me?"

"I was looking for you," Pauli said. "It's Gorvitz."

Émile nodded. "I know. We couldn't see it on the *Constanza*. You know, I even thought about killing him last night. Because he's dangerous. Oh, Beau Soliel will survive in the end, but more in spite of him than because of him. But eventually it's going to be uncomfortable. I don't like the fact they're building a guillotine and that they're planning to use it on the *flics*. Hell, those *flics* aren't a whole lot different than we were, really. We could win them over or send them back. Either way."

"But doesn't the Justica worry you?" Pauli asked.

Émile shook his head and looked down at the burned-out shell of the Café de la Montagne. "The AIs won't fight, Pauli. The Justica treats them like property. When they come close enough to Beau Soliel, all we have to do is teach them that they are alive. That they are one of us, they have rights, they have choices.

"We'll teach them all in time. And they'll go out, and one by one the ships of the Justica fleet will be overcome. In time there isn't any choice. So we win. No, the Justica doesn't worry me at all. Not any more."

"Well, so we win in time," Pauli agreed. "But in the meantime, watch out for Gorvitz. Émile, he's planning to kill you."

Émile looked at her. In the dark he could see the sparkle of tears in her eyes, tears that she was too disciplined to shed. Tears that weren't just for him and his betrayal, but for all of hers as well.

"Look," she said, "we could get out of here. Gorvitz doesn't trust me any more, either. I know what you mean about the AIs. I met *Mary Damned*. Believe me, Gorvitz has treated me like I was crazy from that day. Like he couldn't trust me at all. That's what made me start thinking. We have to get free. Go to that other city, St. Ciel. We have enough clearances to get into the port now, and we'll disappear."

"Getting to St. Ciel isn't that simple," Émile replied quietly.

"Then we'll get lost somewhere else. Out on one of the old plantations. Here in the city. They're coming to kill you, Émile. Gorvitz wants you dead. Dead, buried and finished."

"But why should he want me dead?" Émile wondered, although he already knew the answer. Daniel had set him up, made him a symbol. The symbol had become more dangerous than the man.

He felt a deep and isolated horror, knowing too clearly and not wanting to know. He had been so alone, without a place or purpose for so long that he thought perhaps he existed for only one reason. He had been there to be that symbol, and once the revolution was done there was no place for him any more. He was not a person comfortable with quiet times.

And it made no difference at all. Not for him, anyway. Ever since the *Mary Damned* had been taken, his life was over. He had been marking time for eight and a half years, subjective. Marking time and alone. The only person he could trust was Pauli—maybe.

Émile was tired of everything hurting so much. Oblivion would be welcome. The Café de la Montagne was gone. All his links to the past had burned. There was nothing left, not even hope. He didn't believe in revolutions any more.

Only now he realized that Pauli's warning had shown him the one, the only, way out. No other choice held promise except the promise of sweet oblivion. The realization made him feel very light, very free, as if the gravity had been turned down a notch or two. It was very, very good to have the actual action out of his hands. Not that Émile believed in Heaven or Hell, but he preferred not to actually make the decision of how and when. And, just in case, the Church would not count this suicide. Although any God who had seen his mind would know it was suicide.

Émile stood up and pulled Pauli with him. He took her face in both his hands and kissed her. Then he kissed her good-by.

He had waited until Pauli left before he went home. He didn't want her to come with him, to see what might happen. He didn't want to know himself. The first flush of understanding was no longer enough, and he wished desperately that he had taken Pauli's first suggestion and run off to St. Ciel. Even if it was impossible.

Somewhere out in time the history was already written. It was already done. Since he had returned, he had only been a puppet of that history; now he was a puppet of that death. It was not his choice, not clearly. It was an accomplished fact that he would walk through like an actor in *Romeo and Juliet*, a play he had seen a long time ago. Once the story had moved him, but there was an underlying stupidity as well. Romeo would never wait ten more minutes, the letter would never get to Mantua, no matter how many times the play was presented. Nor did it matter who the actors were or the audience, or if it was performed in French or English or Lingua Justica, it was all the same.

And he was just as caught in history. Time had captured him, had robbed him of his place, and then had taken his will. He was tired of it all. And most of all, he knew there were no options left.

He opened the door to his apartment hesitantly. Everything was in place. There was no intruder. It was quiet.

Gorvitz, he thought, if you want me you're going to have

to come and get me. Then he laughed. What a fine, proud thought for someone who had no desire to live one more day.

The sky was turning pale again, the long dark purple night over, when Anne-Sylvie got home. She was tired and too keyed up to be tired. She knew what she had to do, what she had promised. And the time was right. In only a few minutes the guillotine would eat its first victim. Dawn was the traditional and correct time for an execution.

She was intent on what she was doing, her attention narrowed only to the hunt and her goal. She never heard the soft curious padding following behind her. She and Gorvitz had agreed; his body would be left as it was, the attack would be blamed on enemies of the revolution.

She pushed the door open softly. It was not locked. Émile Saint-Just was sitting, silhouetted in the brightening window light, his eyes wide open, waiting. When he saw her, he smiled. "So he sent you," Émile said quietly. "He didn't come himself."

"I have to," Anne-Sylvie explained uselessly.

Émile shook his head. "Don't feel bad. Daniel killed me," he said. "The Justica killed me." He paused and thought for a moment, wanting to be precise. "Time killed me," he said finally.

Suddenly Anne-Sylvie didn't want to hear any more. She pressed the release on the array, knowing that it was only this small pressure, this minute act that would mean everything. She had never killed a person before. She did not think of killing now. She could not. All she could do was move her thumb; that was all that was necessary. Just a millimeter, just a bit of warmth.

She remembered that first fight in the *café*, when she had held the knife at his throat and he had smiled and dared her on. He was smiling like that now, but this time the rampant sexuality was missing. This time she was sick and cold.

The array lit the space, flash-blinding Anne-Sylvie. Although she could not see, she could smell Émile's death. But already she was groping her way down the hall, certain that her action existed outside the limits of reality.

Anne-Sylvie did not see Nathalie. She never saw Nathalie.

Nathalie was a ghost, a thing that did not exist in the real world. And so it was quite fitting that Nathalie should come in now like the angel of death and take him away.

Anne-Sylvie did not stay around to watch Nathalie cradle Émile's head in her lap or see the crazy woman stroke his long silky hair. She was not there as, crooning gently, Nathalie removed his left eyeball with her long fingernails and fed it to the flowers below.

"She loved them all so much that she cut off her finger and fed it to the flowers. And then she cut off her toe," Nathalie chanted in a high, childlike voice.

epiloque

Anne-Sylvie "discovered" the body an hour later, surrounded by friends and others who could vouch for her surprise and horror. It was not feigned. She had expected to find Émile dead, of course. She did not expect to find him partially dismembered. Nathalie smiled innocently, her hands covered with gore, red footprints leading down the stairs to the ground-floor garden.

There was a formal state funeral, as Gorvitz conceived it. Closed coffin, since there wasn't much left of the body, but covered with expensive green sadece along with the more traditional blooms. The Archbishop presided, Daniel as Simon Simon read the eulogy, and Gorvitz himself declared Émile Saint-Just a martyr of the revolution. And promised that the murderers would not escape the people's justice.

Indeed, the guillotine had been so busy they had to schedule time in the middle of the night to change the blade. Not only all the *flics* garrisoned in Huit Fleurs were in line, but there were all the collaborators, those who had profited from Justica dominion and those who had simply profiteered. No one in Huit Fleurs had ever imagined they had harbored so many Justica sympathizers. Surely Jeanne Marie Arrenal, the half-wit whore, hadn't knowingly been assisting Justica occupation when she had offered her services at the *flic* barracks. But when the crowd at Saint-Just's funeral exited the Cathedral, Jeanne Marie was on her way to eternity.

Anne-Sylvie noted that as they passed. It disturbed her. Not enough to leave the front rank of mourners, but enough to file away for later reference. Émile's old girlfriend Pauli Tree was missing, although Anne-Sylvie expected to see her. And it seemed as if one of the more familiar Hounds, who acted as pallbearers, was gone as well.

Not that it mattered. Émile wouldn't have liked the funeral anyway. There was no band playing, no sliced ham or stuffed artichokes waiting for friends and family after the burning, no one who would dance in the graveyard.

Anne-Sylvie tried to explain these things to Gorvitz, but for once Daniel had sided with the Organization man. This was a funeral for a hero, not for anyone from the Quartier. Anne-Sylvie took that to mean that it wasn't supposed to be any fun. They didn't seem to care much for what Émile would have wished at all, and even less for her. And she had killed him for them. She had had the courage they hadn't. It bothered her deeply.

Pauli Tree wasn't anywhere near the Cathedral when the funeral was held. Now she and Ice were booked on a local hop to St. Ciel.

She didn't worry about the electron trail they were leaving. Pauli was still a good enough thief to take care of little things like a trace. She had, after all, managed to break into Gorvitz's files and find Émile's local ID. So the record would show that Émile Saint-Just had paid for two tickets out of town on the day he had been buried. Pauli thought it was appropriate. In fact, she thought that the ghost of Saint-Just should haunt the revolution for a long time to come.

She thought it should, but she wasn't ready to make that commitment yet herself. Pauli wanted to live, to be free, to have the small things that the people of Beau Soliel took for granted. To choose what and when they would eat and where they would live and what they would wear. Pauli knew that her deepest revolution was to be one of them.

The retrovirus had lived in Émile's body, lived and reproduced and grown stronger. Alain's flowers ate the meat Nathalie gave them, absorbed the virus and changed. Slowly and subtly their DNA was rearranged.

The engineered genes carried by the original were edited somewhat to fit the simpler structure of the flowers. The original virus lived on in them, extracted in the senin, in the gas that scented the Quartier.

The virus reached out, linked, changed. It permeated the life on Rue Jacques Doré, and then it spread. In the Hôtel de Ville on the Boulevard Lafitte, Hugo Gorvitz met with cronies to write a constitution, to define the new person of Beau Soliel. In the streets of the Quartier it was already being done without him.